A Very Kinky Christmas

Book IV
of
The Dudley Files

The Lovely Lucy Ladley, Dudley and his cousins are big fans. Have A Very Kinky Christmas.

[signature]

Dudley 🐾

A VERY KINKY CHRISTMAS

BOOK IV
OF
THE DUDLEY FILES

by
Cary Robinson

ALSO BY CARY ROBINSON

Sold Out Without The Holdout
Burp Gun Bandit
Soul Heeler
Monsters In My Yard
Woody Wooferson Lost His Woof
The Plott Hound Thickens

Copyright © 2020 Cary Robinson

Golden Hound Press

info@goldenhoundpress.com

www.dudleyfiles.com

All rights reserved. No part of this publication may be reproduced, stored in a retrieval system, or transmitted, in any form or by any means, electronic, mechanical, photocopying, recording, or otherwise, without the prior written permission of the author.

Profits from the sale of this book will be donated to animal shelters and rescue groups housing Dudley's friends.

ISBN: 9780578239354

Cover design: Cary Robinson & Adam Sward

Editor: Mike Levine

This is a work of fiction. Names, characters, places, and incidents either are products of the author's imagination or are used fictitiously. Any resemblance to actual events or locals or persons living or dead, is entirely coincidental.

Printed in the United States of America

FOREWORD

A *Very Kinky Christmas*, Book IV of the Dudley Files, represents some of Cary Robinson's best work to date. He remains talented, prolific, very readable, and blessed with a light hand on the tiller. He also has the arcane gift of getting into the head of a dog about as well as anyone I've ever read.

In the world of constipated, humorless mystery writers, who smoke meerschaum pipes and wear their hats at jaunty angles, Cary Robinson stands out not only as a uniquely unpretentious author, but also as a man with a great spirit of generosity. You see, all profits from the sales of his books are donated to animal shelters and rescue groups housing Dudley's cousins. Some may not fully appreciate this gesture, but I say God bless Cary Robinson for opening the gates of Heaven a little bit wider.

You will find many colorful characters in this book. Some are two-legged. Some are four-legged. Some almost seem to leap off the page. This is perhaps because Robinson with an economy of words, is a bit like someone telling a story. His style is deceptively simple, yet highly engaging. Raymond Chandler, the great mystery writer, once said, "Nothing in literature is worth a damn, except what is written between the lines." To fully appreciate Cary Robinson, read between the lines.

Kinky Friedman.

We find our true selves once our reflection is seen through the eyes of the canine. For not only is their soul revealed at that very moment, ours is on full display.

—Careless

I opened my eyes. I must have been out for a while. I can't remember jack. Except for Jack Daniels. I can always remember Jack Daniels, my coffee additive of choice. Everything seemed very blurry. I could see lights and the outlines of figures moving about. I did hear voices and knew E.D. was present. I could smell as well as hear her! She smelled as sweet as a fresh spring day. Her voice sounded like angels singing. I'm not sure I've ever heard an angel sing but somehow felt like I had. E.D. is my beautiful blonde neighbor who lives just above me at Big Rock Lofts. Over time we have become very friendly and my soulmate Dudley stays with her sometimes when I am away. My vision started to clear, and the first thing I saw was Dudley. I love that dog more than anything in the world. He's my golden-colored hound dog who I adopted from the SPCA. The best move I ever made. My hand was resting on his head, and he was staring intently into my eyes. I could not avert his gaze. I felt like I was looking into his soul, and he into mine. It was as if we had been connected for an eternity, or at least since I had been alive, though I had only met him just a short while ago.

"You scared the hell out of me, Careless," E.D. said. Careless is a nickname given to me in college when a group of my friends discovered the meaning of life from a bottle of Jack Daniels. We decided it was imperative that we add the word "less" to the end of everyone's name. I have been Careless ever since. "Don't you EVER do that again." She was just inches from my face, and I shifted my attention from Dudley's handsome golden-colored form to E.D.'s nicely shaped form and beautiful face. Her shining blonde hair was unkempt and flowed freely, partly covering her eyes. But I could see tears flowing from them. I tried to say something but couldn't find my voice. My throat felt sore.

I looked around the room and saw my grandfather, Papa, smiling at me. He had an El Producto cigar hanging from his mouth, like he was having some sort of celebration. It wasn't lit and still looked as new as when it came out of its clear plastic wrapper. My brother and business partner, Ross, was standing next to him, and Birk and Sarge were huddled close by. Birk is a business associate friend of mine. He's a good ol' boy redneck who drives what we call the Cowboy Cadillac. Others call it the Ford F350 Crew Cab Dually. Sarge is my next-door neighbor at Big Rock Lofts. He's a gentle soul, an avid reader, very intelligent, and often partakes in eleven herbs and spices. But mostly the herbs. They were all smiling. I wasn't sure what was going on, but I didn't like it. Were they playing a joke on me? Was there some elaborate hoax going on? Were we having a surprise birthday party? I don't think it was my birthday, but, honestly, I can't even remember what day it was. I then realized I was lying down, not sure why, and decided to sit up and address the situation from a better vantage point.

When I tried to sit up, I felt intense pain in my chest and collapsed backwards. I looked around and realized I was in a hospital room. And I was the patient. I tried figure out how I landed here but couldn't remember a darn thing. A doctor walked in and looked very surprised. Happily so.

"When did he wake up?" the doctor asked.

"Just a minute ago," E.D. said. "Can you believe this? It's a miracle. A Christmas miracle. Even though it's only Thanksgiving."

Well, now I knew it was Thanksgiving.

"I'm Doctor John Fisher and you are a lucky young man. One eighth of an inch to the left and that bullet would have pierced your heart. Other than leaving a nice sized hole in your chest, it entered and exited pretty cleanly." I didn't remember a thing about being shot or how it happened. The lingering pain was my evidence. I had never been shot before. I hope to not ever repeat it. Talk about no fun! I looked at Dudley and instinctively knew he was the reason I was still on this earth.

However, when I put my hand on his big, beautiful golden-colored head, it came back to me. I had been shot and saw him and E.D. standing over me as the life drained from my body. Then I saw paramedics pick me up. The next memory was vague and confusing. I was sitting out by a wide river with Dudley by my side. I had my arm around him, like I normally do. The river was clear, the surface smooth as glass. It beckoned me to cross it, and as I stood up to do so, Dudley stood up, stepped in front of me, and refused to let me enter the river. He thought it was a one-way trip. Perhaps it was. I relented. The next thing I remembered was waking up in this hospital bed. It must have been a dream. But Dudley didn't think so.

The doctor walked over to me and looked into my eyes. He shined a small flashlight in them. It was uncomfortably bright. Dudley eyeballed him and started a low growl. I looked at him and shook my head. He is my protector, but he quieted down, still keeping a watchful eye on Doctor Fisher. The doctor checked my wrist for a pulse. Apparently, I still had one. "Do you know your name?" he asked. I shook my head up and down. "Do you know the people in this room?" Again, I shook my head up and down. "Do you know where you are?" I let him know I did. What's with all the trick questions? "I'm amazed at this but his vitals are really pretty good, and he seems cognizant of his surroundings. I think it's safe to take his trach tube out. I'll send the nurse in. Excuse me for one moment." He began writing something on the chart while walking out of the room. I hoped his handwriting is better than his bedside manners.

Moments later, a nurse came in with Doctor Fisher. She unhooked something, took my pulse, and said, "Take a deep breath." Just as she said this, it felt like she was yanking my spine out, similar to separating an ear of corn from its husk. Tight fit and pretty unpleasant to say the least. My throat felt scratchy, but I tried to talk. Nothing came out but some squeaks and whispers. She placed an oxygen mask over my nose and mouth, smiled at me, and walked out.

"He's still going to need a lot of care. You can have a few more minutes with him, but then I'm going to have to ask you all to leave so he can get some rest."

They all stood around looking at me and smiling like I was some kind of prized animal in a zoo. It made me a little uncomfortable. But not Dudley. He had his eyes trained on me and didn't even blink. It was almost as if he knew I was okay and expected me to be alive. He knew alright.

Thankfully, Doctor Fisher anxiously glanced at his watch and said, "Okay, let's give him some time to relax. You can come back tomorrow during regular visiting hours."

Papa walked over to me, bent down, and put his hand on my head as if he was blessing me. Perhaps he was. Nothing like being blessed by the patriarch of the family! He said in a strong Russian accent, "Don't worry, everything's going to be all right." He smiled down on me and turned and walked away.

Sarge said, "What he said," while pointing at Papa. He smiled and walked out of the room.

Birk walked over, put his hand on my shoulder, and said, "Welcome back, Careless. You really had us on pins and needles." He smiled and walked out, with Papa behind him.

I realized I had been shot but I had no idea why they were welcoming me back. Did I go somewhere? Maybe I was just groggy from the drugs leaching into my veins.

E.D. reached down and kissed my forehead. "I'm going to take Dudley home. I'll come back tomorrow and we'll have a long talk, you and I. Get some rest." I still had my hand on Dudley's head. He hadn't budged or stopped staring at me, except for that brief moment when he warned off the doctor. As far as Dudley was concerned, the doctor was not in. At least in the small group of humans he calls friends – which isn't many. E.D. tried to walk away with him while pulling at his leash. She got snapped back like a middle-aged husband's neck when caught by his wife checking out a pretty, bikini-clad young girl at the beach. Dudley was not moving or going anywhere. He was like a statue. E.D. was not amused. "Come on boy, we have to let him rest."

I smiled at him and whispered in a slow, raspy voice, "It's okay boy." Then the strangest thing happened. With my hand still on his head, I realized I was feeling his thoughts. It was almost like a movie playing in my head. I could see he didn't want to leave me. In fact, he was contemplating jumping in bed with me. Without saying another word to him, I looked him straight in his beautiful brown eyes and commanded him to go with E.D. I let him know I would be home very soon. He stubbornly agreed and walked away with E.D. He turned his head backwards while walking forward. I nodded my head to keep him moving forward. He made sure to keep his eyes on me till he reached the door. The love this dog had in his heart was the size of Texas.

E.D. said, "How did you get him to come with me? I can never get him to do something once he makes up his mind not to do it." I shrugged my shoulders and winced from the shooting pain. No pun intended. For a brief moment, I had forgotten I had been shot. I couldn't use my inside voice yet.

I have no idea how I understood his thoughts. Maybe this was some kind of weird dream. Perhaps I was still back at my place, sleeping one off. Probably too many Careless Coffees. That had to be the explanation. Why would someone shoot little ol' loveable me?

When the door closed behind them, the doctor said, "Okay, Careless, I'm going to give you something for the pain, and it should help you rest. Tomorrow will be a big day. You're going to start PT." I had no idea what he was referring to, but my mind reverted back to when I was a teenager chasing girls. There was no way I was in any condition to even think about something sexual. I must have looked confused because he said, "PT is physical therapy. You've been in a coma for two months, and your muscles haven't been used since then. We're going to re-train them to get you going. It'll be a little tough at first, but we have one of the best physical therapists in town. He'll get you up and going in no time. I nodded my head up and down. I was thinking my version of PT was probably a lot better than his. That was one muscle I definitely hadn't used. Poor Big Pete! I wasn't too keen about Doctor Fisher's version of PT. It seemed a lot like exercise, and really, I'm not a fan of exercise. My eyelids were getting heavy. I slowly closed my eyes and drifted off to sleep.

I dreamt that I was sitting on that river bank with Dudley. His beautiful golden-colored fur was shimmering in the sun. I had my arm around him and his head was leaning on my shoulder. Across the river was a beautiful mountain with a breathtaking, beautiful white bluff on the face. I slept well that day. I'm glad Dudley saved me. There was much to be done before I got called home.

When I woke up, I smelled something odd and saw a plate of food sitting in front of me. Red Jello and something I couldn't readily identify. It reminded me of something a mother bird would chew up and yack back out to feed her young ones. My throat was still a little scratchy, and seeing what some might refer to as food wasn't doing it for me. I made a face to show my disdain. "Oh, you're going to eat it," someone said with conviction. I was startled because I normally notice everything and everyone around me. I guess I was a little off my game after being shot and pumped full of all types of drugs. I turned my head and saw a fairly large man sitting in a chair next to me. He was about middle-aged and had a big smile on his face.

"So, not a fan of the hospital food, are you?" he asked. I was feeling better, and my voice, although raspy, had returned to me.

"Only way I'm eating that Jello is if it has a shot of Jack Daniels in it. Know what I mean, Hoss?"

"Well, Careless, you're drinking days are over for now. I'm Ralph Gardner, and I'll be your physical therapist. You're probably not going to like me much, but I'm going to get you up and moving around again. When you're all better and leave the hospital, I'm sure you can commence with the festivities. But for now, I need you to eat that delicious hospital food so we can get your digestive system working and so you can build up enough strength for what I have planned for you."

Sounded like he had torture planned for me, starting with me eating the hospital food. "Oh, I loved your cousin, Jennifer Garner, in that movie, *Elektra*. You think she can give me PT instead?"

"I'll look into that. And the name's Gardner, not Garner."

I must admit I was a little nervous about Nurse Ratched's insistence that I eat the hospital mush. It didn't appear he was going to take no for an answer. We had a brief but intense staring contest. Sadly, I lost. In my defense, I was in a weakened condition and lying in bed. Normally, I can stare down the best of them. I started to lift the utensils to eat the grub on the plate when the door swung open. It was E.D. and Birk. They brought in a bag of something that actually smelled delicious.

"Hi Honey, we brought you your favorite soup from China Garden," E.D. announced to everyone in the room, but especially Ralph. Strangely enough, he seemed okay with it. Maybe he wasn't as bad as the staring contest had led me to believe.

Ralph said, "I'll leave you guys alone while he eats. I'll be just down the hall if you need me. We're going to get you walking today, Careless." He got up and walked out of the room. Birk walked over and grabbed my hand.

"I'm so glad to see you awake," he said.

"Me too," I replied. When I said that, E.D. started crying.

"I missed that voice. Don't you ever scare me like that again, Careless." She poured some hot and sour soup in a bowl, put a spoon in it, and handed it to me. "Carol at China Garden made it herself and asked me to bring it to you." I struggled but still managed to eat it. Believe me, it never tasted so good. As I ate it, I actually felt my strength beginning to return. The ancient Chinese soup recipe. The human body is a wonderful thing.

Both Birk and E.D. watched me eat with big smiles on their faces. I suppose they are entertained rather easily but it reminded me a bit like when adolescents ogle the manhood of the David statue in the Vatican. Don't worry. David has nothing on Big Pete.

"You know, Careless," E.D. said, "you've been in a coma for two months. We weren't sure you were going to make it. That jackwad, Dick, Wanda's husband, shot you with one of his hunting rifles. He was mad because when you solved your last case, all his funds and toys were taken away from him and given to the rightful heirs of the family. He claimed he did it for revenge. It didn't take your friend, Detective Present, long to track Dick down and prosecute the case. All those involved are in jail now, and they won't be bothering anyone for a long time."

"Well, I hope he gets a boyfriend named Bubba and often drops the soap in the shower, if you know what I mean. With a name like Dick…" We all chuckled. It only hurt for a second. I finished my soup as the two of them caught me up on everything I had missed for the last two months. But what I had missed the most was my boy, Dudley. I couldn't wait to settle back into my normal routine with him by my side. A man misses his best friend – his dog. A friend like no other.

Just when we were done chatting, Ralph walked in. "You finished eating?"

I had but replied, "No, not really."

"Great, let's get going. I hope the two of you will excuse us, but we're going to get Careless up and do some walking around the floor now."

He saw right through me.

This seemed like an opportune time to explain my philosophy to Ralph. "You may not be aware of this, but I happen to have a condition that makes me highly allergic to exercise. It's a real condition. I'm sure someone must have written it up on my forms when I was admitted to the hospital. Don't worry, it's not contagious." E.D. placed her hand over her mouth and began to laugh. Birk seemed amused as well. I think they really missed me.

"Okay, I'll check with Doctor Not Buying It, but in the meantime, let's get you up and using those muscles," Ralph said.

E.D. kissed my cheek and said, "Goodbye, I'll come check on you later."

Birk and I shook hands, and he said, "Later, Careless."

Ralph helped me out of bed. Surprisingly, I did okay. I was a little weak but did the old man shuffle toward the bathroom.

Ralph said, "Where do you think you're going?"

"El Bano?"

"Well, I have to go with you, just in case you fall down."

"I don't know how to tell you this, but I need to drain the main vein and I won't be able to do it if you're staring at Big Pete," I said.

"Tell you what, I'll look the other way. Big Pete won't even know I'm there. Fair enough?"

"I suppose so, but Big Pete may protest."

"Big Pete may be a little uncomfortable. While you were sleeping, the nurse removed your catheter."

Great! Now everyone knows about Big Pete. I took care of business, and he asked me to walk around the hospital hallway with him. He stayed right by my side, waiting for me to slip and fall. I didn't. I did, however, ask him, "Does this hospital gown make me look fat?"

"No," he said, "but you may want to tie up the back of it, or some of the nurses may start asking for your phone number." He made me laugh. It only hurt a little. I could tell I was going to like this guy. We made a big circle around the hospital floor. The first day, just one lap around really wore me out, and I had to retire to the hospital bed. Every day after that, we added another lap. Ralph talked to me about every subject under the sun. He was especially crazy about his golden retriever, Lexi. He loved her like I love Dudley. As we talked and walked, I realized he was not only giving me physical therapy, but mental therapy as well. Lord knows, I could sure use it after all I had been through. Speaking to him took my mind off of the effort of walking as I struggled to build up my muscles. I still believe my version of PT would have been better than his, but that's a whole other subject.

E.D., Birk, Sarge, Ross, and Papa came by daily and kept me company. Thankfully, they brought food from my favorite restaurants: China Garden, Kenny & Ziggy's, Kim Son, Blue Onyx Bistro, and Tapester Grill. I highly recommend them to everyone. They also bought me plenty of decaf Katz coffee, but minus the central ingredient – Jack Daniels, due to doctor's orders. I love Katz Coffee, but it just wasn't the same without the Jack.

The one thing I learned about hospital stays is you become quite good at Jeopardy and Wheel of Fortune. I knew I had recuperated when all I could think about was getting Vanna in my cabana. I'd like to buy a vowel, please.

After several days, I frankly became stir crazy. I had mostly regained full use of my body and no longer needed to be felt up from the belt up by the doctors and their students. Some of the cuter ones, I didn't really have a big problem with. That's how I knew it was time for me to take my leave. You say libido, I say libado. Doctor Fisher came in one day and somehow by the grace of God, I convinced him to release me. He did make me promise to take it easy, not go back to work right away, not partake in alcoholic beverages, and not smoke. I agreed to his terms because I don't smoke, so technically it wasn't really a lie. Of the other restrictions he gave me, what's a little white lie among friends?

When Birk picked me up at the hospital in his Ford F350 dually, which we refer to as The Cowboy Cadillac, I was so excited I could barely stand it. Suffice it to say, there is no place like home. I couldn't wait to get back there. I knew my boy, Dudley, would be waiting for me with open paws and I couldn't get there soon enough. Of course, with Birk driving, soon enough came sooner than I thought. He has a bit of a lead foot.

I even enjoyed the chicken cackle Birk calls singing as he did his best to sing along to the songs playing on the radio. It's funny, the things that go from annoying to endearing when life is almost snatched away from you. That's something I think I shall always remember.

As we pulled up to Big Rock Lofts, I saw Dudley's nose pressed up against the window on the second floor. The frigid December wintery weather of sixty-five degrees really fogged up the window pane. Again, one of those things I truly missed. Birk stopped the truck, and we jumped out and slowly walked into the building. E.D. was waiting for us, so I suppose they had coordinated my arrival. Fair enough, this is what good friends are for. She hugged me and locked her arm in mine as we carefully ascended the stairs to the second floor. An elevator right about now would have come in mighty handy.

"Now, I have everything set up for you. I've stocked your refrigerator and pantry with food, and there's plenty of coffee for you. Your favorite, Katz coffee, Midnight Blue. Also, per doctor's orders, I removed the Jack Daniels from your cupboard. He said no drinking for a while, and you didn't have much left anyway."

My frown refused to turn upside down. Birk was amused and began full out laughing, until E.D. shot him a look that shut him up. We got to my door, and I heard Dudley making noises behind it. I'm sure he could smell and hear me. Birk opened the door and Dudley blasted out like a tornado ripping through Kansas. He jumped on me and hooked his paws over my shoulders. Then the lick fest began. In between licks, he made inhuman noises of joy. I must say, it didn't bother me, other than a tinge of pain here and there.

When Dudley was finally finished, I made some iced coffee and reached for the Jack Daniels. Old habits are hard to break. Disappointed would be an understatement of how I felt right then. I sat on the sofa, unfulfilled. Dudley scrunched up next to me and leaned in with everything he had. I put my arm around him and sipped my coffee. It was still delicious – even without the whiskey. Birk and E.D. slipped out, and I just sat there. It almost felt surreal, but I just wanted to enjoy the moment. I had beaten the odds and just took it all in from my happy place.

Several weeks later, I was up and about. My body was now in good working order. Dudley and I would walk outside together several times a day, and I just hung around, being fairly unproductive and bored out of existence. Sometimes, we would watch Animal Planet together, but he really liked the Cooking Channel. His favorite show was *Nadia G's Bitchin' Kitchen*. While I was busy checking out her booty, it turned out he was a closet foody. I guess I was back to normal, whatever that is. I would occasionally flip it over to watch Vanna, but that usually irritated him, so we didn't watch Wheel of Fortune too much. No accounting for taste. If I actually knew how to get the TV to show split screens, we could have had the best of both worlds. But I'm not a high-tech Texan.

    The next day I was awakened by the telephone. "Dudley, would you please get that for me?" I asked him. Normally, I don't let him answer the phone because his phone skills are atrocious, but I was feeling a little lazy. His mouth engulfed the phone, and goober started flowing like a river. He mumbled something but I couldn't make it out due to the extreme moisture content of his mouth. He's definitely not a morning person. I got out of bed and placed my hand on his very handsome head. He looked up at me. I was immediately able to read his thoughts and knew E.D. was on the telephone. I asked him to hand me the phone without saying a word, and he did. This was pretty awesome even though the phone was somewhat slobbery. We could hear each other's thoughts. When I removed my hand from him, our link was severed, and I had to rely on reading his body language. Whenever we touched we knew what each other were thinking. This definitely was going to come in handy for our future cases, but I dared not tell anyone about it or they'd think I was crazy.

Maybe I am crazy. But since the shooting, I could definitely hear Dudley's thoughts when I came into contact with him. It helped that he's a touchy-feely kind of guy. Not that there's anything wrong with that.

"Careless, I've decided we're going on a road trip. Even though you're making great strides on getting back to normal, it's obvious to me that you need a little more time to rehab before you get back into the swing of things. Your friend Rod called to check on you. He's terribly worried about you, and we decided that it may be good for you to spend some time up at Highland Ranch with him. He said the leaves are turning fantastic colors and are just beautiful. Of course, I'll drive. You're in no condition for that. I'll have to use some of my sick days at the magazine, but that shouldn't be a problem. You can relax and get yourself better."

"Will Dudley be attending?" I inquired.

"Of course. I would never separate the two of you. Frankly, I'm not sure you could function without him. Although he did just fine with me while you were away. Didn't you, big boy?"

He must have heard her. I had my arm around him, and I immediately envisioned him curled up in her bed, practically on top of her while snoring away. I must admit, she was very beautiful while she slept, and I was a bit jealous. As usual, since someone addressed him and spoke his name, he said something. I felt a little guilty because it was almost as if I was spying on her. Oh well, what mamma don't know won't hurt her.

"Rod, Rick, and Chico will be waiting for us. The weather is nice and cool out there in the Hill Country, and we can sit out by the fire pit while Dudley and Chico go roam the property and hunt for critters. We'll have a great time. Let's head out tomorrow morning. What do you say?"

"I say great. Let's do it." Immediately, I had visions in my head of driving up the hill to Rod and Rick's house. Dudley saw what I was thinking about as well. His tail started spinning around in circles, in helicopter fashion. I saw he was thinking about sitting around the fire with Chico, chewing on some elk antlers. Chico is a big furry Briard dog. He may be Frenchy French, but Dudley and I like him. He's a good boy and one of Dudley's best friends.

I hung up the phone, and Dudley and I went outside so he could do his business. He ran around for a while and did his thing. We ate lunch when we went back up to the loft and pretty much just sat around doing nothing. We watched TV and later had dinner. While I love being with my soulmate, I'm not going to lie, I was bored out of my mind. I needed something to do to keep my mind active. Ross and Papa insisted that I stay home and rest. The doctor agreed. They also didn't want me working any police cases for Detective Present or on any of the Dudley Files cases. I knew they meant well and wanted me to get back to normal, but I was never really normal to begin with. I'd oblige them for now. The thing is, I was beginning to feel useless. A man has to have a purpose, or he just aimlessly wanders through his entire life searching for that one thing he can never quite lay his fingers on.

We eventually went to bed. Dudley circled around several times and lay down with his head resting on my chest. I put my arm around him and found him thinking of somewhere I had never seen. He was swimming in a river chasing ducks. It must have been somewhere from his past. I chuckled a little because he never caught a duck. Oh, sure, he came close a couple of times, but no dice. He said something when he realized I was laughing at him. Tomorrow couldn't get here soon enough.

The next morning, we did our usual ritual. I tried to sneak out of bed, but Dudley tried to permanently attach himself to me. Whenever I tried to push him away, he pushed back with an equal but opposite force. I eventually got out of his Kung Fu grip after much effort and some very flexible contortions. I call this Newtoning, after Sir Isaac Newton's theory of relativity. Plus, I like Fig Newtons.

I showered up, got dressed, and packed a bag for our road trip. I imagined E.D. was going to drive her big blue jalopy she calls Betsy. I was still a week away from being able to drive – doctor's orders. I couldn't wait to get behind the wheel of the Power Wagon again. It's funny how you miss the little things in life while recovering from a coma resulting from a gunshot wound. Like driving. Or sipping some Jack Daniels mixed in with your Katz iced coffee.

I made some scrambled eggs and prepared some iced coffee. "Okay, Dudley, let's pray before we eat. Give me your paw." He placed his paw in my hand. He's very spiritual. "Oh Lord, won't you buy me a Mercedes Benz? How long will it be till I have Jack Daniels again? Worked hard my whole life with Dudley, my friend. Oh Lord, I can't wait till my recovery ends. Amen." What Dudley then said sounded like an amen to me. I gave half of the eggs to him, which he immediately hoovered up, and I ate the rest and drank my coffee. Even though the aroma and taste of the Katz Midnight Blue were fantastic, it was a little light in the loafers without the whiskey. I was determined to last another week without my special ingredient. Of course, it wasn't going to be easy but I felt as if I could accomplish this monumental feat.

When we finished breakfast, there was a knock on the door. Dudley was already standing at attention and staring at it. It was almost like he knew who was behind it. I walked over and placed my hand on his head. A vision came to me when I touched him. He was thinking about E.D., so I knew it was her. I also felt that he could smell her, and that's how he determined who was behind the door. "Good boy," I told him. He briefly looked up at me and then almost immediately focused his attention back on the door.

I opened the door, and E.D. was standing there. She was a vision of loveliness and handed me her bag. "Okay, Careless, you boys ready to go? Be a dear and carry my backpack, won't you? Let's just call it physical therapy." Again, not the PT I had envisioned.

"Sure thing, hon. We're ready to go. Dudley and I just finished breakfast. You know it's the most important meal of the day. And I'm hoping to make it for you sometime when you stay over."

"Well, unfortunately for you, that would go against your doctor's orders. And my better judgement. So that's probably never going to happen," she responded with a cute little smirk on her face. I heard the word "probably" so remain hopeful. That's just the way I roll.

We all walked toward E.D.'s car and Dudley did his business. When he was finished, we hopped in the car. All three of us sat in the front just like The Beverly Hillbillies. I guess E.D. was Ellie May Clampett, I must have been Jethro Bodine, and Dudley was Duke, Jed Clampett's ol' hound dog. We made small talk for several hours while Dudley rested his head in my lap, the back half of him resting in E.D. 's lap. She was not amused. We stopped at a Texas institution, Buc-ees, about halfway there. I let Dudley out to stretch his legs and do his business in a grassy area. Then I had him wait in the car while I filled Betsy with gas and went inside to use the facilities. They were super nice, and I bought some Beaver Nuggets. Golden delicious little corn puffs.

E.D. and I walked back to the car and got in. We drove away and listened to music for a while. Everyone was pretty quiet except for Dudley. He was sawing logs. I rested my hand on him and had a vision of him helping someone carry small logs that had been chopped up. Almost like an instant data transfer. I didn't recognize the person he was with. Must have been a previous owner. Either way, he was good at sawing logs – and carrying them. He must have had a pretty interesting past before I found him at the shelter.

Rod and Rick were waiting for us in their customized safari vehicle. In a former life, it had been a Toyota Land Cruiser. There was no way Betsy was ever going to make it up the steep inclines to their ranch house located on top of a hill.

"How you doing, Honey?" Rod said to E.D.

Before she could answer I said, "I'm doing fine, Sugar, how are you doing?"

E.D. shot me one of her looks and said, "Now I know you're feeling better, smartass. I'm doing fine Rod, how are you boys doing?" She hugged Rod and then Rick. Chico and Dudley were busy smelling each other's rear ends. Why they do that, I'll never know. I decided to do a quick experiment. While Dudley was smelling Chico's rear end, I placed my hand on Chico's back. I could see he missed Dudley and was happy we were back. I even saw and felt how he was feeling emotionally. He was happy Dudley was here and wanted to go hunt critters with him. I'll admit, this was pretty cool. I removed my hand from his back. I wondered if this would work with all dogs. Would it work with other animals as well? I was curious. I reached down and rested my hand on Chico's back again. Suddenly, I saw that Chico and the boys had pancakes for breakfast.

I inquired, "Do you boys have any pancakes leftover from this morning? I feel as if I could eat like a horse."

I shook hands with Rod and Rick.

"How'd you know we had pancakes this morning?" Rick asked. He looked bewildered.

"I think we do have a few left up at the house," Rod said.

"You're getting your appetite back," E.D. said. "Now I know you're feeling better." I actually was feeling better. My strength was returning, and being in the Hill Country eased my soul. The air, the trees, everything about it reinvigorated me.

We all jumped in the safari vehicle and drove up the hill. The view from up there was spectacular, and the only sounds I could hear were the wind and an occasional hawk or raven. We went inside, and I ate some pancakes. They were delicious. Dudley and Chico went exploring outside. I felt sorry for any critters they might come across.

"So, how are you feeling, Careless?" Rod asked. "And I am really interested as to how you knew we had pancakes for breakfast. We rarely make pancakes."

"I'm doing well, thank you."

"Yeah, how did you know about the pancakes?" E.D. asked again, placing her hands on her hips.

Should I tell Rod and Rick how I could read Chico's thoughts? They would absolutely think I was nuts. But they were all staring at me waiting for an answer. "Okay, if you really want to know, Chico told me," I said. Now they weren't just staring at me, they were staring at me in disbelief. I knew it was a bad idea.

"Seriously, how did you know?" Rick asked.

"He's obviously still shaken up from his gunshot wound," E.D. explained to them, trying to make me look sane. Well, more sane than usual…

Chico and Dudley walked in, and I placed my hand on Chico's back. "Yesterday you killed two wild hogs and drove them into Kerrville to be processed. Rod's parents came for dinner last night, and you all ate steak. Chico really loved the scraps but said it was a little bit over-cooked. Nevertheless, he enjoyed it immensely and thanks you."

Rod and Rick turned ashen. Their mouths dropped open. They sat down on a sofa and were speechless.

"You probably knew that because you looked around and deduced it from everything you saw in the ranch house," E.D. said. Rod and Rick got their color back and seemed satisfied with E.D.'s explanation.

I placed my hand on Dudley and said, "E.D., you sleep in flannel pajamas every night, and for breakfast you like to eat grilled cheese sandwiches. You call them Cheesy Pleasy. And you drink hot tea with milk and a spoonful of honey. I didn't know you liked grilled cheese, Dudley. I could start making that for you."

Rod and Rick were watching her as the color drained from her face and her mouth dropped open. She sat down next to them.

"There's no way you could know that, Careless. My mother used to call them Cheesy Pleasy, and she's been gone for eight years. I've never told anyone about that."

"In fact, you did. You asked Dudley if he wanted some Cheesy Pleasy, and he did. He really enjoyed it. I didn't even know you could cook. Beautiful and a chef – that's a great combo."

There was a long, awkward silence.

"I could go on if you'd like," I said.

After a few minutes, they all started asking me questions. Mostly, "How did you do that? How is this possible," and so on.

I told them my story, "After I got shot, I think I must have died. I was sitting out by a river and saw Dudley. I knew I was supposed to cross that river and leave this earth, but he stepped in front of me and stopped me. At that point, I understood everything he was thinking, and he understood what I was thinking. That's when I opened my eyes and found myself back in the hospital room with my hand resting on his head. I didn't realize until later, but I somehow formed a connection with him. Some kind of bond, one I've never felt before. And every time I touched him from that point on, I could feel his thoughts. And he could feel mine. I didn't realize until just now that it would work with other dogs. I know it's crazy, but it's true. I was afraid to tell you because of what you might think."

Now they believed me. I could tell by their facial expressions.

After a few days at the ranch, everyone got over their shock about the pet connection thing. We went on walks every day and just sat around talking and having fun. Then the day I was waiting for finally came. I was allowed to put Jack Daniels in my coffee again. Christmas was right around the corner but had come early for me. When I enthusiastically inquired about it with E.D., she called Doctor Fisher and he gave me his blessing. I couldn't wait for the taste. I don't have a drinking problem. I can give up coffee whenever I want. But today was not that day.

I went to the cupboard to get a bottle of Jack Daniels to make my Careless Coffee. But the cupboard was bare. Unfortunately, whoever used the bottle last had put it back empty. I hate when that happens. Oh, the horror! I looked around, and E.D. just shrugged her shoulders. I asked Rod about the dire situation. He told me his nephew had been there a week earlier with some friends, and they had polished off the bottle. He had planned to go to Spec's Liquor store in Kerrville to replace it but just hadn't had the time.

E.D. said, "You know what, let's take a short road trip to Kerrville and buy another bottle. It's the least we can do for you guys for letting us stay here, and it will be a good outing for Careless."

Rod agreed and we left Dudley running around with Chico as he drove us back down the hill in his safari vehicle so we could drive E.D.'s car to town. Rod told us to call him when we got back so he could drive down the hill to pick us up. He and Rick would stay with the dogs. It was a beautiful drive to Kerrville. The hills were green and lush with a fresh coat of white frost making it look like a Christmas scene on a Hallmark card. Deer were roaming around as far as the eye could see. They almost looked like Santa's reindeer. We were really enjoying it until two small dogs with short, stubby legs scurried across the highway, right in front of the car. E.D. hit the brakes, and the car came to an abrupt stop. It was a close call. One had black, curly hair, the other tan, short, straight hair. They ran into a parking lot. The building next to it had a sign in front, Medina Children's Home. I got out of the car and coaxed them over to me. It didn't take much; they were super friendly. They both jumped into my arms and started licking my face.

E.D. got out of the car and said, "That's exactly why you'll never get a woman. You're always kissing on a dog." I tried thinking of a snappy comeback, but in my defense, I had recently been shot, and my response time had slowed just a bit. Also, I was very busy getting kissed by some dogs, so I was mostly concentrating on that. E.D. smiled.

"We can't just leave them here," she said. "They'll get run over. What should we do with them, Careless? If only we knew where they lived, we could take them home."

I already knew what to do. With my hands placed on both of them, a vision popped into my head as to where these two hooligans had come from and how they ended up at the Medina Children's Home. This unique gift came in pretty handy.

"I know where they live," I chirped. E.D. looked puzzled.

"Are you sure about this?"

"One hundred percent. Let's put them in the car and take them home. I'll show you the way. This one is Louie," I said, pointing to the black one. "And this one," now pointing to the tan one, "is Winnie."

We all got in the car. Both dogs sat in my lap. "Well, where to, Randy McNally?" she asked.

"Drive about fifty yards straight ahead and take the first left you can make." I could clearly see which way these two had travelled to get here. She turned left on a gravel road. "Go straight until you get to the fork in the road. Then veer left at the big old cypress tree." We passed several ranches with exotic game grazing on them and came to a small stream crossing where a huge cypress tree stood. It had some unusual branches coming from it. If you looked at one lower branch just right, I swear it almost looked like the shape of a rhinoceros head, horns and all.

"You are making me very nervous, Careless. How in the world could you possibly know this? Are you making this up? You just got lucky with the cypress tree, didn't you?"

"Turn left please," I said matter-of-factly. We drove for several minutes and crossed another stream. This one was shallow and had water flowing over it. We pulled up to an old ranch-style cabin. "We're here," I said. It had a sign above the front door, Lodge. E.D. stopped the car and turned it off. We got out, and the two small dogs ran over to the cabin. Two other dogs came running out of a doggie door. One was a white and brown colored cocker spaniel and the other was a small white poodle. They ran out of a little chain link half-height gate that was cracked open just enough for them to get through. They ran to the two dogs we found. They all seemed to know one another. When I had touched the tan dog, I realized that she and her cohort Louie had sneaked out of the open gate.

"This is where they belong," I said.

I saw an image of their owner as well. He was a man with black hair, a mustache, and a wife-beater patch of hair under his lip. He was wearing a black cowboy hat, a black shirt and black jeans, black cowboy boots, and a black jacket that stopped just below his knees. I knew I had seen him somewhere before, but I just couldn't place him. He probably never worried about color-coordinating his clothing. But that's just a guess on my part.

A woman walked out of the Lodge and looked us over. She was a middle-aged, attractive woman with red hair. "Can I help you folks?" she asked.

"How you doing? I'm Careless, and this is my friend E.D. We found those two goobers running around on the highway. We were worried they might get run over, so we scooped 'em up and brought them here. They do belong here, don't they?" I pointed at the dogs.

"I'm Sarah, and I'm dog sitting the Friedmans," she said.

She looked at the two dogs we picked up and then looked at me. "Where in tarnation did you find them? We've been looking all over for them."

"In the parking lot at some place called The Medina Children's Home," I answered.

"Well, I'll be! Kinky was so worried about them! How did you know to bring them here? Did they leave you a trail of breadcrumbs?" She smiled.

"In a manner of speaking," I answered.

"Come again?" she asked.

"Never mind. I'm just glad they're home," I said. She seemed okay with that answer.

"Louie and Winnie, come on over here and say thank you to these nice people," she said. They heard their names and came running. E.D.'s mouth dropped open when she heard their names were mentioned. I pet them and the two other dogs when they came bouncing up to us.

"That one there's Mr. P," Sarah said, pointing to the poodle. "The other one's Sophie."

We played with them and tried to say our goodbyes. "Hold on a minute," Sarah said. "Let me get your contact info. I know Kinky's going to want to thank you."

"Who's Kinky?" E.D. asked. "And no thanks necessary."

"Kinky Friedman! Singer, songwriter, and author! He ran for governor of Texas a while back. And, might I add, an expert mystery solver. I live up the road a spell from him and help him out from time to time."

E.D. said, "Uh, okay, here's my number." She pulled out a business card and forked it over to Sarah.

We waved goodbye and took our leave. Sarah seemed pretty happy to have Louie and Winnie back.

After our brief canine encounter, E.D. and I got in her car and drove away. Sarah waved goodbye, a big Texas grin plastered across her face. We made the drive to Kerrville and stopped at Spec's. This is one of my favorite stores, and the original one in downtown Houston is a lot of fun. Yes, I do have a Spec's card because I am a frequent flyer. You never know when you're going to want an upgrade.

The store was fairly crowded. They were giving out samples of many of the fine liquors they have for sale. Being that I had been on a hiatus for such a long time, I hit each sample – twice. I don't know why they didn't find it amusing when I said to each person pouring the samples, "Make mine a double." E.D. wasn't pleased either.

We got to the tequila aisle, and there was a man signing tequila bottles for customers. I knew I had seen him before, and then it hit me. He was the man I saw when I was holding the two dogs we picked up on the highway. He was their human, Kinky Friedman.

E.D. and I walked up, and he looked at us. "Well, gooooood afternoon. Can I interest you two in some of the finest Mexican mouthwash this side of the border?" He put a big fat cigar in his mouth and waited for a response. His eyes studied us, but mostly E.D. because, let's face it, she's hot.

E.D. said, "I'm not much of a tequila drinker. I think I'll pass. Thank you."

He turned to me, and I gave my stock answer, "Make mine a double."

He squinted at me with his dark eyes for a moment and then launched a toothy grin with the cigar still in his mouth, lodged between his upper and lower choppers. He had some pretty nice pearly whites for a cigar smoker. I guess the tequila brightened up his smile a bit. I knew it would do wonders for mine as well. He poured two shots from his Man In Black tequila bottle and handed me one. He held up his shot glass, and I did the same.

"To honor. Git on 'er and stay on 'er," he said. We clinked glasses and downed the Mexican mouthwash.

"Choo, choo, choo, choo, choo, gooooood," he said.

I must admit, I was deeply moved and amused all at the same time. E.D. was not. Maybe it was the tequila and all of the other samples I had been drinking, but I liked this guy. He reminded me of somebody. I just couldn't remember who.

"How many bottles do you want?" he asked.

A darn good salesman.

"I'll take two," I said.

E.D. gave me one of her looks, and I said, "What? One for us and one for Rod and Rick."

Kinky signed two bottles that had his image on the label and said, "Thank you for being American."

I chuckled. The Mexican mouthwash had definitely gone to my head. "I just want you to know Louie and Winnie are safely home now. You don't have to worry about them any longer."

He got a strange look on his face and was about to ask, I can only assume, how I knew about Louie and Winnie, when a lot of customers stampeded in with Man In Black tequila bottles they wanted signed. Popular stuff. They crowded me out and stepped in between us. E.D and I were relegated to the back of the line. It was almost like Man In Black Friday at Wal-Mart, where everyone is trying to buy the one discounted big-screen TV. It had been fun, but we made our way to the bourbon aisle when it became obvious things might get unruly.

I was going to buy a bottle of Jack Daniels to start preparing my coffee, using the correct method of choice. A guy was setting up another sample station right as we walked up. I stopped in my tracks. No way was I going to pass up a free sample. Besides, I wasn't driving home.

"Would you be interested in sampling some fine Texas bourbon?" he asked.

I looked at E.D. and yes, I said it. "I sure as heck would. Make mine a double."

25

He laughed and said, "I'm Dan Garrison, and this is Garrison Brothers Bourbon made in Hye, Texas." Frankly, after all the samples I had tried, I was already feeling a little Hye. "I have three different ones here. I have our original bourbon, our single barrel, and our Cowboy Bourbon. Which one would you like to try?"

"Well, Dan, the name's Careless, and this is my friend E.D. You have such a wide variety here, I'm afraid I just can't make up my mind. I'll most likely have to try them all."

"The customer's always right," he said.

E.D. wasn't really tickled pink about my shenanigans. I tried the first two, and Dan told me all about them and how they were made. The regular bourbon was very good. The single barrel was fantastic. The Cowboy Bourbon was magnificent.

"We'll have two bottles of the Cowboy Bourbon, good sir," I said. Dan was happy. In fact, I just had two servings of the Cowboy Bourbon while writing this and am having a hard time distinguishing the keys on my typewriter. Does anybody even use typewriters anymore? I don't know. The bourbon is one hundred proof. Proof that great writing can sometimes come from the contents of a bottle. But I digress…

"You're obviously a man of fine taste," Dan said. He handed me two bottles of the exquisite bourbon. "Thank you very much," he said.

"I thought you wanted to buy Jack Daniels for your coffee," E.D. said to me.

"You know, I did, E.D., but once you leave Jack, you never go back. Am I right?" I asked. Garrison Brothers is my new bourbon of choice. I know what you're thinking, but it wasn't an easy decision for me. So please support me on this.

"You know, ever since the Mexican mouthwash aisle, you haven't been the same," she said.

"Choo, choo, choo, choo, choo, gooooood," I responded with a big smile on my face. I was feeling pretty good. Did I mention I love Spec's?

We checked out (I actually checked out after consuming the Mexican mouthwash) and drove back to Highland Ranch. I'm sure I had a great night later on but, frankly, didn't remember a whole lot after we got back to the ranch. I woke up with a golden-haired beauty in bed with me. Dudley is his name and spooning is his game. I know, I was almost thinking the same thing you were. But no E.D. Just me and my boy. One thing I know for sure, when you lie down with dogs, you don't get up with E.D.

The next day we had a fine home cooked breakfast and then hiked for a bit with the dogs. I cleared my head from the day before. Note to self: no more Mexican mouthwash. I was back to full strength and everything seemed right in the world. This trip had done wonders for me.

After lunch, E.D.'s cell phone began having convulsions. Dudley became interested and in his usual fashion, attempted to answer it. He grabbed it right out of her purse with his big slobbery mouth and said something. He must have pushed the right button with his tongue because I could hear a goober-garbled voice on the other end trying to communicate with the living. Of course, I was a little worried that Dudley may not be long in the land of the living after his mastication of E.D.'s phone. She was clearly not amused.

"Give me the phone, ya big dope," she commanded. Sure enough, he flipped his head upward, opened his mouth, and the not-so-waterproof phone went flying through the air towards her. The rest of us were amused and it visibly showed as we laughed out loud. I think Dudley may have even laughed – a little, until E.D. shot us some dirty looks. It got quiet real fast after that.

"Yes, sure, I remember you. I'm so glad they are okay. No, no thanks necessary. Well, I'll have to ask him. Hold on one second." E.D. turned to me. "Careless, it's your Mexican Mouthwash Man from yesterday." Now my head was having memory throbs (not to be confused with heart throbs, two very different things, not that there's anything wrong with either). "He wants to take us to dinner for saving his dogs. Do you want to go? He wants to meet us in Kerrville at The Flying Dragon."

"Not really, but I'll do it anyway," I responded.

"Okay, seven o'clock at The Flying Dragon. See you there," she said to the Mexican Mouthwash Man, then hung up the phone and got a paper towel from the kitchen to dry it off. I smiled because, despite his efforts, I knew Dudley would never be that great at answering the phone. I admired his effort. He seemed very determined.

E.D. and I left Dudley with the boys that night and drove into Kerrville. We were on Highway 16 when we saw Kinky driving in front of us. He was hard to miss. He was driving an old burnt orange Cadillac convertible with the top down. It seemed a little cool outside to me, but he was wearing a jacket and didn't seem bothered by the weather. I guess that Mexican mouthwash does wonders to warm you up.

"Can you believe that? How does he keep that black cowboy hat from flying off of his head with the top down?" she asked.

"I don't know the answer to that, but we should do an experiment to research it. I think you should wear a hat with your top down and see if it stays on. I bet it doesn't."

"That's one experiment that won't be taking place," she said with the cutest little smirk. "I should have known better than to try to have a normal conversation with you, Careless."

"Not even with a grant? I just wanted to do it in the name of science. Just think of the breakthroughs we could have." I continued on as we entered the city of Kerrville.

Before she could come back with a snappy retort, a dark unmarked van pulled out abruptly in front of Kinky, and he skidded to a stop. The van came within inches of t-boning him. And still, his black cowboy hat managed to stay atop his head. Now that's talent. E.D. came to an abrupt stop just inches before she almost hit the back bumper of Kinky's convertible.

We were all shaken up, so we pulled to the side of the road right in front of an art gallery, where the van had sped off. E.D. and I got out of the car, and Kinky got out of his. "Are you two okay?" he asked.

"Yes," we both answered.

"I can't believe that guy almost hit The Yome Kipper Clipper," he said, inspecting his vehicle.

E.D. and I looked at one another. I had no idea what he was talking about. Had he been downing Mexican mouthwash? E.D. finally got up enough nerve to ask, "Yome Kipper Clipper? What is a Yome Kipper Clipper?"

"Oh, that's my Cadillac. The Yome Kipper Clipper," he responded with a big, toothy grin, separated by a big lit cigar. This guy definitely had mastered multi-tasking.

"Why do you call your car The Yome Kipper Clipper? Why not a normal name like I did with my car, Betsy here?" she asked while pointing at her car.

"Well, little lady, I call it The Yome Kipper Clipper because it stops on a dime… and then picks it up," he said as he puffed on his cigar.

Not being Jewish, she didn't get the humor. On the other hand, I broke out laughing. Of course, one doesn't have to be Jewish to appreciate good humor, but it doesn't hoyt. I knew I was going to hit it off with him, and from the way he was eyeballing me I could tell he felt the same way.

While we were all inspecting our cars like insurance adjusters, I glanced at the art gallery and noticed it was called the Copper Love Art Gallery. It had a big red and white banner hanging up above the door that read: Merry Christmas. It was then that I noticed the door had been flung open so hard, it had almost completely come off of the hinges. It was wide open, like someone had made a hasty getaway. Kinky noticed the same thing and motioned his head toward the door, which some might confuse with a nervous twitch. But I was pretty sure he wanted us to go in the gallery with him and check out what was what.

I walked in the gallery, followed by Kinky and E.D. It was a big mess. There had obviously been a struggle. There was blood on the floor and some on the walls. Lots of blood. There were also two bodies on the floor. One was a female with long red hair, and the other was a Middle Eastern-looking man sporting a long, bushy, dark mustache. E.D.'s eyes were as wide as the Grand Canyon. My guess is it brought back some not so fond memories of when she witnessed me being shot. Frankly, I wasn't too fond of it myself.

"E.D., you stay back and we'll check this out," I blurted out. I was a little excited – not in a good way. My adrenaline was on full throttle. I didn't think there was anyone left lurking around by the way we had witnessed the getaway, but you just never know.

I quietly and quickly walked over to the man on the floor and placed my forefinger on his neck, but there was no pulse. His expiration date had definitely come and gone. There was a big gash on the top of his head and a bleeding wound just above his ribs. His neck was pretty bruised up as well. I looked at Kinky and shook my head. E.D. covered her mouth.

Kinky was standing over the woman's body and I fully expected the same outcome. But I was pleasantly surprised as her eyes started to flutter, and she began mumbling some incoherent words. I could barely make it out but I thought I heard her say "lamb." She put both arms around him and tried to stand up.

E.D. was busy calling 911. Her voice sounded frantic. The Kerrville Police were Johnny On The Spot. They showed up within minutes, just as Kinky had the woman sitting up, her arms around him.

"Sir, step away from her with your arms in the air," a policeman ordered. His gun was drawn. Kinky lifted both hands in the air, slowly stood up, and backed away from her.

Another policeman had his bead on me and said, "Step away from him with your hands up!" That's exactly what I did.

"Wait a minute, you've got this all wrong. We just got here. Someone almost ran us down in front of the gallery, so we stopped and came in to render aid," E.D. explained.

"Ma'am, just wait back there and don't move," one of the policemen said to her.

"I'll need to see some I.D. for all of you," the other policeman said. All three of us slowly reached into our pockets and produced our driver's licenses. It was a good thing I left Dudley with Chico and the boys back at the ranch. He wouldn't have liked this one bit. And besides, he let his driver's license expire several months ago.

The policemen took our licenses and lowered their guns. The woman stood up and introduced herself. "I'm Copper Love, and I own the gallery." The artwork hanging on the wall was beautiful. The blood splattered on it really added a nice quality to it.

"These folks helped me out. I was robbed. I must have been knocked out because I don't really remember a whole lot until these folks came in and woke me up." A short, muscular policemen with a brown mustache walked over to the dead body, snapped some tight blue plastic gloves on and checked for a pulse. He wouldn't find one unless the guy came back from the dead. That would have been a neat trick. He called for an ambulance and the coroner with his radio.

"Okay ma'am, we're going to need to take your statement," a different tall, slim policeman said. "And you three stay here so we can get your statements afterwards."

The three of us sat on a sofa, and E.D. started recapping what had just happened. Neither Kinky nor I were fully listening to her. We were concentrating on what Copper had to say to the coppers. See what I did there?

Copper said she was packing up some paintings to ship overseas to one of her largest corporate clients, who purchased exclusively online. At that point, the coroner showed up and started taking pictures of the dead body. I wanted to say, "Smile for the camera," but I thought it might be in poor taste and didn't want to possibly incriminate myself. The dead guy was definitely not ready for his close-up, Mr. DeMille. Kinky and I just watched, and E.D. gave us a play by play. They hauled the body off, and an EMT treated Copper for a head trauma.

The shorter policemen walked over to us and gave us our licenses back. He took our statements one by one and our contact information. We all pretty much said the same thing, which was we were driving along on the way to the restaurant when a dark unmarked van almost ran into Kinky. At that point we almost ran into the Yome Kippur Clipper, when he suddenly stopped. After we pulled over to collect ourselves, we noticed the gallery door was wide open. We walked in and found the crime scene – just as the policemen had. That was our story and he seemed satisfied with it, for now. Afterwards, he told us we were free to leave and if they had any further questions we would be contacted.

Copper appeared shaken but not stirred and managed to force a smile on her face while waving goodbye. She mouthed the words, "Thank you."

Since all that excitement made us even hungrier than we already were, we decided to continue on to The Flying Dragon. Kinky drove his Yome Kipper Clipper, and we followed behind him. The parking lot was really crowded – a good sign. We hoped the restaurant would take our minds off of what we had just witnessed.

There was a line of people waiting for tables. "Your usual table, Kinky?" a nice young lady asked him.

"Thank ya very much, yes," he answered in a low, raspy southern twang.

I felt kind of bad cutting in front of all the starving people, but not bad enough to keep me from being seated at Kinky's table. It's all who you know. This time it worked out well for us.

"Do you mind if I order for us?" Kinky asked. "Is there anything in particular you don't eat?" E.D. and I looked at one another and shook our heads. "Perfect, we'll have the Daddy Dragon for the table," he told the waitress who was anxiously standing by.

"You got it Kinky," she said as she sprinted off to get the order in.

"Wow, what an exciting evening," E.D. said. I can't get over what happened. I've never seen a crime scene like that, not to mention a dead body. Just crazy."

The waitress brought some Wonton soup.

Kinky was quiet. I could see the wheels spinning around under his black cowboy hat. I too had questions about what we had seen earlier, but I waited and tried the soup. It was delicious.

"You know," Kinky said, "in a former life, when I lived in New York, I solved many mysteries. I gave it up years ago when I moved to Texas. Now I just perform concerts and write books. I tell you, after tonight, this almost makes me want to bring the Kinkster out of retirement."

"That's so funny," E.D. said. "Careless sometimes consults with the police department back in Houston and has solved several cases for them. You two should work together. It would be a perfect match. You sure already think alike and act alike."

The waitress brought the Daddy Dragon Dinner to the table. I didn't recognize any of the food, but it sure smelled good. What the hell? When in Rome... I snagged something deep-fried and forked it into my mouth. Damn delicious.

Everyone was eating so I responded to E.D.'s observation, "Yes, Kinky, we could start the Reese's Peanut Butter Cup agency," I said. "Which one would you want to be, the peanut butter or the chocolate?"

"Don't get all racial on me, Careless. Waitret, oh waitret, may I get a new plate – and some more water please? You were saying, Careless…"

I'd never heard anyone use the word "waitret" before. It threw me off a bit, but I answered, "I don't know, something just didn't add up at the gallery tonight. I can't quite put my finger on it, but it just didn't feel right."

"Don't get all paranoid, Careless. According to the police, it was a simple robbery gone bad. You'll have to forgive Careless, he's had a recent run-in with The Grim Reaper and hasn't been the same since. Have you, Careless?" E.D. patted the back of my shoulder like she was my mother.

"Well, sounds to me like he may need a checkup from the neck up, if you know what I mean," Kinky said with a grin. I could tell from the expression in his eyes that he agreed with my assessment of things not adding up. He's got a great face for playing Texas Hold 'Em.

"Listen, I really just wanted to thank you two for finding Winnie and Louie. Those two little boogers snuck out while I was away, and I'm so glad they made it safely back home. You know, most people would have just left them on the highway to fend for themselves. It takes a special person to stop and help out an animal in need. I wish more people were like you. So, I'm in your debt. I hope you like the dinner. It's on me. It's the least I can do."

"We're just glad it worked out, aren't we, Careless?" E.D. said. I wasn't really paying attention to the conversation. I was still trying to figure out what a checkup from the neck up meant and if perhaps I needed one.

"Careless, cat got your tongue?" E.D. asked. I never understood that phrase. I'm not really a cat person.

"Thank you for dinner, Kinky," I said once we'd eaten the last of the Daddy Dragon Dinner. "It was really good. Unfortunately, we have to drive back to Houston tomorrow, and I left my young man, Dudley, back at the ranch with my friends. So I've got to get back to him before he starts missing me and having a bout of separation anxiety. Then he might need a check up from the neck up."

"Oh, so, you're a Homo Erectus? I didn't connect this," Kinky said. This guy was pretty sly – working his song lyrics into the conversation. That takes talent. Yes, I looked up his songs and books on the internet after we met him at Spec's.

"You know, Kinky, sometimes I think he is," E.D. chirped as she began to laugh out loud. She lovingly patted me on the back.

"First of all, I don't play for the other team. Not that there's anything wrong with that. Second of all, Dudley is my dog and soulmate, not that there's anything wrong with that either. I just don't want him eating another sofa, just as he's done in the past when I left him alone for too long. What a mess he made of that sofa. I still haven't found all of the pieces. It's a mystery where some of them are."

"Oh, I completely understand. I have to get back to the Friedmans as well. They really don't like it when I leave them for too long. It was nice meeting you both. I hope to see you again. Maybe you can come to one of my concerts when I'm on tour again. Your names will be on the list."

"That would be wonderful. We'd love to," E.D. said.

With that, we parted ways. Kinky drove off into the sunset wearing his black cowboy hat, driving his Yome Kipper Clipper, and we drove off in Betsy. Why do people name their cars? I don't get that. I'm pretty sure I heard an "Ay Yeeeee…" coming from Kinky off in the distance.

We drove back to Highland Ranch. Thankfully, Rod and Rick's sofa was intact. Dudley met us at the top of the hill. He jumped up on me and placed his paws over my shoulders. While we were hugging, I placed my hands on his back. I instantly saw what he had done while I was away. He and Chico ate a nice homemade dinner of chicken and rice Rick made for them. Then they went outside and chased a few rabbits. They didn't catch any – but it was close. Then they chewed on some antler bones Rod gave them. They had a great evening, but not as exciting as ours.

"Dudley was fine while you were gone, Careless," Rod said. "He ate dinner and played around outside with Chico. He did great." Of course, I already knew all that but didn't want to spoil Rod's fun of telling me or make him think I didn't care. I held my tongue. "How'd your dinner go with Kinky?" he asked.

"You are not going to believe this," E.D. said. "On the way to dinner, we almost got smashed into by a speeding getaway van. And then we witnessed a crime scene at an art gallery, where someone died. The police arrived later, and it was just wild. I've never seen anything quite like it." Rod and Rick were totally engrossed. I listened halfheartedly. Something about the crime scene stuck in my craw. What were the robbers after? Why did Copper Love mumble something about a lamb? There was no lamb at the gallery, not even a painting of a lamb. How did she manage to stay alive when it was obvious she was outnumbered? There was one dead robber and at least one other driving the getaway van. These were the things that popped into my head – besides the obvious things, of course.

"What do you think happened, Careless?" Rod asked after E.D. finished her tale. She was all excited and certainly seemed all wound up.

"Well, it's exactly as E.D. described. It was a pretty brutal crime scene. But the Daddy Dragon meal was pretty darn good. I highly recommend it."

"Huh?" Rick asked.

"Oh, never mind him. He's talking about the dinner Kinky ordered at The Flying Dragon," E.D. said.

"Ah, got it," Rick said. The TV was on, and a news channel was showing a video feed of a missile blowing up on a launch pad. The caption underneath it read: *Missile malfunctions and blows up on launch pad in North Korea*. I started thinking that some scientists and military personnel were going to be fed to the hogs tonight in North Korea.

"But what did you think about the crime scene, Careless?" Rod asked. "Surely your expertise with the cases you've solved gave you some ideas."

"Yes, tell us what you think happened, Inspector Clouseau," E.D. chimed in while smiling.

"Well, I think it was a robbery gone bad, and someone ended up dead. Now it's a police matter."

"Isn't that exactly what I just said?" E.D. asked.

It was, but that's not all I suspected. That's just what I divulged.

"Why, yes it was, my dear. You have a keen eye." She had an air of satisfaction about her. It suits her.

"And dinner was fabulous," she said. "The food was great, and Kinky got us in without waiting in line. He even paid for it."

"That's the part I liked best," I said.

"Did you know he solved mysteries when he lived in New York? Now he tours and he even invited us to one of his concerts. I think he and Careless should start solving mysteries together. I think they'd make a great team. What do you guys think?"

Rod and Rick nodded in unison and said they agreed with her.

"Well, we'll see what the future brings," I said. "Tomorrow, we'll head home, and I'll settle back into my life. You guys have been wonderful hosts. We had a great time, and I'm feeling like my old self again. And Dudley always loves to see Chico."

We stayed up for a while talking about this and that. I tried to pay attention for the most part and participated when necessary, but the events of the day made my mind wander off. Questions, I had all of these questions circulating in my head. Why did I get shot after my last case? Why did I almost die? And how did Dudley show me the way back? After I awoke from my coma, how was I able to read dogs thoughts when I touch them? And how did Copper survive the robbery when someone obviously killed one of the robbers? Who killed him? These are the questions I wanted answers to, and in no particular order. Since I wasn't driving tomorrow, I made a Careless Coffee for a night cap. But this time, I used Garrison Brothers Cowboy Bourbon instead Jack Daniels. Variety is the spice of life. Am I right? Cowboy Bourbon Careless Coffee is my new favorite.

We all said our goodnights and went to our respective bedrooms. Thankfully there was a hottie in the house so I wouldn't have to sleep alone. He followed me to my bedroom and snuggled in bed with me. Dudley's the best security blanket a guy could have. I had almost dozed off when I heard the bedroom door creak open. Dudley's tail started slapping the bed in rapid fashion. I put my hand on his back and I saw that he smelled E.D.

"Why didn't you guys put a hanger on the outside door knob if you two wanted to be alone? Do I have to teach you everything?" For a minute I thought I was back in college. By the way, that hanger thing never really worked. The sock wrapped around the door knob, on the other hand, had about a fifty-fifty shot. And I didn't have any hangers in college anyway.

"I can ask Dudley to wait outside if you want me to get a hanger out of the closet," I offered. Dudley said something. Apparently, he didn't like that idea.

"The only thing coming out of the closet is probably you, Careless." Well, I did give her the perfect set-up for that snappy comeback. I blame myself for that. She appeared to be rather amused with herself.

"Alright, Amy Schumer, what's going on? Why'd you sneak into my bedroom in the middle of the night?" I asked.

"To be honest with you, I'm a little worried about you. You just haven't been yourself since the shooting. And that thing you do with the dogs, that's just unnatural." I shrugged my shoulders. Funny girl had disappeared and concerned girl was now staring me in the face. "What's going on with you?"

"I'll be honest, I have the same concerns you do. In fact, I was just thinking about that earlier. But I feel great. In fact, I feel like I'm one hundred percent. The dog thing? I can't explain it. I don't know if it's temporary, or what. I'm just going to look at it as a gift. Please don't tell anybody about it. I don't want people thinking I'm weird."

"People already think you're weird, Careless. A little late for that. I mean, people call you Careless." She smiled. I guess the comedienne was back.

"I'm fine. Don't worry about me. Let's get some sleep. We have a long drive ahead of us tomorrow. Unless you're reconsidering that hanger thing." Can't blame a guy for trying.

"No hanger necessary. I'll see you in the morning." She came closer and kissed me on the forehead. Then she grabbed Dudley's big head with both hands and planted a very loud, extra-long smooch on his handsome head. At least I know where I stand with her.

12

I woke up with my partner in crime staring at me. Just like he always does. He made it hard for me to extricate myself from his Kung Fu grip and get out of bed, but I weaseled my way out. I went to the restroom, drained the main vein, and showered. Then I walked outside with Dudley so he could do the same. E.D., Rod, and Rick were waiting for us with coffee (less my special ingredient), watching a magnificent Hill Country sunrise. Friend, that never gets old. And even when I'm old, it still won't be old.

Dudley and Chico ran around like mashuganas (it's Yiddish – look it up) and did their business. We didn't say much, mesmerized by the sunrise. When we finished our coffee, we loaded up the safari vehicle. We hugged one another and said our goodbyes. Dudley licked Chico's snout. Rod drove us down the hill and we transferred our things to E.D.'s car. Rod said, "It was great having you guys over again. Come back whenever you want. And you too, Dudley." Dudley of course said something. We laughed. It had been a good trip.

As we travelled back to Houston, E.D. asked me a lot of questions about the crime scene we had witnessed at the art gallery. "What do you think the robbers were after? How did Copper Love survive that brutal attack? Do you think something was stolen? Who killed one of the robbers? Have you ever seen a murder before?"

I tried to answer her questions as best I could. I really did not have a lot of information to go on, so I kept it vague and nebulous. And I can't believe I just wrote the word nebulous. I figured at least that way, there was a better than average chance I wouldn't be wrong. What really concerned me was the dark gray, late model sedan that had been following us since we got back on the highway. It was a BMW 5 Series with the windows blacked out. Whoever was driving it did a masterful job of trying not to be noticed. They would pull behind an SUV or motor home for good measure, but they were definitely following us. I didn't tell E.D. No need to make her nervous.

We stopped about halfway home at a fabulous gas station and grocery store in Luling to stretch our legs and use their exquisite facilities. I kept a watchful eye on the sedan. As we exited the highway, it sped ahead. I guess I was just being paranoid. I was relieved to be wrong. Even though we had Dudley to protect us, I didn't need any more chaos in my life – especially after the outcome of the last case I had worked on.

E.D. went inside and I filled Betsy with gas. I let Dudley do his business in the lush, grassy area dedicated to dogs. The sign at the gas station read, "You have to pee it to believe it," about their restrooms. Dudley definitely peed it and he looked like he believed it. When he was done, I turned around and did not like what I saw. It's hell being right. The sedan was parked right next to E.D.'s car. A Middle Eastern looking man emerged from the passenger's side front seat and was walking toward Betsy. I froze for a moment. When he reached for the door handle, E.D. came barreling up with drinks and food, tying up both of her arms. Oblivious to what was transpiring, she almost walked right into this dude. Her eyes widened.

"Just what do you think you're doing?" she forcefully exclaimed. He turned and looked at her. He wasn't backing down, and I could tell he meant business. Dudley was standing right next to me and saw the same thing. The hair on his back was standing straight up.

I lightly tapped him on the head with my fingers and commanded, "Go get him, boy!" He didn't even look up at me. He made a beeline for the man making threatening gestures towards E.D. She wasn't backing down either. Before he could react, he had a ninety-five pound, very muscular Black Mouth Cur hanging on to his pants leg. He lifted his shirt and was about to brandish a handgun concealed in his waistband. When I saw what he was contemplating, I hauled ass over to him. No way was he taking out my best friend. E.D. was oblivious to the handgun and was still loudly yacking away at him.

He saw me coming in rapid fashion, and I could tell he was quickly and methodically surveying the situation. He made the correct decision to flee and swiftly ran back to his car, dragging Dudley with him. Dudley planted his feet and shook his head back and forth, which severely slowed him down. He made it to the car when his pants legged ripped. Dudley had a big hunk of pants in his mouth as he quickly slipped back into the BMW. I whistled to Dudley, and he galloped to my side with his prize dangling from his mouth. The car sped off. I couldn't see anything inside of the vehicle.

Now I was certain there was more to the robbery at the art gallery than met the eye.

"Good boy, Dudley," E.D. said. "Thank you for protecting me." She put the drinks and food on the roof of her car and bent down and hugged him. "Did you see that, Careless? Dudley was really protective when that strange man tried to break into Betsy. You just never know what kind of people you'll run into at gas stations. I'm going to report this to the manager. I'll be right back." She walked back into the store. I took the section of ripped pants from Dudley's mouth, rolled it up, and stuck it in my pocket. It might prove to be useful later on.

We were driving back to Houston and E.D. was all abuzz. She kept recounting how she held her own against the strange man, of course with the help of Dudley. I just nodded and agreed with everything she said. Something was very wrong, and someone was obviously after us for a reason I didn't know–yet. It must have been something to do with the robbery we stumbled into. The dead man at the gallery looked Middle Eastern, just like the man with the gun at the gas station.

I didn't see the car following us anymore. When we finally made it home and got out of the car, I scanned the distance but didn't see anything unusual, unless you count Sarge. He's slightly unusual and came strolling up with a bag of groceries. Dudley did his business, and I carried E.D.'s bag upstairs for her. Dudley and I went to our loft, and I fed and watered him. He ate and drank and promptly went to our sofa for a snooze. My mind was stuck on something, but I couldn't quite figure out what. Something was bothering me.

I called Detective Present with the Houston Police Department. I had consulted for him on many cases, and he owed me a few favors. "Good afternoon, may I please speak with Detective Present? The name's Careless and yes, I'll hold for him." Dudley was watching me with one eye open, so I pointed to the telephone with my index finger and said in a quiet voice, "I'm on hold." Why I was speaking to a dog about this, I didn't know.

"Hi Detective Present. Yes, I'm doing well. And you? I'm feeling much better. Listen, I think E.D. and I stumbled into something this weekend that has me a little perplexed. There was a robbery and a death at an art gallery yesterday in Kerrville. No, we didn't witness it, but we walked in at the tail-end of it," I said.

"There was a dead man who was most certainly Middle Eastern and we were followed almost the whole way back to Houston by a dark gray sedan. Yes, I'm sure. In fact, a Middle Eastern looking man who was a passenger in the car stopped when we were getting gas in Luling and tried to rifle through E.D.'s car. He was obviously looking for something. He wasn't successful. E.D. walked up on him before he got into the car and when he wouldn't back down, Dudley tried to take a chunk out of his leg. I think he mostly got pants but who knows? And Detective Present, he was carrying a handgun. A Baby Desert Eagle. I got a good look at it when he started reaching for it."

"That does sound very unusual," Detective Present said. "It was probably just an attempted robbery, but I'll make some phone calls to the Kerrville and Luling police departments and see if we can get a little reciprocity. Just keep in mind, it is out of my jurisdiction, so don't be surprised if they don't cooperate. We may not get any answers."

"Work your magic, sir. Let's see what they come back with. Also, is there any way to analyze this sample of pants Dudley ripped off of the guy at the gas station?"

"I'll give it my best shot. Send the pants sample over and I'll have the lab take a look at it."

"That's all I can ask for. Please let me know what you find out."

I hung up the phone and sat on the sofa with Dudley. My fear was we hadn't heard the last of this. And I was hoping that this time I was incorrect.

Birk, Sarge, and E.D. came over that evening. I'm sure they just wanted to see how I was doing. They even brought dinner from China Garden. Nothing like a little Lemon Chicken to get you as right as rain. They probably thought I was nuts because I claimed I can read dogs thoughts just by touching them. A claim, which by the way, that happens to be true and verified. I don't really read their thoughts. It's almost like we're having a conversation without words. Of course, if I were Birk, Sarge, or E.D., I might just think I was a nut job as well. But this nut did have a job. And I would need to go to sleep early enough to make it there by the crack of dawn tomorrow. After we ate and went over and over the details of the robbery and the incident at the gas station, I told them all to scram. When Birk was leaving, I handed him the sample of cloth Dudley had separated from the pants leg of the guy at the gas station. I asked him to take it to Detective Present at the police station in the morning. He agreed to do it.

Later that night, I fed and watered Dudley and took him outside to do his business. When we got back inside, the answering machine was blinking like it had a nervous tick. I hit the button and this is what played over the speaker, "Careless, it's Kinky. Careless, it's Kinky. Kinky here. We've got a little problem. Call me at the ranch." Once I heard our names mentioned together, I wondered how in the blazes of Hades two grown men could have such strange names. But I digress…

The message was recorded at 10:30 pm. It must be urgent if he called that late. I picked up the phone and called him. "Kinky Richard Big Dick Friedman here. Start talking."

"Kinky, it's Careless. I got your message. It sounded kind of urgent. Is everything okay? What's the malfunction?"

"Well, I did run out of cigars, so that's pretty tedious. But also, I played a benefit concert for a local animal shelter, and when I got back, my place had been completely ransacked. Looked like a hurricane hit it. The Friedmans are fine, but not too good at being watch dogs. Watching appears to be all they did. Not a damn thing was taken, but whoever was here sure tore the place up looking for something. I really think it has something to do with that robbery we came across yesterday. What do you think?"

"I think we need to get you some more cigars, and you're one hundred percent correct about the robbery. In fact, someone was following us yesterday in a dark sedan almost the whole way back to Houston. And I feel like I've been watched ever since I've been back. Maybe I'm paranoid. But something very strange is going on."

"Hey, Careless, someone's beeping in on my call waiting. Can you hold for a minute? I'll be right back."

"Sure thing, Kinky." He put me on hold. What the hell, I guess if I have a hard time waking up tomorrow, I'll just have to be a few minutes late to work.

The line clicked and all I heard was a dial tone. Now I was thinking the worst. What if Kinky was followed as well? And what if that Middle Eastern looking dude was holding a gun on him? Or worse? I quickly hit the redial button.

"Kinky Richard Big Dick Friedman here. Start talking. Careless? Oh, I still haven't mastered the art of call waiting. Sorry about that. But you won't believe this. That was Copper Love, the owner of the art gallery in Kerrville. She said she's missing an item from the gallery and wants to hire us to help her track it down. I haven't done any private eye work since I left New York and am itching to get back in it. What do you say? Are you interested?"

"I say hell yeah. It would be an honor to work with you."

"Well, let's git on 'er and stay on 'er," he said. I guess I set myself up for that one.

"Did she tell you what was missing?" I asked.

"She sure did. A painting that she had sold to an overseas client. And it was supposed to ship the night it went missing. Very strange."

"It sure is, Kinky. It sure is."

Kinky had a concert coming up in Houston in two days. He told me he would call Copper Love and take the case, depending on how much she was willing to pay. I agreed and told him I would meet him at the concert.

Dudley and I fell back into our routine and went to sleep. When we woke up, we went to breakfast at Papa's house the next morning. Then we went to the office. It was a normal day. Dudley went outside through his doggie door to take care of business and harass truck drivers – many of whom probably deserved it. I took sales calls, but for some reason, every time I picked up the phone, I heard clicking noises on it. I called the repair number on the telephone bill, and they said they would run some tests and get back with me. I was sure they would do nothing about it – or just not in my lifetime. The complaint department is never that enthusiastic.

Later that afternoon, Detective Present called.

"Hello Detective Present. How are you today?"

"Better than you Careless."

"What does that mean?"

"Well, for starters, you know the aftermath of that robbery at the art gallery you witnessed?"

"Yes," I said.

"I called the chief of police myself, and there is no record of it. Zero. Zilch. Nada. It's as if it didn't occur. And worse, I called the gas station where you said you had the incident with the Middle Eastern gentleman. When I asked for a copy of the videos they always keep for security reasons, I was told that the video recorder must have malfunctioned that day because no recording existed. I just have to ask this. I know you had a close brush with death, and I'm glad you're feeling better, but do you think all of what you told me really happened?" I could hear the hesitation in his voice and knew he was sincerely concerned, while trying to remain helpful.

"I'm as sure of it as any case I've ever worked on. In fact, I was just retained by a colleague to recover a missing painting for the gallery owner. She claimed it was stolen during the alleged robbery that very night. Why would I get hired to locate a stolen painting if the whole thing never happened?"

"I don't know. I can't explain that. What do you mean alleged? We have a really bad connection. Why don't I stop by your place after work and we'll have a drink and talk about your mental state?"

"Okay, you know where I live. But I can assure you, after a few drinks, my mental state may be suspect. And speaking of suspects..." I paused. The phone line was really acting up with static. "I haven't been drinking much lately due to doctor's orders, so I'm really going to need to build my tolerance back up. You can help me with that, can't you?"

"I'll give it my best shot, Careless."

"Speaking of shots, I've got a new bourbon I'm trying on for size. I'll get your take on it when you get here."

"Hey, did Birk drop off the sample of cloth to you that Dudley separated from the man at the gas station?"

"We got it, Careless. The boys in the lab are analyzing it as we speak. Are you sure it came from someone's pants leg and not something your dog just found somewhere?"

"Pretty sure. Let's talk tonight." I hung up the phone.

I couldn't believe he was doubting me. That was out of character for him. After all of the cases I successfully worked on and solved for him, I can't believe he would even ask that. Well, we'll have that conversation when he comes over tonight.

Dudley and I finished up a rather uneventful day and went home. We did our usual routine. I broke out the Cowboy Bourbon and sampled it in my iced coffee in advance of Detective Present's arrival. I just wanted to make sure it was still delicious. It was. It majorly enhances the taste of my other favorite – Katz Coffee.

Dudley alerted me he was at the door before he knocked. I opened the door and he looked surprised. "Come on in, Detective," I said. Detective Present is a tall, thin, fairly muscular man. He's got light brown hair and a short, cropped beard of the same color. He was wearing a wrinkled gray suit of mediocre quality. "I've got the Cowboy Bourbon ready to go," I said. He held his hand up, briefly waved, and walked in.

I closed the door and poured us a couple of glasses. At over a hundred proof, I thought it should be on the rocks to let it simmer down a bit. But it is full flavored and darn tasty.

We both took a few sips and he started talking, "I've checked into the incidents you called me about, and since I can find no evidence of either actually occurring, my suggestion to you is to let this one go. There will be plenty of other cases for you to work on. This one is just a dead end."

I raised an eyebrow. "What about the cloth sample? How did that turn out?"

"Ah, yes, well, it turns out there was a little snafu at the lab, and somehow the sample you sent over got misplaced," he said sheepishly and somewhat concerned.

I raised both eyebrows. "And you don't find that odd?" I asked. I could hardly wait to hear his response. Something really stunk about this case. You'd have to be High On Jesus to not see all of the strange things going on with this case were not connected.

I started to vocalize a few more inquiries, but before I could, he held up his hand to stop me from talking. He pulled out a pad of paper, wrote something down, and said, "This is some damn good bourbon. Where did you get it?"

"I found it at Specs in Kerrville. I met the owner of the distillery, and he was very nice. So, I bought a couple of bottles. It's my Jack Daniels replacement therapy." While I was talking, I was reading what he had written down. *You are being surveilled by the Feds. Your phones are probably tapped. When I started looking into what you asked me about, I was quickly and decisively told to drop it. No ifs, ands, or buts. Just say you agree with me that you won't proceed. You need to be really careful on this one. It's something major. Nod your head if you understand.*

I nodded my head. "Would you like another round?" I asked.

"Sure, why not. You're paying," he said, laughing nervously.

"You know, you're probably right. I'm going to let this case go. If there's no evidence, then what's the point of me banging my head against the wall? I'll just wait for the next case to present itself," I said. I didn't mean a word of it. Now I was even more intrigued.

"I think that's a wise decision, Careless," he said, nodding his head to approve of my performance. "Well, thanks for the great bourbon. I'm going to head home now. Sorry I couldn't be of more help."

"No worries. You've been a big help. As always, much appreciated."

He finished off his drink and took his leave. His cheap gray suit was even more wrinkled than before, if that's even possible. Mistakenly, I thought the Cowboy Bourbon might straighten out some of those wrinkles. It does that with me. Dudley kept his eye on him as he left.

15

A couple of days passed. I never mentioned the case to anyone. My telephone line was still tapped. I could hear the clicking and noise on the line. In my head, I was formulating a plan.

Dudley and I found soon ourselves at the end of a work week. It turned out that Kinky had a concert that night in Houston. I took Dudley home and fed and watered him. I got gussied up to go watch Kinky's performance. He was playing at a venue I hadn't been to before, The Redneck Country Club. An interesting name. I was curious what it looked like. I was envisioning a parking lot filled with monster trucks and the like. I couldn't have been more wrong.

I left Dudley at the loft. He really wanted to come, but I forcefully told him no and left him some treats and the stuffed toy we call Baby. His place is of course by my side, and he knew that and longs to be there. I could appease him temporarily, but it wouldn't take long for him to start wondering where I was and when I would be returning. My fear was he would consume another sofa. And good sofas are hard to come by. My last one didn't stand a chance in his digestive tract.

The Redneck Country Club parking lot was not made of dirt and gravel, but beautifully paved. The primo building was made of tin and wood. The parking lot was filled with pretty nice (and expensive) vehicles. Much nicer than the Dodge Power Wagon I was driving. Inside, the building was magnificent. Everything was beautifully done. It was made to look like an old, distressed building, but with new materials.

Speaking of distressed, the concert had already begun and I had missed part of it. I hate when that happens. I heard Kinky singing in the background. I saw him strumming a Gibson guitar. He was decked out in all black, from his cowboy hat, down to his waist length jacket, pants, and boots. The concert had already started. I walked up to a cutie pie behind a counter, and she said, "Good evening, are you here for the Kinky Friedman concert?"

I said, "Why yes, I am. I'm on the list."

"We don't have a list, sir."

I looked puzzled and shrugged my shoulders.

Then she laughed and said, "I was just kidding. I love doing that to people. What's your name, Hon?"

"Good one. You really had me there. The name's Careless."

At this point, I usually start asking for phone numbers, but just as I was about to work my magic, I noticed two gentlemen sitting at a table outside, pretending to have a beer. Their heads snapped around while trying not to make it too obvious. Their clothing seemed chosen to fit in, but they certainly stood out. I pretended not to notice them but they had my full attention. I was ready for trouble. I knew this had something to do with the case, but these two were Asian, not Middle Eastern. I walked inside a large room where the concert was happening. They got up from their table and followed me.

"Now this one is on my new CD," Kinky said, "which is on sale at the table in the back. And I'll be happy to sign it for you. I'll sign anything but bad legislation." Everyone laughed. The audience was large and enthusiastic.

He did run for the governor of Texas a while back but was beat by a guy he calls Governor Good Hair – because he had a beautiful head of hair.

"This one's called *A Dog Named Freedom*, not Friedman, Freedom. A dog named Freedom." He was on a big stage with an American flag in the background. "*Looking back, a long time ago, for the people that I used to know. Lost a friend, in a war that wouldn't end. And Bob was singing 'Blowing In The Wind'. Now it's me and a three-legged dog named Freedom. And a sign that says Texas or bust. We got a long way to go, but good Lord don't you know, there ain't no quit in either one of us...*" The audience was mesmerized.

It was a great song. I kept the two men who followed me into the venue in my peripheral vision. One of them was watching me, and the other was watching Kinky. We were absolutely being surveilled. Kinky sang a litany of new songs like *Me and My Guitar, and Jesus In Pajamas*. He's very creative. He went through all his classics –like, *Sold American, Ride 'Em Jewboy* (a haunting song about the Holocaust), and *Old Ben Lucas*. He read from one of his books and told jokes. The crowd was eating it up. It was rather entertaining. Kinky is like a modern-day Mark Twain. But now, he has also resumed his role as a mystery solver. When he finished his performance, he walked backstage. I followed him. So did the two men who had been eyeballing us.

I followed Kinky to a small room behind the stage. As I got closer, two rather large, muscular men halted my forward momentum. Kinky turned and said, "He's with me. Those two aren't." He pointed at the two men following me. I guess he had noticed them as well. I passed between the two mountains of men and they quickly closed ranks. The two men following behind me stopped in their tracks, sized up the situation rather quickly, and sneered at the two bouncers. Kinky turned around, and he and I carefully studied these guys. They stared at us for a good several seconds. It was a standoff. I could tell they were thinking about taking on the bouncers but wisely chose otherwise.

They exited, and a few other bouncers from across the room followed them. Kinky sat down in a nice, oversized, comfortable-looking chair. I sat in one right next to him. The chairs were so large they made us look like children. He poured a couple of shots of Men In Black Tequila from a bottle waiting for him on a table between the chairs. He picked up a glass and so did I. We clinked glasses and downed the shots. "Smooooth," he throated in a low raspy voice. I was still trying to find my voice and catch my breath. I wasn't used to drinking straight up Mexican mouthwash. I always tempered my liquor with coffee. That's just the way I like it.

He poured another one and said, "Spill it." Then he pulled a cigar tube out of his jacket pocket, took the cigar out of it, cut it with a cigar cutter he pulled from his other pocket, and screwed the top back on the tube. He lit it up and smoke wafted up toward the ceiling. He put the cigar tube back in his jacket pocket.

I told him about being followed on the way home from Rod's ranch and that someone tried to break into E.D.'s car when we stopped for gas. I told him about my phones being tapped and all evidence from the crime scene and video tapes of our encounter at the gas station vanishing. I also mentioned that my contact at the police station was ordered to stop looking into the case. And of course, he already knew about the two men who had just tried to have a close encounter of the turd kind with us.

He looked at me and matter of factly exclaimed, "Cover up."

I was thinking the same thing and said, "And somebody is looking for something. I don't know what, but they obviously haven't found it yet."

"Well, I know what." He re-opened the cigar tube, turned it upside down, and a small microchip spilled out into his waiting palm.

I looked at it. I was puzzled. It looked just like any other microchip except that "L.A.M.B." was stenciled across the top of it in very tiny military-style letters. I held out my hand, and he gently placed it in my palm.

"My friend Floyd was driving into Kerrville a couple of days ago. I asked him to take several items to be dry cleaned. One of which was this jacket I'm wearing. You know, you just sweat through these things during a concert."

"Wasn't that the jacket you were wearing the night of the robbery at the art gallery?" I asked.

He raised one eyebrow at me to confirm my observation.

"Speaking of dry cleaners, didn't I just see on the news that there was a robbery gone bad at a dry cleaner in Kerrville where someone was shot and killed?" I asked.

He raised an eyebrow again, still not saying a word.

Things were getting freaky.

I turned the chip over. There was very small military-style lettering on the bottom too, easily missed by the naked eye. But I didn't miss it. It read: U S Government. This couldn't be good. I handed the chip back to Kinky, and he placed it back in the cigar tube and put it in his jacket pocket.

"What are we going to do?" I asked.

"Well, you, me, and that hound dog of yours are going to take the case from Copper Love and find her painting. Then we're going to get paid and turn this chip over to the government before we end up like the dry cleaners. I'm going to miss them. Who will do my dry cleaning now? Do you know how to dry clean?"

"Well, you've seen me drink, so you know I'm not dry. And I like to think of myself as clean. I don't know, maybe I'm overthinking this."

"You think?" Kinky asked, a smirk on his face. "I'm going to head back to the ranch. We're going to need to be careful with this one."

"Okay, I'll head back to the loft and start formulating a plan. Let's see if we can find out more about the L.A.M.B. chip."

"I'll call you in the morning," he said. We walked outside, and he climbed into the Yome Kipper Clipper. I got in the Power Wagon. As he was driving away, he took his black cowboy hat off with one hand and waved it around in a circle to say goodbye. Then he placed it back on his head and disappeared into the night. Something about him made me smile. I can't explain it. Perhaps he just has what is commonly known as the LTL Syndrome. Larger Than Life.

When I got back to the loft, I noticed the door was ajar. There was also a trail of fresh blood from the doorway into the loft. The blood trail stopped at the hallway. That got my Spidey senses tingling, and I drew my weapon from my inside-the-waist holster. My weapon of choice? The Glock 30S. A mid-size .45 ACP, a delightful little fella. I like the take-down power of the .45 ACP. I raised my pistol and slowly swung the door open. My main concern was Dudley. He was nowhere to be found. The loft had been ransacked. Furniture was turned over. Papers were all over the ground. I swept the loft and found no one. I holstered my weapon and searched for Dudley. I checked every inch of the loft.

When I finally found him, he was laying on the floor on the far side of our bed. He was awake but quiet. He looked up at me and tried to raise his head, but he couldn't. I wanted to be outraged with anger, but wasn't able to. All I felt was empathy and sadness. How could someone do this to him? I couldn't imagine my life without him. I fell to the ground and held him for what I was hoping would not be the last time. His tail wagged as I stroked his head and told him he was a good boy. He had dried blood on his jowls and mouth, but he was not bleeding. It was someone else's blood.

As I held him, I felt his thoughts. I saw him standing at the loft door. He heard and smelled people outside of the door. He didn't recognize them and was waiting for them to enter. He would protect his home. He saw the locks twist open and the door knob turn. His hair was raised on his back and he was agitated. When they opened the door and walked in, he lunged forward with water dripping from his jowls. These were the same two Asian men who had tried to accost Kinky and me at the concert, before the bouncers had turned them away. They were taken aback but entered the loft anyway. He felt their fear. They held their hands forward while saying, "Good dog. Good dog."

Dudley was having none of that. He jumped forward and knocked one of them down. He bit into the man's arm and twisted his head back and forth. Blood rushed everywhere. It was then he remembered this was not the first time he had tasted blood. The man was screaming from the pain Dudley inflicted upon him. No words, just loud screams in a language other than English. As he was disabling the intruder, the other one snuck up behind him. Dudley saw him and was about to turn his attention on him, but just before he did, he felt a sharp pain in his chest. He turned loose of the man's arm and was going to take care of business but then felt another sharp pain in his chest. The other man had kicked him full force – twice. Dudley doubled over in pain. He knew something was wrong. He limped over to where I had found him and collapsed. His breathing was short and labored. All he could do was listen.

"Kim," one of them said, "get up and help me search for the *Laser Acquired Missile Barrier* chip. It must be here somewhere. Go get a towel and wrap your wound up." The other man got up and tended to his dog bite. Then he joined his partner in going through all of my belongings and tearing everything apart. They never found the chip – because it was not there. Little did they know it was resting inside of a cigar tube, sitting in Kinky's jacket pocket. "It's not here. Let's go."

"What about the dog?" the other one asked.

"Who cares about the dog. It's not like he's going to tell anyone."

"Yeah, you're right. Let's go."

But they weren't right. Dudley had just told me everything, including one of their names. I speculated they were Korean. And now I knew what L.A.M.B. meant. Laser Acquired Missile Barrier. This was all well and good, but there was something very wrong with Dudley. I lifted him up and literally felt his pain. I carried him to the Power Wagon and gently laid him down on the back seat.

I called my vet and luckily there was still someone on call. I told them what happened and rushed Dudley over there. I parked in the emergency entrance, lifted him up, and ran inside with him. I could feel his life slipping away. Even so, he was just happy to be with me. He had no fear of dying. I was his joy, and he was mine.

A vet tech met me and carried him to the back. I sat and waited, then stood up and paced. I couldn't think about anything except Dudley. And the revenge I would enact on these two Koreans when I found them. And find them I would. Ten minutes later, my vet, L.D., walked out and asked, "What happened? Was he hit by a car? It looks like he was hit by a car. His spleen is ruptured, and he's bleeding out into his abdomen."

"Yes, he must have been hit by a car," I responded. I know it wasn't the truth, but it would have been really hard and taken way too much time for me to explain what actually happened. And I really couldn't tell him how I figured out what had happened. Plus, after seeing what I had seen, I didn't want to involve anyone else in this risky business.

My innards were burning up with the desire for revenge. My muscles were tight and all I could think about was finding the men who had done this. I did my best to sock it away so I could concentrate on fixing up my best friend.

"Well, we're going to have to remove his spleen if you want to save him. And we need to do it right now. Do you want us to proceed?"

"Yes, yes, of course. Please work your magic. Let's save him."

He quickly walked away and I sat and waited. Then, I paced again. I waited for what seemed like forever.

17

Several hours later, L.D. walked out in his scrubs. "Careless, we took what was left of his spleen out, washed out his abdomen with saline solution, and suctioned the blood out. You got him here just in time. He can live a normal life without a spleen. He's resting now, but he'll need to stay here for a couple of days so we can manage his pain and observe him. This was a pretty major operation. He'll be out for a while, but you can come visit him whenever you want."

"Okay, L.D., I've got some business to take care of. I'll come back tomorrow. I really appreciate everything you did for him." He nodded his head and I walked out of the building. I left and started to dial Kinky's number on the way to the Power Wagon. I had found out quite a bit from Dudley and wanted to share it with him. I was sure he would have some ideas as to how to proceed. I also had a score to settle with two Korean men. What these guys had done to Dudley wasn't going to go unanswered. This is Texas. We take care of our own. I was going to track them down for sure and show them what pain really is. While I was waiting for Kinky to answer, a large, dark SUV roared up and quickly stopped. Two men in dark suits jumped out, both armed and wearing ear pieces. They looked so similar, they could have been clones. Definitely the feds.

"Sir, we'd like you to come with us." The door to the SUV was open, and they had their arms outstretched, coaxing me in that direction.

They seemed to be asking but weren't really asking at all. There's no other choice available. I wasn't getting out of this one. "Okay gentlemen, but I'd like to see some ID first, if you don't mind."

Their eyes were glued on me. One of them slightly pulled his jacket open to reveal an FBI badge affixed to his waist, right next to a holstered Glock. This was serious business. I was thinking about wise-cracking like I normally do, but opted not to.

"And we'll relieve you of your firearm," the other one said while holding his hand out. Of course, they knew I had a firearm. They probably had been watching me, and anyone who has a concealed handgun license is registered with the FBI. I very slowly lifted my shirt, pulled it from the holster, and handed it to them – grip first. They were on red-alert during the handover, but seemed to settle down once the transaction was completed.

I got in the SUV, and they slammed the door shut. One sat in the front passenger seat, the other in back next to me. There was a third clone behind the wheel. They all looked straight ahead and said nothing. I did the same.

About thirty minutes later, we pulled up to an old abandoned warehouse that looked like it hadn't been in operation for years. The name painted on the outside had faded and I couldn't make it out. A large warehouse door rolled up, and we drove in. It closed behind us. It was well lit inside, and I could see a bunch of people standing around. All of them exited the SUV and my door was opened for me by one of them. I jettisoned myself from the vehicle.

"Please come with me, sir," one of them said. I was already looking around to map out my escape – just in case. Again, they asked me politely to go with them, even though I had no choice in the matter. I went with them.

They walked me into a room where Kinky was sitting in a chair behind an old beat up metal table that looked to be from the 1950's. Standard government issue. The room was small and windowless. As usual, Kinky was wearing his black cowboy hat. He smiled when he saw me, which didn't seem to surprise him, and said, "Damn glad to see ya, mate."

I sat in a chair next to him and asked, "What the hell is going on?"

"We're about to find out." He slightly tilted his head toward a one-way mirror on the wall in front of us. We were being watched.

Just as he finished saying that the door opened up and another fed walked in. He was wearing a dark suit and tie. This guy was tall, thin, and middle-aged. I didn't trust any of these people. He plopped a manila file folder down on the desk right in front of us. It was so fatly stuffed with papers it needed three thick red rubber bands around it to keep it from upchucking its contents. Neatly typed on a label in the top left-hand corner was a label: FBI. Under that in big red bold letters was stamped: TOP SECRET.

"Good evening, gentlemen, I'm Agent Brian Moeller with the FBI. I'm sorry to pull you away so hastily from what you were doing, but we have a serious situation on our hands, and we're going to need your cooperation. Do we understand one another?" Kinky and I looked at one another and looked back at him and nodded.

I quickly retorted, "The truth is out there, Agent Moeller." I was beaming with joy because I finally got to use a line from the hit show, *The X-Files*. And believe me, I had been waiting years for that moment. What can I say, I'm entertained rather easily.

"Terrific. That's what I like to hear. In fact, that's exactly what I want from the two of you – the truth. Gentlemen, I need to know who you are working with. And please be forthcoming. We have ways at getting to the truth, and believe me, you do not want to find out what they are. Now, who are you working with?"

Kinky and I looked at one another. He didn't appear to be as confused as I was. He said nothing. I looked at Agent Moeller and said, "I work for my family steel business."

Kinky smiled. The agent did not.

Kinky said, "I'm a singer, song writer, and author. You may have heard of me. I toured with Bob Dylan with his Rolling Thunder Revue and have played concerts all over the world. And I once ran for mayor of Kerrville, Texas. Unfortunately, at that time the Kerrverts were just not quite ready for a forward-thinking man such as myself. I even ran for governor of Texas once against Governor Good Hair, Rick Perry. Lost by a hair." Then I smiled. The agent did not. "You don't happen to have some ID on you, do you, partner?" Kinky asked.

Agent Moeller slyly smiled, then frowned. I couldn't tell if he was amused or getting ready to lower the boom on us. These guys were really hard to read. Normally, it's no problem for me to read body language, but these people were different. They must have had extensive training in suppressing their emotions. He whipped out an FBI badge, showed it to us, and put it back in his pocket.

"Okay, you want to play it like that. We can do that. I was hoping you'd make it easy on yourselves. Where's the chip?" he asked, slamming his fist down on the table. Now he was showing some emotion. He was not a happy camper. Someone was getting a bit agitato, or at least acting that way.

Kinky asked, "What are you talking about? What chip? A potato chip?" He was one cool customer.

"Gentlemen, I'm not going to ask you again. I've got half a dozen agents out there who are very proficient at gathering information. They are very thorough, and very good at what they do. If you don't start talking and tell me what I want to know, I'll lock you up for a very long time and let them work on you. At least until you cooperate."

We said nothing.

"Okay, have it your way," Agent Moeller said as he stood up from the table and walked away. "I'll see you guys in about twenty years."

"Are you talking about the Laser Acquired Missile Barrier chip?" I asked. I had no idea what that even was, but Dudley heard one of the Koreans say it, and I needed to give this agent something before the two of us wouldn't see daylight for the longest time. I didn't think either of us needed to take on a girlfriend with facial hair named Bubba in prison – not that there's anything wrong with that. I could see from his facial expression that Kinky looked surprised by my response. The agent was not.

He stopped dead in his tracks and remained motionless with his back to us for a few seconds. He was probably deciding how best to handle the situation and communicating with someone behind the mirror. His cell phone chirped, and he pulled it from the inside pocket of his jacket and glanced at the screen. He quickly whirled around, bent down to face level, and angrily said, "Where's the chip?"

Kinky looked him square in the eye and said, "We're not saying shit until you start explaining why you've brought us here and tell us what's going on. And we want an attorney!" A bold move. I liked it. Kinky whipped out the tube that contained the chip and slid out a fresh, sweet-smelling cigar. I found it odd that he was going to give up the goods without even fighting to see what we were up against. But he coolly slipped the cigar between his lips, placed the tube back in his pocket, took out a lighter and began the ignition sequence. Very clever. He put the very thing they were searching for right in front of their faces so that wouldn't even see it.

"This is a no smoking facility," Agent Moeller snapped. I thought he was going to smack that cigar right out of Kinky's mouth, but instead he quickly snatched the cigar just before it was lit. Agent Moeller had the reflexes of a cat.

Kinky said, "Smoke 'em if you got 'em."

I looked at Kinky and said, "What the hell?"

"Be patient, grasshopper." He winked at me.

A few minutes later, a young, attractive woman walked in, and Agent Moeller walked out. She had jet black hair pulled up and tightly rolled into a ball at the top of her head. I believed it to be the *I mean business* hairstyle. I found it somewhat appealing. She was decked out in a nondescript black suit, white starched shirt, and a black tie like everyone else at the facility. Somebody really needed to teach these folks about fashion.

"I'm Supervisor Chelsea Tirone with the FBI. You'll be dealing with me from this point forward. You should have listened to your friend at the police department when he told you not to pursue this case. It's too late now. Since you already seem to know way more than you should, I'm going to tell you some things. I've cleared everyone out of this area because this is so sensitive and top secret in nature, that it's above most of my agents' pay grade. What I'm about to tell you is classified, but you already know that, don't you? If you ever speak a word of it to anyone, we'll know. And we'll lock you up for the remainder of your lives for treason and espionage. Do I make myself clear?"

We nodded. This woman meant business. Good cop, bad cop, I guess. Except they all seemed like bad cops at this point.

"Fine! The L.A.M.B. chip was designed by some of the finest minds at the Defense Department. As you so eloquently mentioned, L.A.M.B. is the acronym for Laser Acquired Missile Barrier. Did you happen to watch the news about the failed missile launch in North Korea yesterday?"

We both answered, "Yes."

"When the L.A.M.B. chip is put into our laser delivery system, the beam can be directed at a missile on a launch pad or even a missile in flight. We have devised a means for preprogrammed nanobots to piggyback a ride on a directed laser beam to any missile of our choosing. Once the nanobots reach their target, they rapidly disperse and enter the control system of the missile, where they disrupt the guidance system, disarm the warhead, and initiate a self-destruct sequence. And once their mission is completed, the nanobots are programmed to self-destruct. So, even if anything is left of the missile, there is no trace of outside interference."

"Are you saying the North Korean missile failure was due to the L.A.M.B. chip?" Kinky asked.

"That wasn't the first time. We've used it on many occasions. It's how we control rogue nations who feel the need to launch missiles. And until recently, they had no idea the chip existed. They just assumed the missiles were defective. We had a traitor leak the information to a foreign government, and we believe the Chinese, Koreans, Russians, and Israelis are after the chip. They don't know for sure that it truly exists, but they are speculating it does, due to the leaks. To date, we have denied its existence, and there is no proof that it does. But that hasn't stopped foreign governments from trying to obtain it. Right now, we only have a prototype. When we finish testing it, we will mass-produce them. If all goes well, this could effectively end dangerous missile launches and even prevent wars. Unfortunately, the prototype was stolen from a secure facility several weeks ago. We're not even sure how they got in. We're in the process of building another one, but it's weeks away. We need the chip back ASAP so we can stop any future hostile missile launches. And we don't want it reverse-engineered by other governments. If it were to fall into the wrong hands, it could be used in really nefarious ways. It could affect airplanes, ships, trains, cars, you name it. The nanobots can be programmed to do just about anything. So, you see the dilemma. Now you know the whole story, so I'll ask again. Where is the chip? We know you have it."

Kinky had a blank look on his face, like he was having withdrawal symptoms, longing for his confiscated cigar.

Supervisor Tirone stared at us. I had no idea what Kinky was up to. "Here's the thing, darlin'," Kinky said. "I did have the chip. Of course, I had no idea at the time what it was. We just happened to stumble into a robbery gone bad at an art gallery, and later that night when I took my jacket off, I found someone had secretly placed the chip in my pocket. I reached my hand in for my lighter, just like I normally do, and there it was, as plain as day. Someone must have thought it was still in the jacket pocket because when my friend Floyd took the jacket to the dry cleaner for me, I saw on the news the next day the dry cleaner wound up dead."

"We know all that, Kinky. We were surveilling the art gallery, waiting for the sale of the chip so we could reacquire it. A Russian agent at the gallery was smuggling stolen technology incorporated in artwork she would ship to "customers" all over the world. That's when the two Iranian agents entered the gallery and got their asses handed to them by the Russian agent, who goes by the name of Copper Love. You saw what she did to the dry cleaner? We had to bring in one of our cleanup crews for that. The same thing could happen to you if you don't cooperate with us. Where is the chip now? I'm not going to ask you again." She was very demanding.

"We have a little problem," Kinky said. This was news to me.

"What would that be?" She had a stern look on her face.

"Well, through no fault of my own, and before you people unceremoniously brought me here against my will, Copper Love came to my hotel room tonight. One thing led to another and, well, let's just say she lived up to her last name, Love, and leave it at that."

"You did not," I exclaimed while smiling. We fist bumped. "You dog, you."

"Mr. Friedman, she is a very dangerous woman. We know she has killed at least thirty-seven operatives worldwide. You're lucky she left you in one piece."

"She can certainly put away the tequila. I didn't do too badly myself. Can't remember a damn thing."

"Did she get the chip?" Supervisor Tirone asked.

"I'm afraid so," he responded "In my defense, at the time, I wasn't privy to any of what you just told me."

"Well, that's just fine, pal! And you, how did you know the name of a top-secret chip? That's not public knowledge and has never been printed or reported anywhere. It is not even written on the chip. I may have to keep you here for further questioning, unless you have a very good explanation." She held up her index finger just inches from my face.

"You wouldn't believe me if I told you," I responded.

"Try me. And it better be convincing."

"Dudley told me. There, I said it, okay?" Kinky closed his eyes and shook his head. He was obviously not impressed.

"Who's Dudley, and why do we not know about him? What agency does he work for?" She pulled out her cell phone and did some digital digit work in rapid fashion.

"Dudley's my dog, who, by the way, those Korean dipshits beat pretty badly. He's at the vet right now. They're trying to save his life."

She stopped texting abruptly and looked up at me.

Kinky looked at me as well and said, "I'm so sorry, mate. I hope he's going to be alright. I've got a baseball bat that we can fix up those Korean goons with. That is just so wrong!"

"I know. As soon as I get out of here, I'm going to take care of business," I said.

"I don't know," Supervisor Tirone said, "if you gentlemen remember where you are and how much trouble you're in, but you're not going anywhere or doing anything. In fact, you may NEVER get out of here."

Kinky said, "Nelson Mandela is a personal friend of mine. I know all about being held in prison for doing justice."

Supervisor Tirone frowned at him and said, "This is a matter of national security. Now, tell me again how you knew the name of the chip, and it better not be that your dog told you."

"Listen up, Chelsea. May I call you Chelsea? Dudley is my dog and he did tell me. Several months ago, an attempt on my life was made by one of the perps in a case I was working on. Which I solved, by the way. But unfortunately, I almost died. I was in a coma for months. When I awoke from the coma, I found that when I touch a dog, I can read its thoughts and it can read mine. It's almost as if our minds are linked together. I know it sounds bizarre, but it's the truth."

Kinky asked, "Is that how you knew where to bring Winnie and Louie home when they were lost? I do believe you, Careless."

"Thank you, Kinky. I didn't want to tell you because I thought you'd think I was crazy."

"I do think you are crazy. But I believe." He took out another cigar from his jacket pocket and gingerly placed it between his lips. Thankfully, this time he didn't try to spark it up. Supervisor Tirone held firm while Kinky grinned with his cigar firmly placed between his front teeth. Talking and grinning with a cigar in your mouth takes talent. I'm not afraid to admit it, I was impressed.

"Okay, I'm going to lock you guys up till until I get a satisfactory answer. I hope you won't miss sunlight or decent food." She shuffled and stacked some papers together she had taken out of the folder. Looks like she was about to wrap things up. And lock us up.

"Look," I said. "I'm telling you the truth. There's no other way I could know what the letters L.A.M.B. stood for. It's not public knowledge, right? I don't have access to any government documents. You have to believe me. Also, I was never a huge fan of sunlight, but the food thing, I don't know about that…" Frankly, I didn't relish the idea of going to jail. In addition, the thought of Kinky recycling his jokes on me while we were locked up for some time together didn't sound amazingly appealing either. Nobody wants that.

"Okay, I'll tell you what. Against my better judgement, we're going to do a little experiment. If you pass, I'll set you free – with conditions. If you don't pass, I'll lock you both up and throw away the key. You good with that?" I love a woman who plays hardball.

I looked at Kinky, and he shrugged his shoulders. I turned to her and said, "It's not like I've got a choice. Let's do it."

"No, you don't have a choice." She picked up her cell phone and quickly sent a message to someone. She had fast fingers. I hoped she didn't have an itchy trigger finger. Then she stared at me, showing no emotion. Her phone chirped, and she said, "Supervisor Tirone here, do we have any K-9 units in the building today? Diablo? Sounds perfect. Please bring him to interrogation room one." She put the phone back in her pocket. "You're in luck. We have available the meanest, most badass dog in the K-9 Unit we've ever trained. He's on duty today. Let's see how you do with him. Then we'll talk." she said. I thought Kinky looked a little nervous in the service – event though I'm still trying to figure out what that means. Whatever it means, I was nervous in the service as well. And would probably need a check-up from the neck up after all of this was over. A lot of things could go wrong. I was feeling a little unsure of myself.

Moments later, the door burst open and a large, burly FBI agent with the insignia FBI K-9 on his black t-shirt entered the room, along with a dog I took to be Diablo. They stopped just in front of us, and Diablo sat down without even a command. Diablo was a pretty big, all-black Shepherd. His head was huge, and he had pointy ears. His coat was gorgeous and shiny. He seemed very well mannered. He stared at Kinky and me.

"Okay, Mr. Robinson, this is our K-9 Unit specialist, Agent Tom Wocken. He's Diablo's handler. Let's see how you do. Tell me what Diablo is thinking."

"That's not how it works. I have to actually be touching the dog."

"Probably not a good idea," Agent Wocken said tightly holding Diablo's leash. I could see his fist clench even tighter. "He doesn't like to be handled by strangers. Most of the time when he's around the civilian population, we have to muzzle him, just as a precaution."

"It's okay, Wocken, I'm sure Mr. Robinson won't mind if Diablo is off leash with no muzzle," Supervisor Tirone said.

Kinky was studying the situation. I saw him giving the agents and the dog the once-over. While I was busy wondering if I was going to get the shit bit out of me, I could tell he was busy formulating a plan.

Agent Wocken dropped the short, leather leash and said, "Go!"

Diablo dragged the leash and quickly walked over to where Kinky and I were sitting. He smelled Kinky up and down – especially the cigar hanging from his mouth. Thankfully, it wasn't lit but Kinky was now anxiously chewing on it. Then he sniffed me up and down too. I was sure he smelled Dudley. While he was preoccupied, I slowly and cautiously placed my hand on his back. For a split second, he tensed up, just as his handler did and had said he would. His hackles raised up, and I saw in his mind that he was about to switch into attack mode. The handler started moving forward as if to avert a disaster, but Supervisor Tirone silently held her hand up for him to back down. He stopped in his tracks.

Diablo had really soft fur. It didn't take long for me to establish a connection with him. It was almost instantaneous. He stopped sniffing me and looked me square in the eye. I learned from him that he had been smelling us for drugs and explosives. He had been extensively trained for that purpose. I could clearly see that now. He knew from my thoughts that we had none and were not a threat to him. I invited him to sit in front of me, and he did. I started rubbing his ears and he completely relaxed. Diablo was really just a big sweetie pie.

"He's not supposed to do that. Come, Diablo," Agent Wocken said. I knew he wanted to go to his handler, so I told him it was okay. He walked away and sat by Agent Wocken's side.

Supervisor Tirone was impressed but not convinced. Kinky was watching with great interest.

"So, tell us what the dog is thinking, won't you?" Supervisor Tirone said.

"Well, he likes his job and it gives him a purpose. He enjoys his training, but is just a big sweetheart. He also likes a good belly rub."

"That's all general information. Anyone could have said that and been right. I don't believe a word you're saying."

"Well, how about this? Agent Wocken is having an affair with another agent named Sam, not that there's anything wrong with that. Oh, and Sam is very attractive. She's also married. You do have rules against doing that sort of thing, don't you? Yesterday, Diablo sniffed out three bricks of black heroin at the big airport. It was being smuggled into the states by a man travelling from Qatar. He also really likes the treats Agent Wocken keeps in his right front pocket to reward him when he's doing a good job. In fact, he'd like one right now, if you don't mind."

Diablo was sitting at attention in front of his handler. The agent looked him squarely in his eyes waved his hand in his direction while commanding, "Down!" Without hesitation or making a sound, Diablo lay down in front of him and didn't take his eyes off of him. He promptly reached into his pocket, pulled out a treat, and gave it to him. Diablo took it very gently.

"And Diablo loves crunchy peanut butter, don't you, boy?" I held both arms out, invited him to come to me, and he did. He lay down and rolled over, and I gave him a fantastic belly rub.

Agent Wocken was red in the face from the embarrassment of being outed about his affair and of Diablo's misbehavior. But dogs don't misbehave. Owners do. Hey, all's fair in love and war. And I most certainly didn't want to go to jail. I'm pretty sure Kinky didn't either.

Supervisor Tirone looked at Agent Wocken, who confirmed everything with a nod. He called to Diablo. I hugged him, told him it was okay, and he walked back to his handler and sat by his side. He was a good boy.

"You're dismissed, agent. And I want you in my office in one hour with a complete report of what just transpired."

"Yes, ma'am," he responded. He leashed Diablo and walked out.

"Okay, Mr. Robinson. That was pretty impressive. I'm still skeptical, and I'm not totally convinced the two of you have been completely forthcoming, but I'm going to cut you loose–for now. We'll be watching you. If you come across any information about the chip, I'll want to know right away. Here's my card. And if you speak to anyone about this, you'll be doing twenty years in jail. Do I make myself clear?" We both nodded.

Kinky said, "Crystal clear."

She looked towards the one-way mirror, and the door swung open. FBI agents escorted us out of the building. They put Kinky into one SUV and me into another and drove me back to the vet to pick up the Power Wagon.

I drove back to the loft and poured myself a Careless Coffee. To achieve this feat I mixed in a little Garrison Brothers Cowboy Bourbon into my Katz Midnight Blue decaf coffee, for good measure. I drink decaf because it doesn't keep me up at night but for the first time in a while, I was without my sidekick in the loft. I wouldn't be sleeping anyway. It's no fun sleeping by yourself. I couldn't imagine not having him watch over me every night. Plus, I was worried sick about him. I sat on the sofa deep in thought, drinking my Careless Coffee. I felt like I had let my best friend down. And I most certainly did not want to lose him

The phone started doing the Mexican Hat Dance. I debated whether to answer it. That Cowboy Bourbon really dulled my senses – in a good way. I needed that right now. "Careless," Kinky said, "I'm on my way back to Medina in the Yome Kipper Clipper. What did you think about the FBI hauling us in?"

"I'll be honest with you, Kinky, I'm not sure what to make of that. I don't really trust them." I knew our phones were probably tapped, but I'm sure they already knew we didn't trust them. So, it wasn't like they were receiving valuable, secret information from us.

"Me either," he said.

"And I can't believe you slept with that woman. I mean, she's a ginger, for God's sake."

"She truly is, Careless. She truly is." We both laughed at the same time, though it did seem like a little too much information.

"If you say 'git on 'er and stay on 'er again,' I may have to come over and smack that cigar out of your mouth." I said. We both chuckled again. It was kind of funny. This was taking my mind off of Dudley, at least for a little while.

"Anyway, I have a lead on those two goons that broke into your place and roughed up Dudley. How would you like to meet me in Kerrville tomorrow and grab a bite to eat? For lunch tomorrow, we'll be serving a dish I like to call payback. I'll bring my Louisville Slugger. Did you know I played baseball at the University of Texas? What do you say?"

"I say batter up! What time do you want me?"

"Let's meet at noon at The Flying Dragon. You remember where it is, don't you?"

"I'll be there," I responded. I'm not really a violent person, but I can take care of myself. It's just that I didn't take care of Dudley this time, so I certainly do have some payback to distribute.

I called my brother, Ross, and told him I wouldn't be at work tomorrow. He was fine with that. Ever since the shooting, I hadn't really gotten back into the swing of things at work. He and Papa were more than capable of running the business while I was away. And since I had been gone for so long, they had hired a new young fella named Jake to do a lot of my job. Tomorrow, two Koreans were going to account for what they had done to Dudley.

I went to bed, but mostly just tossed and turned. I studied the ceiling for a long time. I didn't really learn anything interesting, other than I missed my boy spooning me all night. He was my security blanket for sure. Normally, I don't remember my dreams, but this time I kept going over the details of everything that had happened during the past several days. I'm sure I was missing something. I just couldn't place my finger on it. And the L.A.M.B. chip? Where was it? Who had it? Did Copper Love really ganiff it from Kinky? Ganiff? It's a Yiddish word, look it up. I learned it from Dudley. He's a non-practicing Jew. Or was Kinky holding out on me? I replayed it over and over in my head. Finally, I closed my eyes and fell asleep.

The next morning, I woke up, brushed my teeth, showered, got dressed, and left the loft without bothering to call E.D., Birk, or Sarge for a ride-along. I didn't want them to see the ugly side of me. And chances are, it was going to get pretty fugly. Fugly? Not a Yiddish word, look it up. I jumped in the Power Wagon and began my drive to Kerrville. Normally, it's a four-hour drive, but I put the pedal to the metal and shaved off about twenty minutes. I was a man on a mission.

I was a smidge early. I parked across the street from The Flying Dragon and waited. From my vantage point, I could see both the front and the side exits of the building. The side exit spilled out into an alleyway. I listened to the radio while I watched, trying to decide what I was going to do if these two Koreans walked out of the building. A Johnny Cash song played on the radio, and all I could think about was how these two animals, who had beat my dog, were going to burn, burn, burn in a ring of fire. I called Kinky. "This is Kinky, Richard, Big Dick Friedman, you know what to do…" Then I heard beeeeeep. I wondered where he was. He didn't seem like the type of person who missed appointments.

Around 12:30, the side door in the alley swung open. The two people I had been waiting for walked out. There was no time to call Kinky again, and I wasn't going to wait around for him. I got out of the Power Wagon and swiftly headed toward them. They were looking at one another while walking in deep in conversation, speaking in a foreign language that sure sounded Korean to me. I don't speak Korean, but I do eat Korean food. If I had to guess what they were saying, it was about either spicy kimchi buckwheat noodles they probably had just consumed or the ass-whipping they were about to receive. Probably the latter but that's just a guess on my part. These were definitely the two who had hurt Dudley. I intimately remembered them from when I connected with Dudley after they left our loft. I positioned myself in front of them, blocking their exit from the alleyway. They finally looked ahead and spotted me. They seemed a bit surprised.

"You boys hurt my dog. This is Texas. You're going to pay for that." I made a fist with both hands. I've never killed a man, and I was hoping to keep it that way. But I had never felt this amount of sheer anger and need for revenge. It was coursing through my veins. I was going to punish them for what they had done to Dudley. Unfortunately for me, one of them reached inside of his jacket and pulled out a handgun with a suppressor screwed to the tip of it. That wasn't the only thing screwed. I guess I hadn't thought this through. But in my defense, I was a little emotional at the time.

"Where the chip?" said the one with the gun trained on me. I was pretty well out of options now and stopped in my tracks. I was trying to formulate a plan on how to extricate myself from this situation but was coming up short.

Unfortunately for them, they didn't hear Kinky silently walking up behind them with his Louisville Slugger. I smiled at them, and they seemed a little confused. I raised my eyebrows and nodded my head up and down in anticipation of what was destined to occur. Kinky mightily swung his bat, connecting with the wrist of the one holding the gun. I definitely heard a bone fracture. The gun dropped to the ground, but not before it went off.

I did a package check and, thankfully, had not been shot. Getting shot twice in a lifetime was something I really wished to avoid. I got a determined look on my face, flattened my lips, and gave Kinky a certain look. He quickly glanced at me, raised his eyebrows, and shrugged his shoulders. I was trying to be mad at him for being late, but he had just saved my bacon.

He swiftly swung his mighty bat again and took out the other guy's knee. He hit the deck. "Swing away, Merrill," I said as Kinky smiled while using his bat to incapacitate the gunman. I had been waiting to use that line for years. I guess he also was a fan of the movie *Signs*, starring Mel Gibson. The man has good taste, what can I say? And he has a dynamite swing.

With his good hand the other Korean reached into his jacket for what was probably another handgun. Kinky didn't see him because he was busy with batting practice. I took care of it. Uppercut to the chin. It was solid and landed with a thud. His legs became wobbly. Then I delivered a blow to the solar plexus. I heard the wind leave him. He hit the ground, and I relieved him of his weapon. An FN 5.7. Nice! I'll just hang on to it for good luck.

"And this is for Dudley," I shouted as I kicked him in the ribs. Both men were writhing in pain on the ground. Kinky kissed his bat and laid it on the ground while I trained the gun on them.

"If either of them move, shoot them in the leg," he said.

"With pleasure," I responded. I had no problem with that.

He pulled some large zip ties from his pocket and tied their hands behind their backs and bound their feet. Then, he zip-tied the two of them together, back to back as they lay on the ground. He seemed like he knew what he was doing. "A little something I learned in New York from my friend Rambam," he said.

Kinky rifled through all of their pockets while they squirmed to try to stop him. He pulled out passports and wallets. "Ah, Mr. Jeremy Reigel and Steve Halpert," he read – the fake names from the passports. He had a smirk on his face.

"I know that one's name is Kim," I said as I pointed to the one who's partner used his name in front of Dudley. I bet he never thought that would come back to haunt him, seeing that most dogs don't talk. But Dudley did talk. He was always saying something. And not only that, he shared his thoughts with me.

"They're all counterfeit," Kinky said. "Some of the nicest forgeries I've ever seen. And I've seen plenty in my former line of work." He threw the passports and wallets on the ground next to the two goons. They struggled to retrieve them but were just all tied up at the moment.

Kinky picked up his bat.

"Why did you hurt my dog?" I screamed. "What were you looking for? Was it the chip? Tell me about the chip." They just looked at the ground in silence.

"You're not going to get anything out of them," Kinky said.

One of them looked up at me and smiled. "Your dog is a filthy animal. In my county, he would make a good meal," he said. Then he spit out some blood and smiled again.

I walked closer and "put the gun against his head to pull the trigger now he's dead." A lyric from "Bohemian Rhapsody" by Queen kept playing in my head. It made a real impression on me when I was younger because it was played at the very first concert I had ever been to with my friend Jeff Horowitz. I knew what needed to be done. Should I? He definitely deserved it. Kinky walked up to me, put his hand on my shoulder, and said, "Don't do it, Careless. Don't do it. He's not worth it. Don't be like him. Just walk away. If you do it, 'you've gone and thrown it all away.'"

Strange, it was almost like we were connected at that moment. That sure sounded like Bohemian Rhapsody to me. It kind of short-circuited my thinking and what I was about to do. I mean, it sounded right but my feelings were trying to override my brain. He took the hand I was holding the gun in and gently moved it away from the Korean's head. "Give me the gun, Careless. Do the right thing. Just put it in my hand." I eventually started thinking clearly again and agreed with him. I placed it in his hand, grip first.

"You have no honor," the Korean said.

"Here's some honor for you," I said as I kicked him in the gut. That shut him up and would have to do as my revenge for what they had done to my boy, Dudley – for now.

Kinky whipped out his phone and dialed someone up. "Supervisor Tirone, yes, Kinky Richard Big Dick Friedman here. Well, I'm doing fine. No, I haven't fled the country. But you already knew that, didn't you? You have GPS tracking capability, don't you? Terrific. I'm leaving a package for you, right here. No, I won't be here when you arrive. You're welcome." He dropped the phone on the ground next to the Koreans, without hanging up, and we walked away.

"Hey, are you going to leave your cell phone there?" I asked.

"Oh, it's not my phone, I lifted it off of one of the Koreans when I was zip tying them together. Let the Feds deal with them. They'll get deported and probably be fed alive to some hogs for failing their mission. So, you see, you'll have your revenge and no blood on your hands. 'It's too late, their time has come. And you need no sympathy. Easy come, easy go.'" Obviously a fan of Queen. I'm liking everything about this guy.

20

"You hungry?" he asked.

"Famished! Beating the hell out of people really makes me work up an appetite." I made a fist to fist bump him, but then realized my fist hurt from the fistfight. Yes, I like using the word fist. But enough about me. I withdrew my fist because it was a little sore. Plus, I wasn't sure Kinky was a fist bump kind of guy. He probably didn't like fist bumps or shout outs.

"We're here at The Flying Dragon," he said. "Let's eat." We walked around to the front entrance and went in. It was only half full. We were seated right away and Kinky ordered his usual, the Daddy Dragon. "I could use a drink. How about you?"

I nodded my head and said, "Pretty much."

"Two Men In Black tequilas, please. Oh hell, just bring the whole bottle, Hop Sing."

I had never heard the name Hop Sing before. It was kind of unusual. While we were waiting for our drinks, two waiters brought out a bonanza of food on the Daddy Dragon order. Hop Sing brought the bottle of tequila and two glasses. Kinky poured two shots. "You know," he said, "after we solve this case, we should take an alcoholiday. What do you think, Careless?"

"I think, why wait? Let's start right now. Bottoms up," I said.

"Okay, mate," he responded.

Not a minute after we downed the first shot, I saw from the window several SUVs pull up and make an abrupt stop in front of the alley. Quite a few FBI agents wearing dark suits and ties quickly jumped from the vehicles and nabbed the Korean packages we left for them. They tossed them in the SUVs and drove off. We watched from our table and continued our alcoholiday while we ate. I guess they didn't notice us through the window.

My telephone rang. I wasn't really expecting a phone call. It was coming from a blocked number. Probably just someone wanting to sell me a free cruise or save me a lot of money with Geico Insurance. "Aren't you going to answer it? That ringing noise is pretty tedious," Kinky said. It was actually harshing my mellow. He seemed to be expecting the call.

"Okay, I'll get it. Crisis hotline, please state crisis. And for your enjoyment, this line may be recorded." I answered like I normally do. I detected a grin on Kinky's face while he was in between tequila shots.

"Mr. Robinson, Supervisor Tirone here, I hope you're enjoying the tequila with your friend. I don't think they have tequila in prison. What do you think?"

"I really couldn't say, Supervisor Tirone."

"Well, you're about to find out, Mr. Robinson. And so is your friend, Mr. Friedman. If I don't get that chip back, I'll make sure of it." I was busy thinking of a snappy comeback but before I could even utter a word I heard a loud click as she hung up the phone. Kinky was chowing down on something I couldn't identify. He didn't seem surprised at all by the abrupt conversation I had with Supervisor Tirone. I suppose I shouldn't have been surprised that she had my telephone number, even though I had never given it to her.

Without looking up, he said, "So, how's Supervisor Tirone doing? She still looking for the chip?"

"Yep." I took a bite of something that resembled chicken. But it didn't taste like chicken. I got fooled on that one. "I don't know what we're going to do. I don't know where the damn chip is."

"Well I do." He was looking at me full on.

"I thought you said Copper Love swiped the chip from you."

"She thought she did. Right about now, she's probably figuring out what she really stole was an old microchip I had sitting around from my Compaq Computer. I hope she knows how to play Pong." I heard him snicker.

"Interesting. So you have the L.A.M.B. chip?"

"Let's just say it's in a safe place and leave it at that for now. Until we know who to trust, I think we'll have to use some caution. Okay? Now eat your food. Somewhere in Korea, someone is contemplating eating a dog.

And possibly Venezuela." Funny, that's what I always tell Dudley when he's playing around with his food. I started playing with my food. I was trying to avoid eating the mystery meat. Kinky gave me a stare, raised his eyebrows, tilted his head up slightly, and pointed his empty fork at the Daddy Dragon. I'm guessing he wanted me to 'open the hanger'. I reluctantly took a bite of the least visually offensive looking food on the plate and forced a smile while he eyeballed me. While chewing, my mind wandered off to Dudley and how he was doing. I was sure he was doing okay. I knew he was in good hands.

We finished our meal and our conversation about the chip. "It's getting late. Why don't you come to the Lodge and spend the night with me and the Friedmans? I'll let you sleep with Mr. P."

"Well, how can I resist spending the night in a strange place, with a cute white poodle named Mr. P. What the hell? Why not? I mean, I'm on an alco-holiday, after all. Sure, I'll spend the night at your place. Just don't call me easy. Oh, and don't call me late for breakfast," I said, trying to be funny.

"Let's go, smartass. We've got a lot of planning to do."

He slapped some money on the table and said, "Keep the change, Hop Sing. See you next time."

"Oh, Kinky, but the bill has been paid in full. Someone from the U.S. Government called in and gave us a credit card. And it's a valid credit card. We checked. Here's the receipt, Kinky. The lady on the phone ask me to write a note on it to you. What you got yourself into this time?" Hop Sing asked as he turned and walked away, muttering something in Mandarin.

Unlike my friend Birk, Kinky actually paid his tab, or at least tried to. I could get used to this. I looked at the receipt. "Approved by Supervisor Chelsea Tirone. Packages received." Not great tippers. Kinky picked up his money and placed it in his pocket. I followed him outside. He drove off in the Yome Kippur Clipper, and I followed him in the Power Wagon. When we got to his place, several dogs came running out of a doggie door. They were really excited to see Kinky. "Winnie! Sophie! Louie! Mr. P! Go say hi to Careless." The whole pack ran over to me, and I reached down and pet all of them. "Mr. P, you'll be sleeping with Careless tonight. Try not to snore." I gently placed my hand on Mr. P's back. I could see he wasn't amused. Neither was I. But now he knew he would be sleeping with me. He didn't seem to mind.

The Friedmans followed us into The Lodge. I sat on a sofa, and Kinky took his cowboy hat off and lit up a cigar. "Want a drink?" he asked. Before I could answer, he poured two glasses of bourbon. I recognized the bottle from the liquor store.

"Sure, why not? I can't remember the last time I've had a drink." I laughed because we had we polished off the majority of a bottle of tequila with dinner. It was a distant memory. So, I was determined to make new memories. After a few more drinks, I really wouldn't remember them anyway.

There was an old camp song we used to sing. Let me see if I remember it. Oh yeah, it goes something like this. *Make new drinks, but keep the old. One tequila's silver and the other gold...* I love that song.

"Cigar?" he inquired.

"Why not?"

He handed me a cigar and a cutter. I chopped it's head off and lit it up. I can see why Pappa enjoys his cigars so much. It was kind of relaxing. And I needed that after the tense night we just had.

"I picked up this bottle of bourbon," he said, "when I was signing tequila bottles at the liquor store. Normally, I'm not a fan of bourbon, but this one is pretty good." he said. It was Garrison Brothers Cowboy Bourbon, my new favorite. Don't get me wrong, I love my Jack Daniels. The Cowboy Bourbon just barely edged it out. Of course, I'll still drink both. Any port in a storm, right? Besides the good taste, what stood out about the Cowboy Bourbon was the big silver Texas star stuck smack on the front of the bottle.

"So, where's the chip?" I inquired. Before he could answer, I walked up to a lamp, unscrewed the shade, removed a small bugging device, and reattached the lamp shade. I walked into his bathroom and flushed it down the toilet. When I got back to the living room, Kinky was sitting with his arms folded. Both my glass and his glass of bourbon were polished off. I looked at him and then glanced toward the empty glasses. "Make mine a double," I said. He was not amused.

"Okay, how did you know there was a bug in the lamp and why didn't you tell me before I started talking?"

"Well, when I put my hand on Mr. P., I saw that Copper Love had been here and placed the bug in your lamp while you were sleeping. You know, afterwards."

"Yeah, I catch your drift."

"You must have forgotten to tell me she had paid you a visit at the ranch.

Mr. P woke up and watched her as she did it. He didn't know what it was but he watched her plant the bug."

"And how did you say you saw this?" he asked again. He was testing me.

"You know, that thing I do, where I touch a dog and we see what each other is thinking. By the way, Mr. P really needs to pee. Mind if I take him outside?"

"No, go ahead. Just one thing. Why'd you say I had the chip before flushing the bug down the toilet. And I never said I had it. I said it was somewhere safe."

"I know, but speaking of flushing, how else would you suggest we flush out Copper Love so we can learn what's really going on?"

"Good point." I took Mr. P outside and the rest of the Friedmans followed. They all did their business. When we all went back in, Kinky had poured two more bourbons. This time, I actually got to drink one of them. Pretty smooth.

"So, where's the chip?" I inquired.

"I never said I had the chip. I said it was somewhere safe. And it is." There was no tripping up this guy. I knew full well where the chip was. He was holding it in his hand.

"Why are you staring at the bottle of bourbon? Do you need another poor?" He was scrutinizing me.

"No, I'm good. I think I'm going to have to take a vacation from our alcoholiday. I think I've had enough for today." I sat down on a sofa. Louie hopped up and sat in my lap. I stroked his fur with my eyes fixed on the big silver star on the front of the Garrison Brothers Bourbon bottle.

He poured me another one despite my somewhat weak objection. "You know where the chip is, don't you?"

I nodded.

"Why didn't you just say so? I guess I can't keep any secrets from you as long as the Friedmans are around. Loose lips sink ships. Isn't that right, Mr. P?" He rubbed Mr. P's head.

"Mr. P really loves when you do that. You have stolen his heart. He told me so himself."

"Did I ever tell you how Mr. P and my paths crossed?" he asked.

I shook my head to indicate no, but I already knew how they met. I knew everything about Mr. P. One touch and he shared his entire life with me. But Kinky didn't need to know that. He seemed like he needed to tell me, and proceeded to.

"A good friend of mine was dying of cancer. He drove all the way out here to the ranch and made his last request. It was that I take Mr. P and give him a great life. I couldn't say no. All of the other Friedmans are rescues, but Mr. P was a dying man's wish. He cared more about his dog than he did for his own life. Mr. P is very special to me. I'm writing a new song about him now. It's called *Dog In The Sky*. Want to hear it?"

Before I could answer, he walked into another room, followed by Mr. P, and returned with a Gibson guitar strapped on his shoulder. He sat down to sing his song to me and Mr. P, who was sitting right in front of him, waiting in anticipation for the ditty.

"Hello, Mr. P., you mean the world to me..." he sang as he strummed his guitar. Mr. P didn't take his eyes off of Kinky. I could see how much he loved this dog. And it was mutual. "Hello Mr. P, it's always you and me. And one day you'll be my dog in the sky..." A couple of minutes later, he finished his song, put his guitar down, drank another shot of bourbon, and lit up a cigar. Mr. P jumped up in his lap. "What'd you think?" he asked while glaring at me.

"Loved it." I would have said that even if I didn't because I could tell he put his heart and soul into it. But I truly did love it. It touched me. A man who loved his dog enough to write a song about him—I understood that because I had that same love for Dudley. I'd missed him terribly since I had to take him to the vet for emergency surgery. If I had any talent, one day, perhaps I'll write a song about Dudley. Maybe even a book. Who knows? I love him that much. But for now, I'll settle for Kinky professing his love for his dog in a beautiful, soulful song.

"Time to hit the sack, mate. You good on the sofa?"

"You bet."

"The Friedmans will keep you warm." He smiled and walked away. Despite us being potential roommates, Mr. P followed him to his bedroom. I snuggled up on the sofa with Winnie and Louie. Not a big deal. I'm used to getting spooned by a dog. That's probably the closest I'll get to sharing a bed with a woman. I could live with that. I closed my eyes and drifted off as the two goofballs sleeping with me sawed logs.

The next morning, I woke up with Louie spread eagle on his back. He was sleeping on top of my head, which led me to some very creative breathing techniques. I had a bird's eye view of his man parts. Not something I necessarily wanted to wake up to. Not that there's anything wrong with that. Winnie, on the other hand, was sleeping right in my crotch, which made it impossible for me to change sleeping positions. I much preferred to sleep with Dudley and get spooned. That was the sleeping disorder of my choice. Once they heard Kinky stirring, they abruptly jumped off of me and scurried away. That was gonna leave a mark.

Kinky walked in with two cups of coffee.

"Morning, Careless, you sleep alright? Did the Friedmans keep you warm? I've got some Kona coffee for you. It's my favorite. I picked this bag up in Hawaii when I was staying with Willie Nelson. We were working on some songs together. One day we'll have some drinks, and I'll tell you of my exploits in Hawaii."

"Didn't we just have some drinks, Kinky?"

"Why, yes, yes we did. Thanks for the reminder. I meant the next time we have drinks. Want a Mexican mouthwash to wet your whistle, Careless?"

"Nah, I'm good right now. But thanks for thinking of me." We both silently laughed at the same time. Great minds…

He walked closer with the cups of coffee, closely followed by the pack of Friedmans. He set my coffee down on a table next to me and walked over and sat across the room in an old wagon wheel chair that looked like it may have come over with the settlers. He sipped his coffee and was deep in thought. I tried to be deep in thought, but Louie was busy licking himself and, try as I might, I just couldn't look away. Not that there's anything wrong with that. I wasn't fascinated with it, more like irritated. But it did keep me from concentrating. Apparently, Kinky had built up some type of tolerance or immunity to this behavior so he didn't find it as disturbing as I did. In my defense, Louie was front and center.

During this tedious time that I will never get back, my phone decided to break the trance I found myself in. It also woke Kinky up from wherever he had mentally wandered off to. I answered it. "Careless, it's L.D. Dudley's splenectomy went well. He doesn't want to eat but is up and walking around. He is in some pain. Instead of waiting four days, we thought it might be better to release him this afternoon since you have such a close relationship with him. I'd like to see if you can get him to start eating. How does that sound?"

"It sounds like I'll see you this afternoon. That's how it sounds." I hung up. Kinky was listening and asked, "Your boy alright?"

"He will be as soon as I get to him," I said while noticing Louie doing something unnatural that I'm sure most guys probably wish they could do. Try not to visualize. I'll take one for the team and do it for you.

Kinky leapt out of his chair so quickly that he startled the Friedmans. He turned on a small television that looked like it had been manufactured around the time *I Love Lucy* hit the airwaves.

The morning news was on, and the President was speaking from the Rose Garden. All of the reporters were buzzing around like little bees, shouting out questions. "As you know," the President said, "North Korea unsuccessfully tried to launch another Intercontinental Ballistic Missile this morning. Fortunately, it malfunctioned and blew up on the launch pad. If Little Rocket Man thinks we will idly stand by and watch as he threatens our allies, and the world, he is sadly mistaken. If he doesn't stop launching missiles and stop working on nuclear weapons, it will be very bad for him and the people of North Korea. We love the North Korean people, just not the leadership. I want to be very clear, the United States will not allow Little Rocket Man to have nuclear weapons on the Korean Peninsula."

A reporter shouted a question at him. "Mr. President, do we know what caused the malfunction?" The President's mouth formed a crooked little smile. It was almost unnoticeable.

"No more questions. Thank you for coming." He turned and walked away with his wife, followed by a whole host of secret service agents. Way in the back I was pretty sure I could just make out Supervisor Tirone.

The news went to a commercial break, "Men, did you know you can be hurt having sex? It's not uncommon. For more information, call 1-800-DUMBASS." I was hoping Louie would take advantage of the situation and make the call. While I was busy contemplating this, Kinky turned to me and we both said at the same time, "There's a second chip."

Either there was a second L.A.M.B. chip or Little Rocket Man was busy feeding one of his generals to the hogs. Perhaps both were true.

"I've got to run, Kinky. I need to pick up my boy, Dudley, and nurse him back to health." I drank my coffee. Kinky was right, it was quite good. I almost felt like I WAS in Hawaii.

I set my cup down on the table, got up to use the head, and shower. When I came back, I saw Kinky still glued to the television, looking for clues.

"Careless, my agent, Cleve, called while you were in the water closet and just booked a tour for me in Israel. The Israelis love the Kinkster. Can you handle things on your own for a while? It's supposed to be a one-week tour. My friend Floyd is going to move in and take care of the Friedmans. It happened really fast. I'm glad but wasn't really expecting it. I'm leaving in two days. They are flying me over and taking care of all of the travel arrangements. It should be a financial pleasure for the Kinkster. Let's talk while I'm on tour. We'll figure this out. You go take care of Dudley. He needs you now."

"You got it," I said. I watched him mix the Garrison Brothers Cowboy Bourbon bottle in with all of the rest of his booze bottles. He had quite the collection. And some of them even had juice left in them. We shook hands and parted ways. All of the Friedmans wished me well. Especially Louie. Somehow, we had become attached. I guess we now had a special bond after sleeping together and after I saved his bacon when he ran off with Winnie. He was going to miss me most of all.

I hopped in The Power Wagon and drove off toward Houston. All that talk about Willie Nelson got me in the mood to sing on the way home. Willie of course has a great voice. I, on the other hand, do not. "On the commode again, just can't wait to get on the commode again…" I sang one of my favorite Willie songs.

22

After four hours on the road, I pulled up in the Westbury Animal Hospital parking lot. As my new friend, Kinky, would say, I was getting a little nervous in the service. I was really worried about Dudley. I was expecting the worst and hoping to get severely disappointed.

I walked in and a lovely young lady asked, "How are you doing?"

My response was the routine, "I'm doing without, how you doing?" But this time I really was doing without. I was doing without my boy, Dudley, for the first time in a long time.

"Are you here for Dudley?" she inquired.

"Why yes, yes I am. Is he doing okay?"

"He's doing a lot better. He's still in a lot of pain and he doesn't seem interested in eating right now. Dr. Eckermann will meet with you shortly. He's just finishing up with a patient. Cason will show you to the room." A nice young man walked up and circled his hand and forearm around like Billy Gibbons in a ZZ Top music video, inviting me in the direction of an exam room. I couldn't wait for Dudley to "gimme all his lovin', all his hugs and kisses too." I walked into a room with Cason and waited. He left through a different door and within minutes he walked back in with my big ol' golden-colored hound dog. L.D. Eckermann walked in behind them.

I got a lump in my throat when I saw his face and his tail rapidly spinning around in helicopter fashion.

"I haven't seen him do that since you left, Careless," L.D. said. "That's a good sign."

I guess he saw the horror in my face when Dudley slowly walked over to me kind of resembling the Hunchback of Notre Dame. He was all scrunched up but managed to muster a smile and licked my face as I fell to my knees to hug him. I didn't cry. I just got some dust or something in my eye. To be quite honest, I had never loved something or someone the way I did him.

L.D. said, "Careless, he's still in a lot of pain. We'll send you home with pain meds to manage that. The main thing you need to do is get him to take it easy, rest, and make sure he eats and drinks. We suctioned a lot of blood out of his abdomen, so it will take a little time for his body to replenish it."

I looked at his belly and noticed a lovely Frankenstein-type scar from his sternum to his pupik. It's Yiddish, look it up.

"I want to see you back in ten days for a checkup. We used dissolving stitches, so they should just absorb into his body. He's probably going to leave them alone because he's not feeling great. Just keep your eye on him and call me if there are any issues."

He extended his hand and I took it in mine. I was happy he was my vet because Dudley was always in good hands with him. L.D. is like a good ol' country doctor – for dogs. As quickly as he entered the room, he and Cason did an about face and left.

Dudley and I walked out of the exam room and went to pay at a desk with two ladies behind it. I remembered how, a year ago, at this very same spot, Dudley had nabbed a whole bag of treats that was for sale. He did it with such lightning speed and accuracy that he was able to inhale the entire contents of the bag before we could process what he had done. But this time, he was just too sore for a repeat performance. I put my hand on his back and I saw his thoughts. He remembered the incident as well and thought it was funny. He looked up at me, and I could see he wanted the bag of treats. I also could see that he wanted to go home and sleep in our bed. I was presented with the bill, which could have doubled as a down payment on a house. However, I was happy to pay it for my best friend. I bought the bag of treats as well. This made him happy. Money well spent.

After I significantly paid down the national debt we left the clinic and went outside. I had to pick Dudley up and sit him in the co-pilot seat of the Power Wagon. This is where he belonged, and he seemed pretty happy, despite his pain. When we got back to Big Rock Lofts, he seemed to be walking a little better while he went around and did his business. I'm sure he was still in a great deal of pain, but sometimes being happy and being home is the best remedy for what ails you.

E.D. and Sarge came bursting out of the front door to greet him. They ignored me like I had the plague, but I didn't care. I was just as happy as can be that he was home and that he would make a full recovery.

I walked up to the three of them. E.D. was on her knees and had her arms wrapped so tightly around Dudley's neck it looked like she was choking him out. She planted kiss after kiss on his big beautiful head. Sarge was standing to the side, stroking Dudley's back. Dudley was too happy to be home and in too much pain to say something. But the look on his face said it all.

"I'm so glad you're back, big boy," E.D. said. "We all missed you."

"Yeah, man, han, han," Sarge chirped in. "What E.D. said."

"How come I don't get this kind of treatment?" I asked E.D.

"When you get attacked while protecting your home and have to get your spleen removed because of it, come talk to me," she said.

I must admit, when I took a bullet and almost died while solving my last case, E.D. was pretty kind to me. So I just smiled and, like Dudley, didn't say something.

"Did you find the pricks who did this to him, Careless?" E.D. asked.

"They've been dealt with."

She nodded her head.

Of course Dudley already knew this, having read my thoughts when I placed my hand on his back at the vet. He saw what Kinky and I had done and was happy justice had been meted out. Revenge is sweet. And best served on a pu pu platter. Like the one FBI Supervisor Tirone had comped for us at The Flying Dragon for delivering a couple of Korean spies to her. Yes, revenge was sweet, especially to people who hurt animals. They are the worst of the worst.

When the reunion was over we all walked into the lofts. I carried Dudley up the stairs to our loft. There was no way he was going to traverse the stairs on his own in his current condition. He drank a bowl of water, which I took as a good sign. But he didn't touch his food. He walked over to the door and sat, staring at it. I placed my hand on his extremely handsome head and saw he had picked up E.D.'s scent on the other side of the door. I reached over and opened it.

"How did you know I was here. I was just about to knock on the door?" she asked.

"It's a long story." I said. She was holding a pot of something in her hands. It caught Dudley's attention. Speaking of pot, I wondered if Sarge would be stopping by as well.

"I made our boy some chicken to make him feel better," E.D. said. "Careless, why don't you try and feed him some?"

He didn't seem interested in eating earlier, but I took the pot from E.D. and took some chicken out of it. It smelled delicious. I knelt down and Dudley walked over and gingerly took it from my hand. I gave him more and more until he had no interest, but at least he was eating again. Poor boy had lost some weight since the operation. I could tell and no, he was not watching his girlish figure like I am.

When he finished, he walked over to our bed and stood looking longingly at it. Then he looked back at me. I walked over, lifted him up, and placed him on the bed. He was in too much pain to jump. He circled around three of four times and then lay his weary head to rest. He was finally at peace and started snoring.

E.D. and I both smiled.

E.D. sat on the sofa and patted the space next to her. I must admit, this did entice me. But not before I poured myself a Careless Coffee.

I mixed the iced coffee and the bourbon together and promptly sat next to the gorgeous E.D. Was she finally about to profess her love for me? Oh, I hope so. A guy can dream.

She turned to me and put her hand on my shoulder. So far so good. She looked me in the eye with her beautiful deep blue eyes and said, "I'm so glad Dudley is okay. I was really worried about him."

Okay, this wasn't exactly what I had expected and was definitely not about me. But I still had high apple pie in the sky hopes that she was going to get there.

"You know," she said, "I almost lost you both this year. I don't think I could have handled losing either of you, and I'm just so thankful you are both in my life."

Now we were getting somewhere. She started moving in to plant one on me, and I closed my eyes for the magical Hallmark moment that was about to happen. I could feel the warmth of her face next to mine. I felt her sweet cherry blossom breath upon me and then it happened. Dudley had the loudest bout of gastritis I had ever heard to date. Being the over achiever he is, I'm sure he'll most likely outdo himself at some point. But the damage had been done. E.D. broke out laughing and pulled away like a Greyhound Bus leaving the station. Foiled again by my partner in crime. I'm pretty sure I heard him snickering. I only hoped it didn't hurt him much because of his stitches.

I opened my eyes, and E.D. appeared to be studying my face. She placed her hand on my cheek and said, "I'm really glad the two of you are okay."

I remained hopeful. I mean, what would a dog-comedy-mystery-spy novel be without a little romance in it?

"Here's the thing, Careless. I don't know if you've been watching the news, but the United States is about to move its embassy in Israel from Tel Aviv to Jerusalem. It's a big deal because many of our presidents have been claiming they wanted to do this for over twenty years. And now this president is actually doing it. It's a major media event and is being covered by all of the news outlets. My magazine wants me to go cover it and take photos. It's a three-day assignment. My usual assistant, Carlos Ortega, was given the assignment with me, but he was involved in an accident on his motorcycle on the way home from work last night and has a broken leg. He's out of action for at least six weeks. There's another photojournalist, Pamela Cardona, who stepped up to go on assignment with me, but her husband has mysteriously disappeared, so she's staying here to work with the police to find him. It's the strangest thing. In fact, your friend Detective Present is working with her to locate her husband. It's almost like the universe doesn't want me to go to Israel. I'm literally desperate to find an assistant, and my office can't spare another person right now."

It wasn't the universe reaching out and touching her. But there was something just as determined at work here. It seemed way too coincidental that both of her assistants were out of action. Besides, I don't believe in coincidence. I did next what the universe called for me to do.

"You want me to go with you?" I asked. It felt right because obviously it seemed something was trying to get me there. And besides, how bad could a trip to the Holy Land be anyway?

"Would you be interested in helping me on the assignment? My office has approved me to choose an assistant to take with me since no one from our office is currently available. I know it's asking a lot, but it would help me out tremendously. It doesn't pay anything, but it's free. I know you like free. The magazine would cover everything. And you would be spending quality time with me. Who wouldn't want that?"

Who wouldn't indeed?

"That is a really interesting proposition. However, the one thing we haven't thought of is what would I do with Dudley. You know I can't leave him right now. He's still recuperating from his splenectomy surgery. And what about work? You know they need me at the office."

"I'm glad you asked that, Careless. While you were off running around with your friend Kinky, I called Papa and asked him if you could have some time off. And guess what? He said you sure could. And my friend Leticia Hess, who I work with at the magazine, is a total dog person. She even volunteers at an animal shelter called Sonoma's Haven. She has agreed to come stay with Dudley while you are away on assignment. So, you see, it's all set. You can go, if you want to."

I had to hand it to her, she did think of everything. Even though I did feel like I had just been set up.

"The work thing I can agree to, but I don't even know this Leticia person. I can't leave my Dude with just anyone. And why isn't Leticia going with you on assignment?" I took a swig of my Careless Coffee. I'd definitely been set up.

"I just knew you were going to say that, Careless. She'll be here in ten minutes for an interview. Just trust me, Dudley will love her. And she is our office manager, so there's no way my boss is going to do without her."

How could I say no? Ten minutes later, there was a knock at the door. Dudley acknowledged it by lifting up his head and watching us answer the door. I guess he was feeling too lousy to snap to attention. E.D. opened the door.

"Hi Leticia, come on in and meet Careless and Dudley." Leticia nodded while otherwise ignoring me as she passed by and went straight over to Dudley to sit by his side. Smart gal. I already liked her. Dudley looked up at her, and his tail spun around in a half circle because the bed stopped him from completing the loop. She patted him on the head and rubbed his ears. He didn't say something, so I knew he probably liked her. But just to be sure, I walked over and introduced myself while placing my hand on Dudley's back. Yes, he definitely liked her. I also found out that Sarge was in the hallway and about to knock on the door. Dudley smelled him.

"E.D., would you mind getting the door for Sarge?" I asked. There was a knock at the door. E.D. and Leticia seemed surprised. Dudley and I were not. E.D. shot me a look and opened the door to reveal Sarge.

"Hey man, han, han, I came to check on Dudley. How's he doing?"

He walked over to Dudley and immediately had a Hallmark Channel connection with Leticia. And I'll be darned if she didn't have one right back at him. Dudley and I could see it and feel it. Ruh Roh!

"Well, hello. I'm Sarge. And you are?"

"I'm Leticia," she said, holding her hand out. I wasn't sure he knew what to do. Would he shake her hand? Would he kiss her hand? Or would he just stand there like Sarge and awkwardly do nothing? He surprised me and took her hand in both of his as their eyes met. One could feel the electricity.

"I'll be taking care of Dudley while E.D. and Careless are away on an exciting assignment in Israel," she explained to Sarge. Even she knew it was prearranged that I would be going with E.D. to Israel. I've learned over time that it is useless to fight the universe. Or a determined, beautiful, blonde woman.

"Oh, I live right next door," he said. "Dudley loves me. I can come help you." My hand was still on Dudley's back. He was listening and not amused.

"That would be wonderful. I'd love that. You know what else I'd love? If you'd give me my hand back." She had a big, inviting smile on her face.

It looked like Doctor Love had just found a match made in heaven. E.D. and I looked at one another and smiled. I was happy because it certainly wouldn't hurt having two people take care of Dudley while I apparently would be away on assignment.

E.D. and I walked Leticia around the loft to show her the lay of the land. Fortunately, at one thousand square feet, we didn't have far to go. Sarge followed Leticia around like a little puppy dog. It was endearing, so I didn't mind. I showed her where the dog food was and showed her Dudley's medicines that he would need for the next ten days. I also showed her the chicken in the fridge E.D. had brought over for Dudley and explained to her that she might just have to hand feed him until he was feeling strong enough and well enough to eat. She said she had no problem with that.

Sarge told her he would show her where to take Dudley outside to do his business, and she seemed grateful for that. She actually liked having him around. I explained to Sarge that he may have to carry Dudley up and down the stairs until his pain subsided, and he seemed good with that.

E.D. said, "We're leaving in four days at 7:00 am, Leticia. Can you be here at 6:30 just to be on the safe side?"

"I'll be here. Don't worry about a thing."

Sarge said, "I'll be here as well. Just to make sure everything goes okay."

"Don't worry Careless," Leticia said. "Dudley's in good hands. E.D. told me how special he is to you and all you two have been through. I house-sit for a lot of clients, and I ALWAYS get repeat business."

I nodded my head in response.

She walked toward the door and Sarge followed her out into the hallway. Dudley stayed in bed just watching and listening. They hugged goodbye and E.D. and I gave each other a look. She was smiling. I did find it endearing but just was happy that Dudley would be well taken care of. And that Sarge finally found a girlfriend and wouldn't have to go on farmersonly.com.

It appeared that a long journey was in my future.

"Careless, don't fool around. I'll need you ready. Okay? You know how I feel about being late. Make sure in four days you get up, take care of Dudley, and be ready to go. I don't want to miss our flight. That means pack up your things and get your passport ready before you and lover boy over there get busy and you forget about it. Okay?" E.D. barked out her orders. She walked over and kissed Dudley on the head. "Don't you worry about a thing, big boy, you're going to be just fine." I could tell he was already on the road to recovery. She walked past me and toward the door. I swear this time I heard Dudley snickering. Yes, he was definitely feeling better.

"Did you forget something," I asked E.D.

"Whatever do you mean, Careless?" She was grinning.

"Well, Dudley got a big smooch, so I felt kind of neglected when you walked right past me and nada, nothing."

"Oh, I was just testing you to see if you were paying attention. You've seemed a little off ever since that art gallery incident and making friends with Kinky." She turned back around, placed both of her very soft, supple hands on my cheeks and briefly kissed me on the lips. But that brief moment seemed to last an eternity, at least to me.

She was, of course, correct. I had changed since the gallery incident with Kinky. That's what going on an alcoholiday does to you.

I lay down to sleep with Dudley. As soon as I got comfortable, he stood up, circled around four times and lay his head to rest on my shoulders. I could tell being home already made him feel better.

I stared at him resting peacefully. Then I decided that I was just not comfortable leaving him with a stranger. Oh sure, Leticia seemed lovely enough, but Dudley had been through a traumatic experience. I felt like I needed to be here with him, just like he was always there for me. Loyalty is a trait that runs strong in my family.

I quietly picked up my cell phone and dialed E.D.

"No, Careless," E.D. said before I could even utter my concerns about leaving Dudley behind. "I'm not coming down for a nightcap. Now go to sleep. Lord knows you need your beauty rest."

"Well, I do like the idea of you coming down for a nightcap. Believe me, I do. But that's not it this time. I'm really having second thoughts about leaving Dudley with Leticia while I travel to Israel with you on assignment. Look, Leticia seems wonderful, and I'm super glad Sarge finally found a soulmate, which in my mind is a Christmas miracle, but I'm just not comfortable leaving Dudley right now after all he's been through. He really needs me right now." I expressed my deep concern. I still heard a clicking noise on the phone line, so I was sure I was still being surveilled.

There was silence on the other end of the line. For the first time since I met E.D., she seemed speechless. Not a good sign.

"Are you still there or are you too pissed off and thinking of the appropriate response to what I said?" I asked.

"You know, Careless, I love you. And I really love Dudley, sometimes more than I think I love you…"

This didn't seem to be going well.

"Look, I understand your concern, I do. And I think Leticia will do a fabulous job with Dudley, but if you are uncomfortable with leaving him now, especially with what he's gone through, I'll understand. I really wanted us to go to Israel together, and I really did need a photo assistant, but if you feel you can't go, I'll understand. That's what friends do. But just do me a favor. Sleep on it and let me know first thing in the morning. Leticia is still on call, and I'm sure she'll understand if you end up staying with Dudley. Just think about it. Okay?"

Wow! This is why I loved her so. I thought she would be angry, but instead she gently let me off the hook. I couldn't ask for a better friend.

"Okay, thank you for understanding. Dudley and I both appreciate this." I was resting my hand on his side and he understood every word I heard and said. He didn't want me to go. I wasn't going to.

But I said, "Okay E.D. I'll think about it and let you know in the morning. Thank you again. And how about that nightcap now?" I think she heard a bit of hope in my voice. All I heard was a loud click after that as she hung up. Dudley cracked a smile. I saw him. And he knew I saw him and didn't care.

The next morning I woke up and called E.D. to inform her I would be unavailable to help her on the embassy assignment in Israel. She was of course disappointed but told me she would try to find someone else to fill in. I was disappointed as well to miss such a golden opportunity, but a friend in need is a friend indeed.

Dudley and I kept our usual routine of going to work and coming home for three uneventful days. The morning of the fourth day, I woke up at 5:00. Dudley was staring at me but hadn't budged from his vantage point of the night before. I placed my hand on his head and saw that he needed to use the little boy's room. So did I. I also saw that he was hungry and thirsty, a great sign that he was feeling better. I got up and used the facilities. He gingerly stepped out of bed and was walking just fine. I fed and watered him. Not a problem at all. His appetite was back. I got dressed, grabbed my cell phone and walked with him by my side. He descended the stairs like a champ. No more walking hunched over. He certainly wasn't walking gingerly anymore and seemed to have a lot of pep in his step again. I'm sure the pain medication I mixed in his food probably helped. Other than the stitches, he seemed just fine.

I took him outside to the back courtyard, and he did his business. While he was smelling everything and making himself at home, my cell phone started having spasms. I pulled it from my pocket and answered, "Miss Cleo's Hotline, would you like me to tell your fortune?"

"Very funny, Careless," E.D. said. "How about I tell you your fortune?

Your wish may be about to come true. My trip to Israel was about to be cancelled. Since I was so desperate for an assistant on the Israel assignment, my office agreed to let Leticia go with me. The only problem is she just called me and told me her aunt was in a car accident in Florida. It sounded pretty serious, so she has to fly down there and stay with her in the hospital. Isn't that awful, Careless?"

"That's terrible," I said. And convenient, I thought. It seemed a little strange and even a tad bit coincidental–again. Or was I just being paranoid since I realized so many people were spying on us? "Well, I guess that settles that. I still can't go with you. What would I do with Dudley? I could never leave him with Sarge. Lord knows what'll happen if I even attempt that. I can't leave him by himself. And Birk is away on business. I guess you're going to try to go it alone. I'm sorry, E.D."

"That's what I'm trying to tell you, Careless. I called my boss and told her I would need a new assistant for the Jerusalem embassy photo shoot assignment. She told me they were short staffed and didn't have anyone else. Since it's such a huge story, they are going to fly us over in a corporate jet. Do you know what that means?"

"Yes, the food selection and quality will be much better than on most of the major airlines."

"Well, yes, that's true but not exactly what I was going for. I said us! You can bring Dudley! My boss is a big dog lover and wouldn't hear otherwise after I told her what happened and his life story. No TSA line to stand in, so I won't get felt up from the belt up–again. We'll get pre-checked and walk right onto the plane with Dudley. Dudley's going to Israel with us. Isn't that amazing? Just make sure to bring all of his vaccination records with you from your vet."

"I stopped listening after you said felt up from the belt up. I was visualizing. Oh, and Tov M'ode." That's Hebrew, look it up.

Dudley walked over to me after he had finished his morning ritual. I placed my hand on his head and he felt my thoughts. He knew he was going on a trip but was a little skeptical about flying on an airplane. The really nice thing was that Dudley would be going back to his homeland. Oh, did I forget to mention he is a member of the tribe? That's right, Dudley is Jewish on his mother's side.

"I've already called Papa, and he has given his blessing for you to take a couple of days off. You're going. Get packed up."

"It's fine," I reassured Dudley. "I've flown hundreds of times. It's no big deal and safer than when your first owner dropped you off at a high-kill animal shelter." He understood. And he let me know as long as he was by my side, he didn't care where we were. We walked back up to the loft. He easily traversed the stairs. I threw some dog food, Dudley's pain pills, and a copy of his vet records in the bag I packed, along with clothes and a few manscaping items. I would have to leave behind my pain pills of choice, AKA whiskey, but I was sure they would have plenty on the airplane.

We walked out to the hallway to meet E.D. She was right on time, just like she normally was.

"Here's my bag, Careless. Be careful, all of my camera equipment is in there, and it is very expensive. Not to mention I'll need it for the embassy opening. I have two press badges for us. Security is going to be very tight. And you," she said as she bent down. "This will be your first time on an airplane. I bet your manners will be better than his. She pointed at me. Let's get a move on. I don't want to be late. I'll drive."

Dudley kept up with us stride for stride down the stairs and seemed back to normal. We walked over to E.D.'s big blue Oldsmobile she called Betsy. I gently placed the luggage in the trunk and opened the front seat door for her and Dudley. They both climbed in and I got in on the other side.

Since it was early, there was very little traffic. Fifteen minutes later, E.D. drove up to the security gate for private jets at the airport. No parking garage for us. A guard checked her driver's license and mine, and she handed him Dudley's documentation from Westbury Animal Hospital. He glanced at a clipboard he was holding. He waved us through as the gate opened and he said, "Please drive straight ahead and park in spot 1A.

E.D. parked the car, and we got out in front of a beautiful jet. I had never been on a plane this small. I got the bags out of the trunk, and a well-dressed, very fit man walked over and said, "Let me help you with those, sir. Welcome aboard one of the finest jets we fly, the Gulfstream G550."

He had a slight Middle Eastern accent but was quite well spoken. Before reaching for the bags from me, he patted Dudley on the head. Dudley said something, but the man didn't seem to pay attention to it. I patted Dudley on his head, and he simmered down. Then I gave him the bags, and he said, "Please follow me."

"E.D., why don't you and Dudley stand in front of the plane, and I'll take your picture with my phone? It will be a great way to start off our trip."

She walked over to the plane with Dudley, turned sideways, and placed one hand on her curvaceous hip and the other on Dudley's big handsome head. What a poser! The man with the bags looked a little uncomfortable with this and stealthily backed his way out of the picture. Although I would cherish a picture of my two favorite people, that was not the reason I wanted the image.

All three of us followed him into the plane. The doorway wasn't terribly large but once we boarded the inside of the plane opened up to reveal a very luxurious cabin with plush leather seats. Dudley helped himself to one that looked particularly inviting and curled up and closed his eyes. The man stowed the bags and disappeared into the cockpit. I heard the door close and lock behind him. Something just didn't seem right to me. E.D. and I looked around, and I could tell she was impressed. I was as well. About five minutes later, a stunning young woman with long brown hair pulled up in a bun and wearing sexy librarian glasses walked in and closed and locked the door. She turned toward us and I was struck by her cat-green eyes.

She said, "Good morning, my name is Kelley and I will be your flight attendant for this trip. Eh, is there anything I can get you before we depart? The preflight check is being done now, and we should be underway in about fifteen minutes." She looked very familiar, but I couldn't quite place her. From her accent, I knew she was Israeli. I had met many Israelis in business. Also, the most common word in Israel is "Eh." They always say "Eh" at the beginning of each sentence. I have no idea why. This whole thing made me very uneasy, and I started to wonder about Kinky because he was already on tour in Israel. Coincidence? I thought not. Why did our paths keep crossing?

"Good morning, this is your captain speaking. We are just about ready for takeoff. We'll be travelling to JFK in New York. That should take about three hours, depending on the weather. We'll make a brief stop to refuel and travel on to Ben Gurion Airport in Tel Aviv. Please make yourself comfortable, and if you need anything, please let Kelley know and she will be happy to assist you."

Dudley's ears were perked up, and he had one eye open during the announcement. I could tell he was a bit skeptical. So was I. E.D. was just as happy as can be, checking out the seats, picking just the right one for her to sit in. She had a big girlish grin on her face, like a kid in a candy shop. She looked back at me and was a bit perplexed by my facial expression. She sat down and patted her hand on an oversized, plush leather seat next to her for me to sit in. And I did.

"Isn't this great, Careless? I feel like a celebrity. I just love it."

"You've always been a celebrity to me, darlin." Brownie points. She smiled. Dudley said something, sighed, and went back to sleep.

Kelley walked over and asked, "May I get you anything to drink before we take off?"

I looked at E.D. and waited for her response.

"I'd love a Mimosa if it's not too much trouble," she said.

"We can do that," Kelley responded. "And for you, sir?" She was definitely studying me.

I was certain I'd seen her before but I just couldn't place it. However, I hid my body language as best as I could and tried not to let on.

"Would you happen to have decaf coffee?" I inquired.

"Yessir, that will not be a problem."

"Terrific. What kind of bourbon do you have?"

"Eh, we have Makers Mark and Jack Daniels."

Easy choice. "Beautiful, would you please put some ice in the decaf coffee and mix some Jack Daniels in it for good measure?"

E.D. chuckled and Kelley's lips made a quick smile before returning to the professional manner she so cleverly maintained. Iced coffee is a staple for most Israelis. They drink it hot in the morning and don't let it go to waste later on, turning it into iced coffee.

Kelley quickly returned with our drinks and excused herself. Dudley kept a watchful eye on her. I saw his nose sniffing her as she passed by him. Her scent seemed familiar to him.

I whipped out my phone and texted Detective Present. I wanted to let him know we'd be gone for a little while and to ask a favor. I asked him to trace the tail numbers of the jet we were on. I'm sure everything was fine but something in the back of my mind told me otherwise. He asked me for the manufacturer and model of the jet. I told him and texted him the tail numbers, which were visible in the image I had taken of E.D. and Dudley with my phone. Of course, I didn't hurt that E.D. and Dudley were in the picture. That brightened it up and was a great excuse to take the picture, but also allowed me to record the tail numbers so I could inquire about them later on. He responded almost immediately.

He texted that there was no plane registered under that number in the international database but that we were on an Israeli jet. His dad had been in the Air Force and was a big airplane buff. The number and letter 4X in the tail numbers meant it was an Israeli aircraft, and the Israeli Defense Forces had been known to fly Gulfstream G550's in the past. A lot of things were starting to fall into place.

"This is your captain. We are ready for takeoff. Kelley will come by and collect your beverages. Please turn off all electronics until we are airborne and have reached altitude." Kelley walked by as I gulped down the last bit of my Airplane Careless Coffee. She smiled and I handed her my glass. E.D. gave her the half-drunk Mimosa. She and Dudley closed their eyes and went to sleep. The plane took off and I sat back and started going over things in my head.

I had no clue why we were on what was obviously an Israeli jet headed to New York and then Israel. I'm sure it had something to do with the L.A.M.B chip. When the plane was at altitude, things smoothed out. I turned my phone back on and was going to text Detective Present to see if he had any further information that might be helpful. I felt the most desirable urge to close my eyes and go to sleep. I turned my phone off. Kelley came over and said, "Let me help you with that, Careless," taking my phone from me as I nodded off.

In my dreams, I found myself back at the Copper Love Art Gallery. I was studying what had occurred when we walked into the bloody crime scene. There was one deceased Middle Eastern man on the floor. Many of the paintings were either damaged and on the ground or hanging crooked on the wall. It was obvious to me somebody was searching for something. It had to be about the L.A.M.B. chip. Was it there? And if so, what was it doing there in the first place? And who was the dead man lying on the ground? What was Copper Love's involvement? She must have slipped the chip into Kinky's jacket pocket when he was helping her. Why would she do that? Was she worried that someone would discover the chip and take it from her? And, finally, who was Copper Love? I studied her facial features and expressions. I distinctly remembered her eyes and mouth. They belonged to Kelley, the flight attendant. The eyes were a different color and her hair was different, but it was definitely her. It was a great disguise. To the untrained eye it would have never been noticed. Now I had even more questions. I hoped I remembered all of this after my snooze.

When I woke up we were already at JFK. I normally don't sleep on airplanes, and I was still kind of tired. E.D. was still sound asleep. Dudley was resting in a comfy seat, but he had his eyes open and was watching me. The plane was motionless, and I could see that it was being refueled.

I woke E.D.. "Morning, Sunshine," I said. I must say, she does look truly spectacular waking up. Well, she looks great all of the time, but especially when she wakes up.

"Morning, Careless. Were you able to sleep? Where are we?"

"Oh yes, I slept. We're at JFK, refueling for the flight to Israel."

The cockpit door was open. The pilot and co-pilot were in their seats inspecting gadgets. The pilot was on his phone, speaking Hebrew. When he heard us stirring, he quickly switched to English and said, "Okay, I understand," and abruptly hung up.

"Good morning, this is your captain speaking. We are doing a quick stop in New York to refuel and should be in flight to Israel in about 20 minutes. If you need anything, please ask your flight attendant, Krysten. She will be along shortly."

"Hey, wasn't our flight attendant's name Kelley?" I asked E.D.

"I don't remember, Careless. It was so early in the morning, and I fell asleep pretty quickly. Kelley and Krysten are really similar names. I just can't recall. Don't worry about it. Just relax and have another drink." She was staring out of the window and seemed preoccupied. I was not.

Now I knew for sure the flight attendant, Kelley, was really Copper Love posing as a flight attendant. I would confront her as soon as I saw her again. Did she work for the Russians? Was she an FBI agent? Or perhaps the Mossad? My curiosity was peaked. And I don't make mistakes on names, or people.

The flight attendant walked up from the back of the plane. She had her back turned, but she definitely looked like Copper Love, or Kelley, whatever name she was currently using. When she turned around I was very surprised. "Is there anything I can get you?" she asked.

I was ready to spring into action, but she was not Copper Love or Kelley. They looked very similar, almost too similar, but this was definitely not the flight attendant from the first leg of our journey. Same hair, eyes, sexy librarian glasses and figure, but this was a different person. The face was similar, but not the same.

"Hi, can you tell me where the other flight attendant has gone to? I would like to speak with her."

"I'm sorry sir, other flight attendant? I'm not sure what you mean. I'm the only flight attendant on this aircraft."

Either I was crazy or someone was trying to pull a fast one on me. I went with door number two.

I was about to confront Krysten with my observations when E.D. elbowed me and said, "Please excuse my friend, he just hasn't been himself lately. Careless, why don't you have a drink and simmer down."

"You're right, of course. I'm sorry, Krysten. It's early, and I haven't had my coffee yet. May I please get a glass of iced coffee with a shot of Jack Daniels in it? That will probably make me feel better." I knew it wouldn't but I didn't want to act suspicious or, worse, have E.D. begin thinking I was going crazy. I knew something was up, but I just didn't let on.

"I'd like a glass of sparkling water, if you wouldn't mind," E.D. said.

"Sure thing, hon, I'll be right back with your drinks," Krysten said. She walked towards the front of the plane. She was as attractive as Kelley, but without a hint of an Israeli accent.

"What is wrong with you, Careless? Sometimes I wonder what's going on in that mind of yours."

"I feel like that's a trick question, and if you knew what was going on in my mind, you WOULD have come down to the loft for a nightcap last night. Just sayin."

"Now, that's the Careless I know. Straighten up and fly right, mister. I'm going to need you on this assignment. Make it happen, Captain."

"Yes, honeybunch. Would you mind if I go over and sit with Dudley for a spell? He's looking kind of needy." I did want to go sit with him, but I also knew he would be my little black box recorder if he had managed to stay awake during the flight. He would reveal anything that happened while E.D. and I were asleep.

"You go ahead and sit with lover boy. I know you two hate being separated." He was watching and of course said something while his tail spun around in circles.

He eyeballed me as I got up and walked over to sit next to him. When I sat down, he repositioned himself so that his head rested in my lap. I gently rested my hand on his head, and boy, was I right – as always. I watched through his eyes as E.D. and I fell asleep during the first leg of the flight. Kelley, the flight attendant walked up to me and said, "Let me help you with that, Careless," as she took my phone. I fell asleep. She had obviously drugged E.D. and me. E.D. was already asleep.

The pilot opened the cockpit door and walked out. The co-pilot stayed at the controls. Kelley was a busy girl and when she finished going through my phone, she turned it off and put it back in my lap. The pilot and she spoke, but Dudley didn't understand what they were saying. They were speaking in Hebrew and gesturing with their hands as they spoke. They were definitely Israelis. Besides using the word "Eh" at the beginning of every sentence, Israelis also wave their hands around while speaking. Probably worse than Italians. Kelley took off her sexy librarian glasses and with both hands removed a wig she had been wearing. Her long red hair flowed down her back. It was definitely Copper Love, if that was even her real name. I was betting she was a Russian double agent for the Israelis. But at this point, who knows?

The pilot directed her to go through our bags that had been stowed away. She pulled them out and thoroughly went through them. She must have been looking for the L.A.M.B. chip. She was disappointed and came away empty handed. She neatly placed everything back in the bags just as she had found the items, closed them up, and stowed them away where they had been. She was darn good at this.

Then they looked and pointed at Dudley. They were speaking Hebrew so he had no idea what they were saying. The pilot said something to her to which she responded very strongly several times, "Lo! Lo! Lo!" while holding up her index finger in front of the pilot, as if preventing him from doing something. Dudley thought she was saying No! No! No! because it sounded a lot like no. She came and sat down next to him, and his tail spun around. She asked with a smile on her face, "You won't tell anyone, will you

Dudley?" Of course, he said something and they both laughed. She stood up and walked away.

But he would tell someone. And he just did. They had no way of knowing that. It seemed like there was the possibility something bad that coud have happened to him. I was glad Copper stepped in. And now I knew everything. More importantly, I was right about the flight attendant, and E.D. was wrong. It's important to be right. Except when you're around women. Then you're usually never right. Ever! When the plane landed in New York, Copper deplaned and Krysten came on board. At least now I knew where I stood. And it looks like the Israelis were also searching for the chip.

The co-pilot came out of the cockpit and closed the door of the plane. He returned to the cockpit and closed that door as the crew prepared for another takeoff. Krysten brought us drinks and some snacks. E.D. drank away. I did not. No, I won't be repeating the same error I had before. No telling what would happen this time.

The captain announced that we had refueled and were ready for takeoff. Once in the air, E.D. and I discussed what we were going to do in Israel. She said we would have plenty of time to tour, but we would have to hit the embassy opening in Jerusalem pretty hard. She was on a deadline, so we would have to work quickly. She told me someone representing her office would meet us at the airport and get us settled in.

Once the small talk was out of the way, E.D. closed her eyes and started to snooze. Dudley did the same. I decided to check my phone and see if Detective Present had sent me any more information. I wasn't too surprised to find out that all of my texts to and from Detective Present were deleted. Imagine that. And the lovely image I had taken of E.D. and Dudley next to the jet had been deleted as well. Too bad for them that the texts still existed on Detective Present's phone. At least, I hoped they did. You never know with these guys. I was getting a little tired, so I tried to get some rest – with one eye open.

I rested up with trusty Dudley, who was sleeping with his head in my lap. I remained vigilant. So did he. He now knew what I knew. You can bet I didn't accept any more food or beverages for the duration of the flight. Most likely we didn't have anything to worry about because all of our belongings had already been thoroughly searched, with no positive results. They knew we didn't have what they were looking for. Now I had to determine if this was a legitimate assignment for E.D. or a ploy to get us to Israel while people searched for the chip. Or both? And what about Kinky? Was he on tour or being set up like we might be? These were my questions.

I played several scenarios in my head, which made the ten-hour flight go pretty quickly. So did having my best pal sleeping in my lap. Little can happen to you when your guard dog is on duty. The plane came to a soft landing at Ben Gurion Airport in Tel Aviv.

"We've landed in Tel Aviv. Please remain seated until the plane comes to a complete stop. Natan will meet you at the plane. He will be your guide in Israel and take care of you from here on. Welcome to Israel." The pilot was very informative.

The plane came to a gentle stop. I was suddenly reminded that the Israeli Air Force pilots are renowned worldwide as some of the best. And the most feared. They are that good. Chances were our pilot either is or was in the Air Force at some point. Krysten walked through the cabin and asked if we needed anything else. E.D. and I both responded, "No." Dudley of course said something.

The cockpit door opened, and the pilot and co-pilot emerged. They looked at us, saluted, and deplaned without saying a word.

"That was odd, don't you think?" I asked E.D.

"I think you're odd. Don't go reading a bunch of stuff into this, Careless. This is just a simple assignment to cover the moving of the Israeli Embassy from Tel Aviv to Jerusalem. That's all. No mystery here. Okay? Now behave yourself and be a darling and grab our bags so we can go to the hotel. Also, I think your soulmate over there needs to go do his business. It looks like his eyes are floating."

She was right, he did need to go. I could feel it. He probably has better bladder control than I do. Especially after a few Careless Coffees.

I stood up and so did he. E.D. was already walking toward the front of the plane. I grabbed our bags and we joined her. We walked out of the plane. It was nighttime, and the airport was lit up like a Hanukkah Bush during Christmas. It was great to be in the homeland. Yes, I am a member of the tribe. So is Dudley, as previously disclosed.

Once outside, Dudley relieved himself on the front wheel of the plane. A young man with dark hair and olive complexion shut his eyes and shook his head from side to side to show his disdain for the evacuation.

"It's a natural biological function," I explained, shrugging my shoulders to possibly alleviate any negative judgement. E.D. elbowed me and placed her hands on her hips, glaring at Dudley and then back at me.

"You'll have to forgive my travel mates. They are unaccustomed to international travel. And manners." The young man cracked a smile.

"I am Natan, I have been assigned to be your tour guide. Eh, anything you need, I will take care of for you. Don't hesitate to ask."

There's that pesky "Eh" word again. Sometimes I think Bugs Bunny may have been Israeli. "Eh, what's up Doc?"

"Eh, let me help you with your bags. I will drive you to your hotel in Jerusalem." He took the bags from me and loaded them in a dark, fairly new Mercedes SUV. Dudley joined us after he drained the main vein. It took a long time because he had been holding it for so long. I guess they'll have to run the jet through the plane wash.

"Well, at least someone here knows how to be a gentleman," E.D. said.

Natan gave a little smirk and stowed the bags in the back of the SUV. He wasn't particularly big. Medium height. Slim. But he was definitely strong for his size.

"Thank you, Satan, much appreciated," I wisecracked. E.D. was not amused. Neither was Satan.

"Eh, it is Natan."

"Oh, I'm so sorry, my ears are still clogged up from the altitude."

"You must put your kelev on a leash," he said, pointing to Dudley.

"My what?" I asked.

"Your dog. You must put your dog on a leash. It is the law."

Dudley said something. I leashed him. He didn't mind.

We all got into the SUV. E.D. sat in front with Natan, and Dudley and I sat in the back. It was very roomy.

"How long is the drive?" E.D. asked.

"About an hour and a half," he answered.

He drove out of the airport and onto a freeway.

"If you have any questions, please let me know. I will point out things for you as we drive." His phone chirped once or twice. He quickly glanced at it and put it away. "We have several national parks, one of them being Castel National Park. It was very crucial to Israel during the War of Independence in 1948."

Of course, we could see very little since it was nighttime, but E.D. intently listened. I was thinking of other things but half-heartedly listened.

"What is that big wall I keep seeing as we're driving?" E.D. asked.

"Eh, that is our security wall. We were having many terrorist problems in our country. You know, we are surrounded by enemies who wish to destroy us. They say they want to drive us into the sea. Can you imagine? A small strip of land only eight-five miles across at the widest point, and the only democracy in the Middle East. The wall stopped all illegal entry into Israel and stopped terrorist attacks. A sad but necessary tool to keep our country safe and secure. You know, we don't just have Jews in Israel, even though it is a Jewish state and all Jews are welcome. We live among Arabs and we all get along fine together. A small group of terrorists are the reason a wall has become a necessity." He was very convincing.

Being from America, none of us in the vehicle except for him knew what that was truly like.

Natan played American music from the 1970's. E.D. inquired about the music selection, and Natan told her the Israeli people love America, love our president, and especially love our music. "I love Santana," he said. I found it endearing. I could tell he was genuine. E.D. continued asking a lot of questions. Strangely enough, she never stumped him. Much like E.D., he had an answer for everything.

We travelled for a while, but the music and all of the *Jeopardy* questions being asked, made the drive go by pretty quickly.

"Eh, we are passing by the embassy right now. The official opening will be in two days. It is very busy, as everyone has moved everything from Tel Aviv to this location. The Americans say it will be fully operational and ready for the grand opening."

There was a lot of action going on, even at night. I saw heavily armed guards in front of staggered concrete barriers in front of a gate. Behind them were steel bollards. People were hustling about behind those gates. I had little doubt that it would be ready in time.

"The U.S. Ambassador, the U.S. Deputy Secretary of State, the U.S. Treasury Secretary, and the U.S. President's daughter and son-in-law are already here to attend the ribbon cutting ceremony. I think they are staying at your hotel. Maybe you will run into them, yes?"

"Maybe. Oh, I hope so!" E.D. said. "That would be great for my magazine!" She was all excited.

A few minutes later, Natan said, "This is the old city. I can take you on a tour of it tomorrow if you'd like."

It was very beautiful. Huge stone walls surrounded the city. Its towers and mosques were lit up. It was breathtaking as well as spectacular.

"I would love that! Wouldn't you love that, Careless? Let's go visit the old city tomorrow. What do you say?"

"How could I say no to you? That sounds great."

"Very well, I will pick you up at the hotel at 8:00 tomorrow morning. A lot of places we will go do not allow dogs, so he will have to stay at the hotel. Also, bring a jacket. Jerusalem can get cold during winter. Snow is forecast for the next several days."

"I don't know about leaving Dudley at the hotel," I said.

"Now, Careless, he can stay by himself for a little while. He's done it on plenty of occasions." She was giving me the look.

"Fine. I don't like it, but it's fine." He didn't like it either, as I saw while resting my hand on his back.

"Okay, then it's settled. We'll see you tomorrow, Natan."

Just as she accepted, we pulled into the hotel driveway. Security was very tight. There were Israeli soldiers, all young men and women about same age as Natan, armed with rifles. They were walking around looking for any signs of trouble. He drove the car around to the front entrance, and a bell man opened the car doors and said, "Good evening, welcome to The King David Hotel." E.D. got out and thanked Natan for the ride. Dudley and I got out as well. Another bell man took our luggage. They were very organized here.

As all of this was going on, several soldiers walked up to Natan. They seemed to know him. He pulled out a pack of cigarettes and offered them to the soldiers. All of them took one and lit up. They started speaking in Hebrew. Smoke 'em if you got 'em, I guess. They made a few hand gestures in our direction as they briefly glanced at us, but I didn't understand a word they were saying. The bell man took our bags inside, and E.D. and Dudley and I followed. Natan and his soldier friends were deep in conversations. It's funny, Israelis only say "Eh" when they speak English. Israeli's also use a lot of hand gestures. They like to talk with their hands. Maybe they're secretly Italians.

"Good evening, may I help you?" a young lady at the front desk asked E.D.

"Yes," E.D. said, "I'm checking in. The reservation should be under Positively Houston Magazine."

"Eh, yes I see two rooms reserved." The phone next to her rang and interrupted her. She picked it up, holding up her index finger – the universal sign for "just one moment, please." "Cane, cane. Todah Rabah," she said as she hung up the phone. "Eh, I see two of our best Old City Suites are available, and they are connected. Would that be acceptable if I upgraded you at no extra charge?"

E.D. looked back and Dudley and me, and I nodded. How could this be a bad thing? "We'll take it," she said.

"Very well, here are your room keys. Your luggage will be brought up to your room. Have a wonderful stay at The King David." She handed the room keys to E.D., and we walked to the elevators. She pushed the elevator button and the doors opened. Dudley walked in with me like an old pro. Of course, he had been in an elevator once or twice before. The first time was a hidden elevator in the Astrodome that led up to some long-forgotten suites. That was the very first case we solved together. We called that one the 'Sold Out Without The Holdout' case. I'm sure one day a book will be written about it. And then there was the elevator in the hospital he had been on when he came to see me after I had been shot. He actually saved my life that day. I'm grateful for that.

E.D. pushed button number five. "Isn't this hotel wonderful, Careless? I just love it here already. Everyone is so nice. It almost feels like home to me."

I nodded my head. It felt like home to me as well, as it would for any other Jew searching for their homeland.

The elevator doors opened and we found ourselves on the fifth floor. As we were walking to our rooms a door further down the hallway opened, and a rather familiar character walked out. It was Kinky! He was all dressed in black, from the tip of his toes in western boots to the top of his head with a black cowboy hat. He was carrying a guitar case. He had an unlit cigar in his mouth.

E.D. seemed surprised. I wasn't. Neither was Kinky.

"Well, choo, choo, choo, choo, look who we've got here. How you doing, honey?" he said to E.D. He hugged her. "How you doing, Careless?" he said to me, reaching out his hand to shake mine. He seemed to want to say something judging by the look he gave me. "And this must be Dudley. How you doing, boy?"

Right on cue, Dudley said something.

"What are you doing in Israel? Did you fly all this way to see the Kinkster perform? That's awful darn nice of you. I'm on the way to the gig right now. Why don't you meet me over there?"

"I have to feed and walk Dudley, and we need to get a bite to eat," I said.

"Well, go ahead and feed him. They serve food at the Kozy Kelev where I'm playing. Meet me over there. Your names will be on the list." He walked toward the elevator. We heard him call out "Ayeee!" He picked his hat up and put it back on his head as he strolled ahead. He disappeared as the elevator doors closed.

"Isn't that strange meeting Kinky all the way over here?" E.D. asked.

"Strange indeed," I replied sarcastically. She didn't pick up on that.

"Let's go see him tonight. What do you say, Careless?"

I said, "Ayeee!"

E.D. walked up to her door, unlocked it, and entered her room. Dudley and I went to ours. It was fabulous, very large with a sitting area, where Dudley promptly sat on the sofa. It even had a full kitchen. The view of Old Jerusalem lit up at night was just majestic. Dudley jumped off of the sofa and sat down facing the door. I walked over and put my hand on his head. I saw that he smelled two things. There was a stranger outside of our door, and Copper Love had been in this room at some point. Dudley is really good about remembering smells. His nose serves him well. And he's never been wrong when it came to scents.

What had Copper Love been doing in the room? We hadn't even checked in yet. I was sure we were being surveilled–again. First things first, I readied myself and flung open the door. The bell man was standing there with our bags and a perplexed look on his face. Perhaps it was fear. It was hard to tell. I probably surprised him, in addition to the eighty-pound golden-colored hound dog staring him down. Dudley knew from my thoughts that it was okay and simmered down in a hurry.

"Good evening, sir, I have your bags," he meekly said.

"Thank you. Please put them over there." I pointed in the direction of the closet. Dudley sniffed him as he walked by. As Kinky sometimes says, it made him a little nervous in the service.

I gave him five dollars, and he quickly and nervously took his leave. I fed and watered Dudley, giving him King David's finest water. Nothing too good for my man!

There was a knock on the door to the adjoining room. Dudley continued eating while peering behind him at the door. I'm sure he knew it was E.D.

"Are you ready yet, Careless?" E.D. said when I let her in. "I'm getting a little hangry. Let's get going."

"Let Dudley finish up and then we'll have to take him for his evening constitutional," I replied.

He played with his food for a while and then made it all disappear. After he drank his water I put him on a leash and we walked out of the room and rode down the elevator. When we reached the lobby, Natan was still talking to a bunch of soldiers outside. I suppose he never left. He saw us walking out with Dudley and abruptly broke off his ongoing conversation, dropped his lit cigarette, and put it out by twisting the tip of his shoe on it. He briskly walked over.

"Eh, do you need to go somewhere? I can take you." He seemed very insistent.

"Oh, no, Natan," E.D. said, "we're just walking Dudley. Then we're going to the Kozy Kelev to eat and watch our friend Kinky perform."

"Eh, you like Kinky? We love him in Israel. I will take you. I know just where The Kozy Kelev is. It's no problem."

I tested him. "That's okay, Natan, we'll just walk once Dudley has done his business." Dudley proceeded to do his business as if on cue. He's just talented that way. Thankfully, it was on the side of the hotel where a patch of grass was located. This was probably the fanciest facility Dudley had ever taken advantage of.

"I insist! You are a guest in Israel. I will wait for you in the lobby. It's fine."

Somehow, I knew he wasn't taking 'no' for an answer. "Okay, we'll go park Dudley and meet you downstairs," I said. Dudley finished up so E.D. and I took him back to the room. "Okay, boy, you stay here, and we'll be back shortly," I instructed. He said something but obeyed and hopped on the bed for a snooze. He was clearly suffering from pet lag. It was a long flight. That's my diagnosis. He had certainly been through a lot lately. He seemed pretty worn out.

E.D. and I went back downstairs and met up with Natan. He waved us over and we walked to him.

"Eh, before we go, our tour guide company wanted you to have this, celebrating your first of many trips to Israel," he said to E.D. He held up a small box that looked like it might contain an engagement ring. It had better not be an engagement ring or Careless would have to take Natan on a little trip to Knuckle Junction. Knuckle Junction may be a tourist attraction in Israel, but I was pretty sure he didn't want to go there.

He opened the box for E.D. to see what was inside, fortunately without getting down on one knee. Probably fortunate for me – in several ways. By the way he was speaking to the soldiers, I assumed he was most likely Sahal. That's army in Hebrew. I wanted to save you time from Googling it. What kind of name is Google anyway?

"It's beautiful. But I couldn't accept such a lovely gift. Thank you, though." She pushed it away with both hands. In the box was a beautiful silver Star of David with a mother of pearl inlay in the middle section of the star.

"In Israel, it is considered a great insult to not accept a gift when it is offered. It is from the city of Tzefat, where many artists live and make beautiful things. Tzefat is one of our gems of the Holy Land."

"Well, I wouldn't want to insult you," E.D. said. "If you insist…" She shrugged her shoulders and then placed her hands back down by her sides.

Natan whirled around behind her before E.D. knew what he was doing and placed it around her neck. It looked beautiful on her.

"Come! I take you to The Kozy Kelev now."

We followed him to his vehicle. He glanced back and forth while we were walking, as if to check if we were being followed, then gave a quick nod to his army buddies. They nodded back. He's pretty sharp.

Natan opened the back door of his Mercedes, and E.D. got in. I was about to join her when he turned to me and said, "Why don't you ride in front with me?" I couldn't tell if he was asking me or telling me. I didn't want to insult him like E.D. had just done, so I sat in front. I thought I detected a little smirk on his face. E.D. was oblivious as to what was going on. She was busy watching the sights as Natan drove.

"So, tell me, what you do in America?" he asked

"Well, I work at a family-owned steel business."

"Eh, very nice. Just you and your brother?" he asked.

Got him! "How'd you know I worked with my brother?" I could barely wait to hear this one.

"Eh, you told me earlier. Don't you remember?" he asked.

"Oh, of course, that's right. I remember now."

He knew I was watching him, and he knew he had screwed up. But he played it well and hid it. He was good. I was better. This WAS about the L.A.M.B. chip.

We made small talk after that, both pretending we didn't know what the other was thinking. A few minutes later, we pulled up in the front of The Kozy Kelev. It was a seedy little joint with a red neon sign hanging just over the door in the shape of a dog. A very generic looking dog. It flashed off and on, making it look like the dog was dancing. I already liked the place. E.D. looked somewhat skeptical. How bad could it be?

"Eh, okay, this is it. Here is my number. Call me when you are ready to go, and I will come back and pick you up." He handed E.D. his business card.

"It's okay, Natan," E.D. said. "You go home and rest up. We can walk back to the hotel. It's only a few blocks away."

"I cannot. It is part of my job. I will get in big trouble if I do not pick you up. You don't want that, do you?" He guilted her. It's a Jewish thing. We do guilt almost as well as Catholics.

"No, we wouldn't want that, would we, Careless?" she asked me, giving me the evil eye, also referred to as *ayin hara*, in Yiddish. You learned something new, didn't you?

"Certainly not," I responded sarcastically. He knew I was on to him.

We exited the car and entered The Kozy Kelev. Natan slowly drove away, eyeballing us in his rearview mirror.

Kinky was getting ready to take the stage. A very attractive young lady at the entrance asked us in an Israeli accent, "Do you have reservations?"

I replied, "No, I'm sorry we don't."

"Americans?"

"Yes, and we don't have reservations, but our name is on the list," E.D. chirped.

"Eh, let me check the list." She picked up a long sheet of paper. I mean, it was as long as my schmeckle (it's a Jewish word, look it up), and that's long. Although I call him Big Pete. My friends all bet me I couldn't work Big Pete into this novel. Oh, how they were so wrong. And long. But I digress…

"What are the names, please?"

"E.D. Sweetie and Careless… What's your last name, Careless…?" she said, while smiling.

Now, I knew full well she knew my last name. However, I was about to blurt it out anyway when Kinky parted the sea of people like Moses and walked over to us.

"These are my friends I told you about, Ahuva," he said. Thank goodness I was able to hold back the secret information of my last name.

"Very good, Mr. Kinky. You may go," she commanded us, while smiling. I knew she was warm for my form. And she hadn't even met Big Pete yet. I smiled back at her. E.D. witnessed this and elbowed me in the ribs. Ahuva laughed out loud and waved us in.

"Come on, you two, I have a table up front waiting for you. I'm about to go on." We followed him through the very crowded establishment to a small table with chairs right in front of the stage. It appeared they did love him in Israel. This place was packed. There wasn't even room to walk around, which was great just in case we had another encounter with some unfriendlies. The only immediate problem I could foresee now was if Big Pete needed to use the facilities. Fortunately for me, my grandfather taught me long ago that a good traveler never passes up an opportunity to get a drink of water or use the facilities. I pass along that knowledge to you now. You're welcome. And don't worry, Big Pete will be fine.

Kinky walked off and the next thing we saw was him walking out on the stage. He was dressed in all black, just like usual. From his black cowboy hat down to his cowboy boots.

The noise level went from moderately tolerable to rambunctiously and tediously loud. Everyone started clapping. Kinky tipped his hat to the crowd and belched out, "Thank ya very much!" He started strumming his Gibson guitar, and the crowd simmered down and it got quiet. I looked around for two reasons. First, I wanted to see if anyone was watching me instead of Kinky. A dead give-away that we weren't out of the woods with this chip thing yet. And second, I wanted to see the reaction of the crowd. Thankfully, no one appeared to be watching me. Everyone was completely mesmerized by Kinky.

"This is from my new CD called *Resurrection*. Willie Nelson sang it with me, and I have to say, it has been a financial pleasure for the Kinkster. I'll be happy to sign CD's after the show. I'll sign anything but bad legislation." Everyone chuckled.

Kinky was on his game. He sang many of his old songs, *Sold American*, *Ride 'em Jewboy* (which if you happen to be Jewish, reaches out and touches your very soul), *'Ol Ben Lucas*, *Asshole from El Paso*, and *The Ballad of Ira Hayes*. Then he paused and told a few jokes. He joked that a native American Indian came up to him at one of his shows and told him the turquoise necklace he was wearing meant that he was an available Indian Maiden. The crowd doubled over in laughter. Then he told them he went to his doctor and his doctor told him he had bad news. Kinky asked the doctor what that was and the doctor told him he had AIDS and Alzheimer's. Then, Kinky told the doctor that at least he didn't have AIDS...

When the enthusiastic laughter settled down a bit, Kinky pulled out one of his books, *Heroes of A Texas Childhood*. The mood of the crowd got serious and so did Kinky. He read about his father, Tom Friedman, who was beloved by countless Texas children from the summer camp he ran. There were so many. Funny thing about children from Texas, they never seem to truly grow up. Oh sure, on the outside they age, but inside, they're all still Peter Pan – not the peanut butter. But I like mine crunchy, just in case you were wondering.

Kinky clearly had great love for his father. Tom always said that Kinky was a modern-day Mark Twain – the travelling storyteller. The people in the audience really connected with him. When he finished reading, he put the book down, and took a shot of Man In Black Tequila. It was touching.

He told a few more jokes and sang a bunch of songs, some of which the crowd sang along with. It was a great show, in a foreign land.

When he was finished, he tipped his hat to the crowd and left the stage. A lot of people followed him. He stayed pretty busy in the back of The Kozy Kelev signing CDs, books, shirts, and even a boob or two. He loved schmoozing.

A young lady came over and asked if we would like to order dinner. I said, "Oh waitret, please waitret, come put down a plate..."

E.D. first smiled, then changed her mind and frowned and said, "You have definitely been around Kinky too long. Now be quiet and let me order dinner before I go hangry on you."

I smiled at the waitret and she handed me a menu. Then she handed one to E.D., who I just found out not to mess with when hangry.

We ordered falafels. They were pretty tasty. It's a very common dish in Israel. I don't know what chickpeas are, which is what falafels are made of, but they're not half bad. We wolfed our food down. Traveling sure can make you hangry.

The Kozy Kelev began to empty out. Kinky came and sat with us and brought three shot glasses and a bottle of his tequila.

"What did you think of the show?" he asked. He poured three shots.

We clinked our glasses together and downed the shots.

"Choo, choo, choo, choo, choo, it's goooood…" Kinky said in a high-pitched voice.

"It was a great show," I said. "Everyone loved it." E.D. nodded.

"Let's get out of here, The Kinkster's tired and you two don't look that fresh yourself." He stood up and picked up his guitar.

I paid the bill and we walked toward the door. Strangely enough the door through which we'd had entered was closed, and a rather larger Middle Eastern man pointed to a side door and said, "Door is broken. Working on it now. Please use other door." He pointed to a side door. His English was broken, but I'd wager the door was not. Against my better judgement, we left through the side door. I hate always being right, but as soon as we walked out, a large black van pulled up, and everything went dark. A bag was placed over my head and a gun barrel shoved into the small of my back.

"Get in the van," someone with a thick Middle Eastern accent said. "If you make noise, I kill you right here." I assumed, correctly, that they had E.D. and Kinky as well. "No talking." I felt E.D. (and not in the good way) get in the van and sit down next to me. At least I hoped it was E.D., not Kinky – not that there's anything wrong with that. All three of us were definitely in the van, and at least three people were speaking to one another in a different language. They kept the chatter to a minimum. I heard the excited, adrenaline-laced desperation in their voices. We didn't travel for long. A few minutes. I listened for anything I could identify but got nothing.

The van abruptly stopped, and I heard the doors open. "Let's go! No talking." I heard a door open ahead of us as we were walking. We were led into a building. The door slammed shut behind us. I could hear E.D. breathing quickly behind me through the hood they had placed over her head. Two men were now conversing in a language that sounded like Arabic.

"Walk down the stairs," the man commanded. This was definitely not going well. Being held by terrorists in a basement was not really what I had signed up for when agreeing to help E.D. on assignment.

I slowly and carefully walked downward. At the bottom of the stairs, I heard another door slam shut, and my hood was removed. I strained my eyes to focus and when things looked sharp I saw we were in a large, dark underground tunnel. E.D. and Kinky were next to me, their hoods off as well. We were pretty shocked and confused. Well, I wasn't. I bet Kinky wasn't either.

"No talking. Walk ahead. Do anything stupid and you die." Two burly men behind me with dark beards were holding handguns. They obviously didn't know me well, telling me not to do anything stupid. But I would have to wait till the time was right. They pushed me forward to keep me from looking at them.

We walked ahead for a couple of minutes. The tunnel was well constructed. Somebody had done a nice job engineering it. A lot of concrete was used to reinforce the structure.

We came to a big opening and were told to stop. A man with a black and white headscarf was standing just ahead, waiting for us.

"Welcome to Palestine," he said while gesturing us forward with a handgun. "Now, let us get down to business. Only speak when I ask you a question. Nod your head if you understand."

All three of us nodded. I was just waiting for go time.

"I understand you have a certain chip in your possession. I do not know how you got it, but I want it, and I want it now. Do you understand?"

None of us nodded.

"You!" He pointed at Kinky. "Where is the L.A.M.B. chip? I know you have it." He pointed the gun at Kinky.

"No idea what you're talking about, mate," Kinky responded.

The terrorist smirked.

"What about you?" Now he was pointing the gun at me. "You want to save your friends, don't you? You will all die here if you do not give me the chip."

"I don't have any friends." I smiled but I could see he was not amused.

"Hey," Kinky said, "I was going to say that next, Careless. Bad form."

The man in the heard garb was pretty unimpressed with our responses. And a smidge unhappy.

"Okay, then. Which one of you would like to die first while the others watch? You think you are funny? Let us see just how funny you are." He slowly took aim at each one of us as if counting sheep. Back and forth, back and forth.

The thing is, I did lie. I did have a friend. Unfortunately, he was probably sacked out in a very comfy bed at the King David Hotel.

"Okay, okay," Kinky said. "I'll get you the chip. Just let my friends go. They don't know anything about it."

The terrorist lowered his gun.

"NO, you will tell me where it is, and we will go get it."

"I have to get it myself." I knew Kinky was just buying time. "It's back in the hotel room."

"You tell me where it is right now or she dies," he said as he pointed the gun at E.D.

The two jokers behind us snickered. I couldn't wait to take them to the woodshed. Unfortunately, right now I was out of options. We were covered by guns from in front and behind.

"Okay, say goodbye to your American whore," the guy in front said, aiming his gun at E.D.'s chest.

It was now or never. Just as I was about to rush the one in front, I heard familiar footsteps behind me. Very familiar. And they were getting ever closer. Allah was not going to smile on these kidnappers. The next thing I heard was a screaming kidnapper behind me and something that sounded like a wolf tearing into a sheep. It was blood-curdling. I looked at Kinky, and he turned and sent a Haymaker to the kidnapper behind us, who was in shock watching his partner on the ground after getting mangled by a golden-colored, eighty-five-pound hound dog, who was now latched onto his arm. It was pretty bloody. He hit the ground after Kinky connected.

I quickly stepped in front of E.D. and was going to neutralize the ring leader. He pulled the trigger. Damn it, getting shot twice in a lifetime was not one of my New Year's resolutions. If I had to take one for E.D., that was just the way it had to be. I didn't hear anything or feel any pain. I did a quick package check, and all was still intact. Looked like dumbass forgot to take the safety off.

Before I could get to him, he started shaking violently and face-planted on the ground. At first, I thought I had made him so nervous that he fainted. He even peed himself. I guess he won't be needing any Flomax. But then reality set in and I saw Natan standing behind him with a Taser gun. The wires were still connected to the kidnapper, and they were hot. Natan then took his finger off of the trigger, and holstered the weapon. The guy on the ground was limp. Natan reached down and zip tied the man's hands behind his back. An easy task since he was incapacitated. Four uniformed soldiers rushed in from behind Natan and grabbed the two sitting on the ground. They zip-tied their hands behind their backs and marched them out of the tunnel. They left a trail of blood. It didn't bother me at all.

Everything happened so fast. Dudley quickly ran to my side, sat, and looked up at me. I placed my hand on his blood-stained head and saw everything. Natan had come to the hotel room and found Dudley resting on the bed. Dudley didn't recognize him and said something. Dudley smelled E.D.'s scent on Natan, so he knew I had to be close by. Natan was talking to someone on a cell phone in front of Dudley. He heard everything.

"Eh, I went to pick them up, but they weren't there. Nobody had seen them leave, so I thought they walked back to the hotel. I am at the hotel now. Only the dog is here. Yes, I have been trying to track them. There is no signal. It was removed or they are underground. I don't know how to find them. Wait. I have an idea. What is the dog's name? Dudley? Yes, I will call you back."

At the mention of his name, Dudley looked up and said something. Natan opened my luggage and took out one of my tee-shirts. Luckily for him, I don't do laundry – at least not very often. He held it up to Dudley's nose and said, "Go get him."

Dudley is a Black Mouth Cur and an excellent tracker. Natan put a leash on him, and they left the hotel. They got in a truck with four army personnel and drove to the Kozy Kelev. Dudley got out with Natan and started tracking me. He followed my scent to a house and stopped. He looked at the house. He didn't take his eyes off of it. Natan called someone and said, "We tracked them to a house close by. Get the coordinates from my phone. They must be underneath the house in a basement. I'm still receiving no signal from the tracking device. Okay, yes, I will go there now."

He handed the leash to one of the others and said, "This is a known tunnel site. I will go to the other end. Wait for my call. When I tell you, enter the tunnel, and we will ambush whoever took them. DO NOT hurt the Americans. Do you understand?"

"Yessir," they all responded.

Natan left. A few minutes later the phone rang.

Dudley heard Natan say, "Okay, go get them."

A couple of the soldiers screwed suppressors to their firearms. They walked ahead of Dudley and kicked in the door of the house. He heard a few muffled sounds and then walked ahead on the leash with one of them. There were two humans lying on the ground. He could smell their blood and knew they were dead. He tracked me to a door. They opened it, and he went down some stairs to the tunnel. While the one holding the leash was walking down the stairs, he stumbled and let go of the leash as Dudley pulled away from him. He ran ahead through the tunnel while the others silently chased him. My scent was getting stronger he knew I was not far away. That is when he came across the two kidnappers holding guns behind us. He jumped and bit into one of their arms and knocked him to the ground. When he appeared to no longer be a threat, Dudley bit into the arm of the other kidnapper. Kinky decked him while he was distracted with a big hound dog hanging from his arm. Blood drenched Dudley's mouth as he kept watch over the two disarmed disabled kidnappers, while by my side.

When the soldiers caught up to Dudley, both terrorists were sitting nervously on the ground, bleeding profusely. It was not Dudley's first taste of blood. I could see that as I read his thoughts.

Natan slapped his hands up and down together as if to show his job was completed. "Eh, I guess that's that," he said with a gratified smirk on his face. "And I guess the cat's out of the bag now, isn't it?" He was peering at us to judge our reaction.

"I guess it is," I said. The cat had been out of the bag well before now. I had already suspected he had to be Israeli military or intelligence. But I'm not really a cat person. Neither is Dudley.

"I'm not sure what just happened," E.D. said with a puzzled look on her face. It wasn't her fault. How could she possibly fully appreciate what had just happened without the knowledge Kinky and I had?

Another soldier walked up and took away the napping terrorist to most likely be interrogated.

"Come," Natan said, "I'll explain it to you. Let me take you back to your hotel."

We didn't leave the way we had come in. I bent down and hugged my little bloody buddy. He was so happy to see me. And once again he had saved my bacon. Also, I like words that rhyme.

31

We followed Natan to a set of steps that led us out of the tunnel. Dudley never left my side. At the top of the stairs we came out of the tunnel and into a house. There was garbage strewn everywhere. It was obvious a struggle had transpired. There wasn't much furniture. The little there was broken and toppled over. We walked out of the house, and Natan said, "Welcome to the West Bank."

We were surrounded by military vehicles. At least a half a dozen Israeli soldiers stood with their M4 rifles trained on us. There were another half dozen standing behind them with their weapons trained on something in the distance. I didn't see anyone out there, but they looked like they meant business. Night vision is a bitch.

"Natan held his hand up to his mouth and said, "Are the charges set? Good, let's move out before we have company." He clearly was sporting an earpiece and was communicating with his counterparts.

"Come, you will ride with me," he said, walking toward a dark colored Humvee in front of us. We all climbed in and just as Natan shut the door, I heard one of the Israelis bark out some orders. We immediately lurched forward and rather quickly built up speed. The other vehicles followed. There was a huge explosion behind us and a flash of light. The ground shook. The house we had just exited completely vanished. We rapidly and stealthily sped away. Nobody talked. Everyone was watching. There was an eerie quiet after the explosion. The convoy sped ahead with the headlights turned off. The drivers were wearing night vision goggles. It was pretty cool. And a must for this type of operation.

Natan must have ice-water running through his veins because he didn't look nervous at all. Neither did Dudley. However, the three of us were a bit on edge. Natan turned away from the window and smiled.

"Eh, I guess they won't be using that tunnel again. So, I suppose an explanation is in order..." He shrugged his shoulders.

We waited for one. I was pretty sure I knew where this was headed. So did Kinky. E.D. was somewhat clueless for the time being.

"Eh, so, you have probably already figured out by now that I work for Israeli intelligence." Kinky and I nodded. We were well aware.

"You were kidnapped tonight after the show by some very bad people. Very bad. They are terrorists who want to get their hands on our microchip that was stolen from us. You know this, don't you?" He studied us. I was a blank slate, as was Kinky. E.D. looked like she was in the dark.

"What in the world are you talking about, Natan?" she asked. "What microchip? And why did those people want to kill us?"

"So, tonight you must have been followed by people looking for the microchip. It was our prototype. We call it the L.A.M.B. chip. The Laser Acquired Missile Barrier chip. We need it back so we can produce more of them. We have tried to recreate the microchip based upon the same exact process used to make the original one, but something's not quite right. We need to study the prototype to fix a few ongoing issues. Word has leaked out that we manufactured such a microchip and that it was stolen. Many nations are now actively searching for it. They will do ANYTHING to acquire it. It must not fall into the hands of our enemies." Of course the explanation was mostly for E.D.'s benefit. I found it odd that the Israelis, if they did invent the L.A.M.B. chip, used an English acronym. I could tell from Kinky's expression he was thinking exactly that. This was something we'd need to investigate a little further.

He continued, "The people who took you tonight are desperate for the microchip. They must not get their hands on it. If they do, we may not be able to defend ourselves when they attack us with missiles. They were fully prepared to kill for it. You were lucky we found you. They secretly dug the tunnel to smuggle weapons and terrorists from the West Bank into Israel. We built walls to stop them from attacking us, so now they tunnel underneath the walls. Instead of spending money to help their people, they use funds to build tunnels to attack us. We always find the tunnels and neutralize them. It is a real shame they waste their time and money on acts of terror."

"Speaking of which, how did you find us tonight?" Kinky asked.

"And not that I know anything about a microchip," I said, "but if they did get their hands on it, how would that stop your country from defending itself?" Hey, inquiring minds want to know, and I was really trying to figure out who the chip truly belonged to and what it would really be used for. I wasn't yet convinced who the true owner of the chip really was. Now we studied him.

"Ah, yes, how did we find you?" he mused. He looked at E.D. and pointed at her chest. It did make me a little nervous. I mean, I didn't need competition from some good-looking foreign intelligence agent with a sexy accent. Not that there's anything wrong with that.

"You see, the night I insisted on giving you that necklace as a gift, it was for two reasons. One, to welcome you to our country, and two, it has a global tracking device built into it." I'll admit I didn't see that one coming.

"As to how the microchip would prevent us from protecting ourselves, well, it's like this. Iran is constantly shipping missiles into the West Bank to the terrorists who reside there. When they have stockpiled enough, they barrage us with the missiles. They continue to launch them until they run out. And because the missiles don't have sophisticated guidance systems, they sometimes indiscriminately fall in very populated areas–where women, children, and families reside. Because it is classified, I cannot tell you how our Iron Dome technology works, but suffice it to say that if the microchip fell into the wrong hands, it would render our defenses useless. That is all I am allowed to tell you."

That made sense. Good answer. From his body language, I could tell Kinky also seemed satisfied.

Kinky said, "Hold the wedding, partner. Why is Dudley here? How does he fit into the puzzle?"

A valid question.

"Eh, you see, when you were taken underground, the signal was lost to us, so we could no longer track you. We went to get Dudley because we hoped he could track your scent. And he was kind enough to do so from the location where we last knew you had been. After that, he went rogue and led us straight to you. Didn't you, boy?"

Dudley said something. I already knew all that because my hand was resting on his very muscular shoulders and I could feel his thoughts. He was ready to come to my aid whenever needed. He let me know that was his job. And he takes his job very seriously. And he's good at it.

Kinky and E.D. seemed satisfied with Natan's explanation.

Natan put his hand up to his mouth and barked out some orders in Hebrew. The entire convoy then turned on their headlights and approached a checkpoint at a large wall.

"We are now entering back into Israel. You will be safe here." I believed him. So did Dudley.

We were hastily waved through the checkpoint. The trucks barely slowed down, and just like that, this nightmare had ended. E.D. started to take off her necklace. I guess she didn't like the lack of privacy.

Natan held his hand up and said, "No, keep it. It was a gift. It really was. A gift that will keep you safe in our homeland." He must have convinced her because she stopped trying to take it off.

Now I had my arm around Dudley. He understood everything that was going on. He was still pretty juiced up about how he had dispatched the two goons who had kidnapped us and were probably now parked somewhere in an Israeli prison.

The convoy of trucks came to an army base and stopped at a heavily fortified guard shack.

"Eh, I must take your telephones from you. We do not allow any images or videos of our bases. As far as anyone knows, they may or may not exist. And we must keep it that way. You will get them back once you have left the base. If, in fact, there is a base." He smiled slyly.

At least he had a sense of humor.

"Please hand them to me now. I insist." He forcefully stretched out his hand.

The three of us reluctantly handed over our cell phones. Either Dudley kept his or he had left it in the hotel room, probably because he left so hastily to come find us. I think his phone is the Jitterbug because the numbers are larger. He has fat paws. Also, he sometimes wiggle butt dials me. It's okay. It gives me an opportunity to hear what he's doing while I'm away.

Our Humvee came to a stop alongside a black Suburban. It had the engine running. The windows were blacked out. The rest of the trucks were driven ahead and disappeared into a camouflaged building. If there was a camouflaged building.

"Please wait here for just a moment," Natan said as he got out. He held his hand up to make sure we understood. The driver remained silent and motionless. He stared ahead and looked pretty serious. Natan walked up to someone dressed in military garb and started speaking to him. He used a lot of hand gestures while speaking. Natan seemed pretty animated and if I didn't know any better I might have thought he was Italian. They stopped talking and the soldier walked away. Natan came back to the Humvee and opened the door.

"Please come with me," he said.

He led us to the black Suburban. We hopped in and he closed the door behind us. He walked to the driver's side door and got in. As he drove us to the entrance of the army base (that may or may not have existed), he said, "I must request that you not speak about anything that has occurred tonight. Not to anyone. It involves our national security. May I have your assistance with this?" He may have asked, but it felt more like he was telling us, not asking.

"As far as I know, it may or may not have occurred," I said, hoping to be humorous.

"No, it did not occur. Period. End of story!"

"Yes, that is what Careless meant, isn't it?" E.D said, while staring at me with her big blue eyes wide open.

"Yes, of course that is what I meant. Of course." I did my best to reassure Natan.

Kinky was not amused. Neither was Dudley.

"I am taking you back to the hotel. I can assure you nothing like this will happen again while you are in our country. We have taken the necessary precautions to make sure there are no more security lapses. Here are your cell phones." He handed us back our cell phones.

Several minutes later, we were back at The King David Hotel. Natan stopped the truck and said, "Tomorrow I will come pick you up and take you to the embassy opening. Before that, it would be my pleasure to personally show you some sights in the Old City. We can go on foot. Would you care to do that? It will be my way of making up for what happened tonight."

E.D. was excited and said, "Sure, we would love that."

I nodded but said, "What happened tonight? Nothing happened tonight." I thought I was being witty.

"Exactly!" Natan replied.

Kinky nodded and said, "I can go on the walking tour with you. But I have a gig later that night, so I will have to get back early to get ready."

Natan said, "Very good." We exited the Suburban and waved as he quickly drove off.

As we walked into the hotel I said, "Wow, that is the most exciting thing that never happened to me." E.D. nodded said nothing. I'm sure she felt the same and was wondering what we had gotten her into. Kinky visually acknowledged what I said but seemed deep in thought. I knew he was putting things together in his mind. That's how he rolls.

We rode up the elevator in silence and walked toward our rooms. Dudley, E.D., and I stopped at our rooms. Kinky kept walking to his and without turning around, let out a prolonged, "Aaayeee!"

E.D. and I looked at each other and smiled. Dudley tried to smile, but he was still all wound up from earlier. I could tell he liked Kinky. Without saying a word, E.D. bent down and kissed Dudley on his very handsome head. That appeared to make him simmer down a bit. She unlocked her door.

"Uh, did you forget something I asked?" Of course, now Dudley was smiling.

"No, I don't believe so. See you boys in the morning."

I said, "Aaayeee!" Not as well or authentic as Kinky, but I gave it a shot. I heard her giggle as the door closed behind her and all went silent.

"Come on boy, let's get you cleaned up and get some sleep." He said something. We entered the room and I toweled the dried blood off his jowls and fed and watered him. I got undressed and sat on the bed as I turned on the TV. The local news was reporting a huge explosion in the West Bank. It was all in Hebrew, so I had no clue about the majority of what was being said but did make out the words "accident" and "terrorist." It seemed they were blaming the explosion on a terrorist who accidentally blew himself up. They showed the pictures of the two men who had kidnapped and tried to kill us but made it seem like they were dead. However, I knew they were in Israeli custody. If, in fact, anything had actually happened tonight. Which it didn't.

I turned off the TV and started dozing off, waiting for my security detail to join me. And he did. He circled several times till he found his sweet spot. He rested his head on my chest, and I placed my arm on him and tried to go sleep. He was still proud of himself for snagging a kiss from E.D. I let him know that I was okay with that. We both went to La La Land.

The next morning, I slept a little late. All that terrorism stuff can really wear a guy out. Dudley, of course, was frozen in place, eyeballing me. I finally managed to squirm out of his King David grip and use the head. I got dressed and walked him downstairs to do the same. We walked on the outskirts of the Old City for a while and he found some grass to do his business on. There were quite a few people walking their dogs that morning. I was guessing some of the dog walkers probably just happened to be Israeli intelligence. Of course, that is speculation on my part.

After our walkabout we returned to the hotel. I ran into Kinky and he said, "Careless, you want to join me for coffee? Why don't you go park Dudley and we'll have a coffee?"

"You got it." Dudley wasn't happy and said something. We went back up to the room and I put out food and water for him. While he was busy playing with his food I snuck out to meet The Kinkster.

"Boker tov," a very cute young waitress said as I walked into the hotel cafe to join Kinky, who was already drinking a cup of joe. I don't know if I mentioned this earlier, but the Israeli women are truly the most beautiful in the world. Right behind where else? You guessed it, Texas. I know it's true because I read it on the internet.

"Boker tov," I replied as I sat down at Kinky's table. Kinky nodded. Probably not a morning person.

"May I get you something?" she said. This sure wasn't no *Highway Cafe*.

She was either a model or an undercover brother intelligence agent. No way was she just "pouring coffee from dusk until dawn."

"Yes, do you have ice?" I asked

"Yessir, we do."

"Tov M'od, do you have coffee?" I asked.

"Yessir, we do." She looked somewhat confused.

"Great, how about Jack Daniels?"

"I'm sorry, sir, the bar is closed." She seemed a little hesitant.

"Well, I'll have a decaf coffee over ice with a shot of Jack Daniels. Can you make that happen? I'll be your best friend." I smiled and raised my eyebrows. I can be charming when I want. Or when I need a drink. Whichever comes first.

"So, you want decaf Iced Coffee with a shot of Jack, is that correct?" She had a big grin on her face. If she wasn't Israeli, she could have easily been from Texas. I guess I could have just asked for iced coffee with a shot of Jack but where would be the fun in that?

"You say tomato, I say Jack Daniels."

"I'll see what I can do." she said laughing. She walked away. She even had a great walk.

"So, what do you think?" Kinky asked.

"I don't know, she's pretty hot." I responded, knowing full well that wasn't what he was asking. Hey, it was early and I hadn't had my Careless Coffee yet. Okay?

He looked at me like I was being scolded by my parents.

"I don't know, Kink. I can't tell who's telling the truth and who's lying. They are all so good at it. I'd hate for the chip to fall into the wrong hands."

"Agreed, let's see how it plays out." He sipped his coffee.

The waitress came back with a Careless Coffee with a shot of Jack Daniels in it. I could smell it. She set it down on the table in front of me. I was like a kid in the candy store.

"I thought you said the bar was closed." I was curious.

"It is. I asked my manager and he said, 'Anything a friend of Kinky Friedman wants, he gets.'" She smiled at Kinky and he tipped his black cowboy hat to her.

"Thank you, little darlin'," he said. She blushed and walked away.

He gave me the look. You know, the one that says, hey, I'm cool, everyone knows I'm cool, and I'm so cool, I don't have to act cool. That look. I guess it pays to know somebody cool. And famous.

"Alright, back down to business. What are your thoughts?" Kinky asked.

"Well, everybody and their mother knows about the chip. It was clearly a prototype. If it doesn't belong to the United States or Israeli governments, then it definitely should. We cannot let it fall into the hands of anyone else. But which one? That is the real question. And are we safe until the chip is delivered? That's the other question. Because I don't particularly feel safe right now."

"That about covers it," Kinky said. "How do you propose we move forward?"

"I don't know. I haven't figured that one out yet. Let's see how this plays out, then get back to Texas and make a plan."

"I like it. Tonight's my last gig and I then fly home right afterwards. It's been a real financial pleasure for The Kinkster. They really seem to love me here."

"I can see that," I said as the sweet young waitret shimmied back over to fill his coffee cup. She even brought me another decaf iced coffee and a shot of Jack Daniels. Served with a smile.

We really didn't have a lot to talk about since last night never really happened. We drank our coffee and waited for the day to start, while we were silently trying to figure out what we were going to do.

Just as we finished up, Natan walked up and sat at the table with us.

"Oy va voy, this can't be good. The two of you sitting around plotting. I don't know if I like this or not," he said while smiling. "This morning I will take you on a special tour of the Old City. And I have a big surprise for you. You will love it. Where is your beautiful friend? We should get going."

Right on cue, E.D. walked up. "Well, thanks for inviting me to the party. You men are all alike," she said, placing her hands on her very curvaceous hips.

"Boker tov," Natan said. "Did you sleep well?"

"I sure did. That concert really wore me out." She winked at us.

"Are you all ready to go for a walking tour this morning? We should get going so you can make it to the embassy opening and so Kinky has time to get back for his concert."

"Let's hit it," I said.

Kinky said, "Waitret, please waitret...", holding up his index finger in the air in order to get her attention.

"Yes, Kinky." She quickly walked over.
"Check, please," he said.
"It's been taken care of," Natan said.
She smiled and walked away.
"Thank ya very much!" Kinky said in a loud, low, exaggerated southern accent. You know, the kind politicians use when trying to trick southern folk into voting for them, while pretending to carry hot sauce around with them. Like southern people are the only ones who like a little spice in their lives. The only difference was that Kinky was sincere. Politicians? Not so much. In one of our very deep conversations, Kinky once told me the word politics is Latin in origin. Poly, meaning many, and ticks, meaning blood suckers. Pretty sure he got that one right.

"Okay, now that it's settled, let's begin our tour," Natan said. "Follow me, please." He walked ahead and out of the hotel. We followed. I was a little disappointed Dudley couldn't come, but after what may or may not have happened last night, I felt like he needed a little time to collect himself and get back to normal. I had never seen him react like that before, if in fact it did actually occur.

We walked around the walls of the Old City. The stones were ancient and in many places were being restored and studied by archaeologists and students. We reached a gate, and Natan stopped walking. He looked around and said, "This is the Lions gate. We are now entering Old Jerusalem." I was sure he had plenty of undercover agents around us. "If you look to your right and higher up on the wall, many of our archeologists have discovered secret Hebrew writing carved into a lot of the stones. It was just discovered and is from thousands of years ago. We are trying to decipher it now. Many believe it is a secret message from scholars. The sun has to hit it just right for us to be able to see it. Ten minutes from now, the writing will vanish, and these stones will look just like every other stone in the wall." We could see it now but would have walked right past it if Natan had not pointed it out. He was a darn good tour guide.

We walked for a while, and Natan informed us, "We have now entered the Muslim quarter. This path we will now walk on is called the Via Dolorosa Tour, tracing the footsteps of Jesus Christ. Some refer to it as the Sorrowful Way. There are fourteen stations. If we keep up a good pace, we will be able to make them all."

E.D. was very engrossed in all of the history surrounding us. Kinky was as well, but I could tell he was thinking of wise-cracking. He had written extensively in his music about this very subject.

We were now walking down narrow cobblestone streets when Natan stopped and pointed to a plaque on the side of a building.

"This is station number one. This is where Jesus Christ was condemned to death," Natan said.

"Well, they ain't makin' Jews like Jesus anymore," Kinky said while almost singing in rhythm to one of his many hit songs.

Like the coffee, earlier at breakfast, I knew this had been brewing. Natan smiled. They do love Kinky in Israel. I smiled too. It was funny. And perfect timing. E.D. was not impressed, and neither were the pilgrims standing there, who were with a different, less lively tour guide. Kinky tipped his black cowboy hat to them, reached in his pocket, pulled out a fresh cigar and proceeded with ignition. I was really starting to love this guy. He definitely ruffles some feathers. The pilgrims walked away. Natan followed them to the next station. We followed Natan. Kinky's cigar smoke lingered behind us for the next group to enjoy. I never really liked history that much, but now I saw how much fun it really can be.

Natan walked with us to station number two. Again, there was a plaque on a very old wall.

"This is where Pontious Pilate gave his Ecco Homo speech condemning Jesus Christ," Natan informed us.

Yep, you guessed it, right on cue, Kinky, the now born-again tour guide, hummed, "Now I'm a Homo Ecco Erectus, got to connect this…"

He really does suffer from perfect timing. The pilgrims, again, were not amused. Neither was E.D. She hadn't put her hands on her hips yet, so there was still room for a few more pearls of wisdom from The Kinkster. Natan and I must somehow have been related because we couldn't wipe the grins off of our faces.

"Let's proceed to the next station," Natan said. This time the pilgrims stayed at station number two. I wasn't sure if they stayed because they were offended or because their tour lecture wasn't finished yet. But I was reasonably sure I knew the answer. People sure do get offended easily nowadays.

We walked on and came to station number three.

"So, this is station number three. It is right next to the Polish Catholic Chapel. This is where Jesus Christ fell for the first time," Natan told us.

Natan, E.D., and I silently waited for Kinky's take on things. We didn't have long to wait. He grinned, showing his pearly whites, took a puff of his cigar, blew the smoke out very delicately, and sang, "Jesus in pajamas came at 3:16 one mornin'…"

This one seemed a little more serious than the last two.

"Help him if you're able. Help him if you can. And God bless you friend, the menu's in your hand," Kinky sang and then abruptly stopped. I had heard him sing this song, "Jesus In Pajamas," before. It was pretty prophetic. This time, nobody seemed annoyed. We walked in silence, following Natan.

At station number four, the first thing I noticed was that it was eerily quiet and completely devoid of people. This was pretty strange because, while not everyone was on a tour, there were plenty of people walking the Sorrowful Way. Natan stopped and stood in front of a very old building. He looked from side to side and behind him. Then he nodded his head up and down. There seemed to be no one around to see it except for us. Or so we thought.

"Eh, this is station number four, The Church of Our Lady of Sorrows," Natan said. "This is where Jesus met his mother."

I know what you're thinking. You're wondering what delightful ditty Kinky was about to deliver. I turned toward him and waited. It appeared to me he had already made a selection. I could tell because he had just finished taking a deep puff of his cigar and was in the process of slowly and deliberately exhaling it. He had a look of enlightenment as he followed the smoke upwards with his eyes. He was about to speak when something unexpected happened and stopped him short in his tracks.

His cell phone began to ring, as did mine and E.D.'s, all three simultaneously. We looked at each other in utter disbelief. After about the third ring, we snapped out of it and all answered our phones. All three of us said, "Hello" at the same time.

The three of us took the phones away from our ears and looked at Natan who was standing in front of us with his right hand outstretched. We gave him the phones. It appeared we had all received the same message telling us to hand our phones over to Natan. This definitely caught us off guard. But not as much as what happened next.

Natan placed the phones in his pocket and said, "Let's go in."

We followed him into a beautiful old church. I don't know how many centuries old it was, but it looked ancient.

"Have you been good boys and girls?" Natan asked. "When was the last time you confessed your sins? I know for at least two of you, it's probably been a long while, if at all. Come."

He led us to a confessional booth and opened the door. At first blush, it sure didn't seem to be big enough for three people. Hell, Kinky's cowboy hat would barely fit in there. You know what they say, everything's bigger in Texas. They also say, size matters. But enough about that. It's getting hard to explain but something was definitely up.

Before one of us could enter the booth, the back wall slid open, revealing a very large room. A light came on, emitting a fluorescent buzz, and then the room got pretty bright. Once we walked forward, the door behind us slammed shut. Then another door in front of us loudly slid open. We walked into another room. Just like before, the lights turned on. Forgive me for drawing this comparison, but frankly, I felt like Maxwell Smart, Agent 86. So, I guess that would make the lovely E.D. my Agent 99.

The door slammed shut behind us and just as it did the whole room shook with a jolt. Going down! Apparently, we were in a rather large elevator. E.D. and Kinky looked confused, but not Natan. He was a smooth operator. And probably a special operator. Maybe even an elevator operator. E.D. was about to ask the million-dollar question when Natan preempted her by holding up his hand and saying, "All will be explained shortly."

As we were traveling downward for what seemed like a very long time, my mind began to wander back to the very first case Dudley and I solved. I ended up calling it Sold Out Without The Holdout. Dudley and I were thrust into the case when country western singer Jake Harm, of Jake Harm and The Holdouts, was kidnapped. We found him being held in a secret room hidden in the top part of The Astrodome. The only way to get to the room was in a small, secret elevator with no lights hidden in a storage closet. When E.D., Dudley, Detective Present, and I rode up in the elevator, Dudley goosed E.D. She thought it was me because we were so cramped together and it was dark. I told her it was Dudley, but she never believed me. Honestly, if I were as smart as he was, I would have thought of it first. I dared not try it now because we weren't cramped in a small space, the lights were on, and Dudley wasn't here for me to blame it on. Oh well, always late to the picnic. While I entertained you with that memory, the boring elevator ride came to a sharp stop.

Another door opened in front of us, leading to what I can only describe as an underground military complex, if it actually existed. Natan walked forward and waved to us to follow him. We did. There were armed military guards stationed everywhere. They were looking us up and down. Natan stopped walking and we stopped as well. I think everyone was too afraid to ask any questions.

Two soldiers with bomb-sniffing dogs walked up and the dogs began sniffing us one by one. They were Belgian Malainois. When one got close enough to sniff me, I let my hand indiscriminately brush against his back as he did his thing. He stopped and looked up at me. We had a connection, and now I knew what he knew, which was everything.

"Do not touch the dog," his handler said. "He can be very dangerous." I guess I wasn't as tricky as I thought I was. But I wasn't worried. His handler barked out an order in Hebrew, and the dog broke his stare and continued walking.

When they were satisfied, we were led into another room that was not as sterile. Several armed soldiers escorted us and remained stationed at the door. There were large computer screens behind a desk and a TV tuned into various news channels. A door behind the desk opened, and a very tough, distinguished looking gentleman wearing a nice fitting suit walked in. He closed the door behind him and stood behind the desk, looking at us. E.D.'s eyes got wide, and Kinky looked intrigued.

"Welcome. Do you know who I am?" he asked.

"Yes, Mr. Prime Minister," E.D. said. "What a great honor."

"Okay then. Please have a seat. Thank you, Natan."

Natan walked out of the room.

"Please, take a seat" he repeated.

We sat in three pretty comfortable chairs in front of the desk. He sat in a plush leather executive's chair.

"Welcome to Israel. I've heard you've had a very exciting trip so far. I hope you are enjoying your stay in our homeland."

All three of us nodded in affirmation. I gave him the raised eyebrow as well to let him know we were very interested.

"Good! Terrific! I trust Natan has taken good care of you?"

Again, we silently let him know that yes, Natan was taking good care of us.

"Where are my manners? Would you like something to drink? Some water? Orange juice?" He looked at E.D.

"Some tequila?" he asked, looking at Kinky.

"Or perhaps some bourbon?" he asked, looking at me.

Nothing escaped this guy or these people. Natan walked in with a tray holding water, orange juice, tequila, and bourbon. He set it down on the desk in front of us and took his leave. These guys were good. Nobody reached for a drink.

"Well, go ahead. Don't worry. If we wanted to give you truth serum, we would have done it when you first came in. Help yourself."

E.D. took a glass of water. I took the bourbon, and Kinky took the what he calls, Mexican mouthwash.

"Choo choo choo choo good," Kinky said. I cracked a smile. So did the Prime Minister. E.D. remained silent, like a meek little mouse. I think she was intimidated by the Prime Minister. There's a first time for everything.

I downed the bourbon. It was a fine vintage. Then again, any bourbon would have been fine in this situation. I'm not really a day drinker, but why not? I now knew for sure we were in over our heads.

"So, let's get down to business, shall we? We believe you have something that belongs to us. It is vital to our national security. We think the Russian agent who stole it probably gave it to you at some point. You may not even know she had. We're going to need it back. We are prepared to buy it back from you. Name your price. But make no mistake, we will acquire the chip." He was pretty intense.

E.D. looked perplexed. Kinky listened intently.

"Let's just say that we did have the L.A.M.B chip," said Kinky. "How do we know that it truly belongs to Israel? And how do we know that, once you have the chip, you won't come after us? We have already been threatened with jail time. How do we know you won't do worse?"

Valid questions.

"You have my word. You are just going to have to trust me. And you will have the undying gratitude of the Israeli people."

I knew most Israelis would never learn about the chip and therefore would never know we did anything for the Jewish state. Still, he was strangely persuasive. Most politicians are, but he seemed different, more sincere.

"Look," the Prime Minister said, "if you have the chip, we need it and want it back. Right now. We cannot wait. Many lives may depend on the return of the chip."

"What I would like to know is how a Russian double agent snuck the chip out of a top-secret lab hidden in the hills, that may or may not exist, and why the chip wasn't recovered when that agent was terminated," I asked. It's amazing the information you can get from a bomb sniffing dog deployed to the Prime Minister of Israel. They truly have exquisite hearing.

Now the Prime Minister seemed both intrigued and alarmed.

"I have no idea what you're talking about," he said. He obviously did.

"Look, time is running out. As you know, we have the grand opening of the American consulate in Jerusalem today. I must go to prepare for that. I would like you to be my guest in a VIP section we have set up for dignitaries. You can bring your camera." He looked at E.D. "Consider it a gesture of good will. Please understand that we need that chip back. If you have it or know where it is, we need to know. We could have forced the information out of you like the terrorists were going to do before we rescued you. But we are more civilized than that. Can we count on you? You would have the gratitude of our entire nation. However, this meeting never occurred and you must not ever speak of these matters to anyone. Do you understand?"

E.D. said, "Yes, Mr. Prime Minister." She had no idea about the chip.

Kinky said, "Clear as a bell."

"So, it is secret gratitude? I'm good with that," I said.

"Yes, secret gratitude," he said. He had been studying me since I mentioned the top-secret lab in the hills, that may or may not exist.

"Well, if you will excuse me, I must go prepare for the opening of the embassy. Natan will show you out. I expect we will be hearing from you very soon." I'm pretty sure he wasn't asking. He stood up and left the room through the same door he had earlier entered.

Natan said, "Let's go. Follow me." We left the building the same way we had come in. Israeli soldiers were stationed everywhere. We finally made it back to The Church of Our Lady of Sorrows and walked outside. The whole thing was so surreal. And I didn't even get to confess my sins. We may be the chosen people but Jews have sins too, you know.

"Eh, the tour has actually taken much longer than I had anticipated, so we will have to cut it short so you can make it to the embassy ceremony on time. I will walk with you back to the hotel and pick you up at 1:00 to take you to the embassy. Do not be late."

"Well," Kinky said, "Natan, ol' buddy, I won't be joining you for that one. I have a show I need to get ready for."

"We'll miss you, Kinky," Natan said.

"We sure will," E.D. echoed.

At the hotel, Natan said "Shalom" and kept walking, peering over his shoulder to a few soldiers stationed outside of the main entrance. They acknowledged whatever message he was sending with a quick nod.

We walked in silence because I think we all still couldn't believe what had just happened. Plus, we weren't allowed to talk about it. I stopped at my door and E.D. stopped at hers. Kinky kept walking and did his usual, "Aaayee!" we had become accustomed to.

"Careless, be at my room at 12:30, okay?" E.D. said.

"Okay, honey, but we don't need to meet Natan till 1:00. I really don't think it's going to take me that long."

"In your dreams, Careless. I have a lot of equipment I need you to carry for me so I can get some good images for the magazine."

"Well, I have the equipment and know how to use it. Besides, a guy can dream. A simple misunderstanding."

"Yes, dream on, Careless. But while you're dreaming just make sure you're here at 12:30 sharp." She smiled and walked into her room. Much like my chance at romance with her, the door slammed shut.

I could hear Dudley snickering on the other side of our door. When I opened it, he jumped up on me so fast he almost knocked me over. His tail was spinning around in circles like a helicopter rotor blade. "I missed you too, boy," I said. "Come on, let's go for a walk." I put him on a leash and we left the hotel. We walked around Jerusalem and he did his business. A few people stopped and wanted to pet him, but, as always, he said something and mostly prevented it. Usually, people thought better of the idea of making first contact with Dudley. When we got back, I fed and watered him. I made myself a Careless Coffee and sat on the sofa trying to make sense of this case. How did we stumble into that crime scene? How did we end up with the L.A.M.B. chip? Why were we hired to investigate the case, and why were so many countries after the chip? That last question I obviously knew the answer to. And meeting the Prime Minister of Israel? That certainly doesn't happen every day.

As I was pondering these things, Dudley finished playing with his food and ate it like a champ. He drank some water to wash it down and then joined me on the sofa. This broke my concentration. He lay in my lap, turned over on his back, and curled up his front legs. I put my hand on his chest, and he let me know he was ready for a belly rub. He also saw everything we had done that morning. He was a little concerned about not being there to protect me, but also a little jealous because he really likes riding in elevators. Especially with E.D. A man after my own heart.

I let him know he would again have to stay in the hotel room by himself, but that I would leave Baby, his favorite stuffed animal, with him. He didn't like the idea of staying without me, but I let him know it wouldn't be for long. We shared all this by me simply touching him. I kind of liked it. I gave him a fantastic belly rub so he would forget about being left by himself. And he did. It's the little things.

We sat for a while as I tried to sort things out in my mind. At 12:25, I rolled Dudley over and escaped his clutches. It sounds easier than it was.

When he wants you to stay, he lets you know. He's pretty good about applying his body mass in a manner that makes it difficult to extricate yourself.

I told him goodbye. He stared at me as I walked toward the door, guilting me, so I walked back, kissed his handsome head, and gave him Baby to play with. He took Baby in his mouth, made some weird unworldly noises, and rolled his eyes back in his head. I took that opportunity to quietly sneak out while he was preoccupied.

Just before I could knock on E.D.'s door, she opened it. She had a rather large backpack and a medium-sized bag leaned up against the wall.

"Oh, you're right on time. You think you can handle these two bags? But you must be careful. I have my cameras and gear in them And I need these images for the magazine."

"Piece of cake," I said.

"Well, let's get a move on. We don't want to be late." She can be rather bossy when she's on assignment.

I grabbed the gear and almost felt like Clint Eastwood. Not the *Dirty Harry* Clint Eastwood, more like *The Mule* Clint Eastwood. We rode down the elevator and walked outside, where Natan was waiting in a black Suburban. We got in, and he handed us two badges on lanyards.

"Put these security badges on so you may enter the embassy," he said.

We put them on and within five minutes we were pulling up to the new embassy. It was a beautiful building made from Jerusalem limestone. A gorgeous, huge glass wall covered one whole side of it. The security was tight. Retracting steel bollards were installed in front of it. However, they were not retracted so we would not be entering that way. I was wrong. A group of heavily armed soldiers stopped the car and spoke to Natan in Hebrew. He showed them his badge, and they looked us over through the window. They exchanged a few more words and then waved us through. The bollards sank into the ground, and Natan drove to a parking lot just to the left of the building. I guess it pays to have friends in high places.

Just in front of the building entrance, a large canopy was set up for dignitaries. Most people were already seated. I spotted the President's daughter and son-in-law sitting in the front row with the Prime Minister and his wife. Behind them were several United States senators and representatives, as well as the Secretary of Treasury.

Natan escorted us to a roped off area just to the side of the podium, then he walked to the side of the building and stood watch. We were with at least twenty other journalists with similar press passes. E.D. grabbed my hand and worked her way to the front of the crowd. She was like Moses parting the Red Sea. I was in awe of how she got away with that.

She asked for her backpack and I forked it over. She opened it and pulled out a camera body and a very long lens. She snapped them together in no time and asked me to hold it. As I took it from her she did the same with another camera body and lens. I was apparently her backup cameraman. She aimed the camera at the podium and began snapping photographs.

Then she turned the camera towards the senators and representatives and took some photos. I followed with my eyes, and sure enough, the Prime Minister was looking straight at us. It spooked me a little bit but didn't seem to faze E.D, who was busy taking photographs. We were definitely in the hot seat.

A band began playing the Israeli National Anthem, and the crowd grew silent. As the Israeli Ambassador to the United States stood up and walked to the podium, a photographer bumped into me. "Please excuse," he said in a thick Russian accent. As he walked away I saw out of the corner of my eye that Natan's hackles were up.

A video of the President of The United States played on a big screen.

"Almost seventy years ago, the United States of America recognized Israel. Jerusalem is the eternal heart of the Jewish people. Moving the embassy has been a long time coming. Jerusalem was the established capital of the Jewish people in ancient times. Israel is a sovereign nation with the right to determine its own capital. Today, we open the embassy in the sacred land of Jerusalem. God bless the embassy and all who serve there. And God bless Israel and the United States."

I watched as The Prime Minister was then introduced by the Israeli Ambassador.

"Today, the embassy of the most powerful nation on earth, our greatest ally, the United States of America, today its embassy opened here. So, for me, this spot brings back personal memories, but for our people, it evokes profound collective memories of the greatest moments we have known on this City on a Hill." He went on to speak about Abraham, King David, and King Solomon, who built their temple in Jerusalem.

The President's Son-In-Law spoke for a few minutes and reiterated what the President said.

E.D. was busy taking photos. She was clicking them off in rapid fashion. She is quite the accomplished photographer.

When the ceremony eventually ended, everyone stood up and clapped and cheered. This was a big deal and it seemed like the Israelis loved the President–almost as much as they loved Kinky. Almost. E.D. packed up her cameras. When the crowd thinned out, we walked over to Natan.

"You ready?" he asked E.D. "Did you get good photographs?"

"Yes, I got some fabulous shots. Thanks for getting us so close."

"It was no problem. Come, I take you back to the hotel."

I picked up E.D.'s bags and we walked back to the Suburban. Five minutes later we were back at the hotel.

"Your flight is scheduled to leave at 10:00 tonight. I will pick you up at 8:00 to make sure you make it on time."

"Funny, I don't remember telling you we were scheduled to leave at 10:00," E.D. said.

"Oh yes, you must have. You probably just don't remember," Natan said rather convincingly.

He drove away. I knew for a fact E.D. never mentioned the time of the flight home to him.

We walked back to our respective hotel rooms. E.D. stopped at her door and said, "Thank you for your help today, Careless. I have to say, this trip may have been short, but it sure has been unforgettable. Now you and your mutt be ready at 8:00 for the plane ride home. You got it? Don't be late. You know I hate when people are late."

"Got it." I heard Dudley milling about behind the door. I reached into my front pocket to extract the key but felt something strange and foreign in there. Hey, get your mind out of the gutter, it wasn't Big Pete.

I pulled out a folded-up piece of paper that hadn't previously been there. I carefully unfolded it and it had these words written on it: "We want the chip. We know you have it. Name your price." There was a telephone number written below the words. I won't disclose the number here because it's probably a KGB-monitored number. Damn Russians! First, they messed with our elections, and now they were trying to bribe a true patriot like myself. Speaking of electile dysfunction, is that a Russian bribery note in your pocket, or are you just happy to see me? Don't answer that, it was a rhetorical question.

I folded up the note, stuck it back in my pocket, and retrieved the key. Dudley gave me a bear hug as soon as I opened the door. I took him for one last spin around Jerusalem. It was getting pretty cold outside. When we came back to the hotel room, I packed us up for the trip home. He was more than happy to be going home. Dogs want and need a routine. It helps them to know what to expect and how to act.

After packing, I sat on the sofa with a Careless Coffee and my best friend. I dozed off for a couple of hours and, sure enough, woke up right on time. I grabbed our bag, put Dudley on a leash and we strolled over to E.D.'s room. I knocked on the door and within seconds the door opened.

"How's my big boy?" she asked.

I was about to answer that I was fine but just as she finished speaking she bent down, gently placed her hands under Dudley's head, and gave him a big kiss on his forehead. Dudley said something.

"Careless, be a doll and grab my bags. I'll walk with my handsome man." She held her hand out, waiting for the leash. Dudley said something again. I handed her the leash and picked up her bags. We walked down to the lobby and met Natan outside. I stowed our bags in the back of the Suburban and Natan walked up to me.

"Eh, I will have the note in your pocket, please." He held out his hand, expecting me to fork it over. I can't say I was surprised. I gave it to him.

"It is good you did not call it." He walked away and got behind the wheel. I climbed in the back seat with E.D. and Dudley.

Natan started driving and said, "I want to take you to the Western Wall. Some of us call it the Wailing Wall because it is said that our ancestors wept here because of the destruction of our temples. I want it to be the last memory you take from Israel. So you remember how vital your help will be to our national security. Many people still weep when they see the Wailing Wall for the very first time. It is that powerful and brings out something very deep within us."

When he finished talking we pulled up to the outskirts of the Wall. We were at an elevated area where we looked down on the entire wall. There were still people congregating around it. Night time had settled in but lights detailed every crack and crevice of the Wall and exposed the many notes to God. People from all over the world come to place their folded up very personal handwritten messages to the Lord in the very small openings.

We all exited the Suburban and stood outside, staring down at the Wall. Natan was right, I did feel something deep within me. And I don't think it was just the Careless Coffee I had ingested earlier. At least I think it wasn't. A cool breeze overtook us as we looked on in silence. It had been a great trip, an interesting trip. I felt somehow forever changed. And then something wondrous happened. It began to snow. The flakes fell from the heavens and stuck to the Wall and the ground surrounding it. I had never seen anything like this. It was very moving, almost biblical. Maybe even a miracle. A Christmas miracle.

"Eh, I have lived here my entire life," Natan said, "and I have never seen it snow here in Jerusalem in December. It rarely snows at all." Dudley was sitting next to me. I dropped his leash and rested my hand on his shoulders. He too was in awe. He also extended his rather large tongue to feel the snowflakes landing on it. This kept him very busy. Then I felt E.D.'s warm hand take mine. The three of us stood there hand in hand (and paw) next to Natan. If someone had seen us from behind, it would have looked like a spectacular happy ending to a Hallmark movie–without the music, of course. This was spiritually powerful. Special moments like this rarely come in a person's life. It's best to recognize them and record them in your mind before they slip away.

"Listen to me," Natan said. "I want to tell you something since you are leaving soon and we will probably never see each other again. I know I was assigned to you for the duration of your trip here in Israel. But for some reason, you have become more than an assignment to me. I feel very close to you. You know what line of work I'm in, so please remember what I am about to tell you. One day when you see a single white dove fly over your head, you will know I'm gone. Please say a prayer for me at that time. Understand?"

I was not expecting that. At first, I thought he was kidding but he had a dead serious, stern look on his face. E.D. was almost in tears and hugged him. For once, I was at a loss for words. I knew he was sincere. So did Dudley. Dogs are very good at reading people. I knew then that the chip must belong to Israel. And if it didn't, it should. I don't get played. Neither does Dudley.

We finally broke ourselves away from the Christmas scene in Jerusalem and got back into the Suburban. On the way to the airport, I had a very important revelation. I suddenly realized the reason I like the Suburban so much is because it ends in bourbon. That has to be it. For obvious reasons, I'm not a huge fan of the Tahoe. But I digress.

Natan drove us back to Ben Gurion Airport. We sat in solemn silence the whole way there. I contemplated this whole trip, and it was perplexing to me. There sure seemed to be a lot of coincidences surrounding the L.A.M.B. chip.

Natan pulled up in front of the airport entrance. We got out of the Subourbon and I grabbed our bags. Natan got out and hugged E.D. I extended my hand, but he walked right past it as if it were invisible and tightly hugged me. No words were spoken. None were needed. We locked eyes for what would probably be the last time. He turned, got in the Subourbon, and quickly drove away.

As the Subourban pulled away, it revealed Kinky sitting on a bench, in front of the airport. He was dressed all in black, wearing his black cowboy hat and black boots. He had a small bag and his guitar case leaned up against the bench next to him. He tipped his hat to us.

"Hi Kinky, what are you doing here?" E.D. asked.

"Well, you see, my performance was over at eight o'clock, and I came straight to the airport to catch my flight back home. When I arrived, they told me my flight was cancelled due to mechanical issues. The next flight isn't until tomorrow at 6:00. I already checked out of the hotel, and all of the hotels in this area are booked up due to the embassy opening. I guess The Kinkster is stuck at the airport till tomorrow morning."

She looked at me and said, "Are you thinking what I'm thinking?"

"I sure am," I said while nodding. I had no idea what she was thinking.

"Great! Kinky, why don't you fly back with us? I'll call my office, but I bet they will be fine with it. The plane is practically empty."

I nodded again as if that was exactly what I thought she was thinking, even though I didn't. E.D. walked away with her telephone up to her ear. Dudley and I sat next to Kinky.

"Well, what are you thinking?" I inquired.

"One thing's for sure, Careless. And that is, the chip clearly belongs to the nation of Israel. When we get back, we're going to need to somehow make sure it ends up in their hands. Not in the hands of any other nations. I haven't figured out how to do that yet, but you and I can brainstorm on the long trip home."

E.D. came back and announced that her office was thrilled to have such a big celebrity fly back with us. We walked into the airport and were escorted to a section for private jets. We sailed through a guarded area where our passports were checked. Then we were escorted out to the tarmac to board a waiting jet. It was the same size jet as the one that had flown us here, but this one looked slightly different and had different tail numbers. I couldn't call Detective Present to check the origin of this plane since we were in another country, not to mention the different time zones. I never really figured out time difference thing. He was probably asleep anyway. I asked E.D., Kinky, and Dudley to pose for a picture to commemorate our trip to Israel. I'll just save this for later, I thought, after Detective Present wakes up and has had his coffee and donuts. I know what you're thinking, not all policemen eat donuts. Or do they? We boarded the plane, and a very attractive young lady named Kayla greeted us. She was moderately tall, pretty muscular, and had long, straight brown hair well past her waistline.

"Welcome aboard. I'll stow your luggage for you. May I get you something to drink while we're waiting to take off?"

This definitely was not Copper Love.

"I would love a Mimosa," E.D. said.

"Sure thing, hon," Kayla replied.

Kinky said, "I'll have a Mexican mouthwash, please. And make mine a double."

That was usually my line, but I was perfectly happy to share.

"I'm sorry, sir, I'm not familiar with that drink," Kayla said.

"Well, little darlin', I can go back there and give you some pointers," Kinky said.

"I'm sorry, sir, passengers are not allowed in the galley. It's company policy."

E.D., Dudley, and I intently looked on. Kinky was very entertaining. Although I must admit, we are entertained rather easily.

"In that case, I'll just have a tequila. A double, if you don't mind.," Kinky said.

Dudley and I silently laughed. Well, almost silently. Kayla took notice and asked me, "And what will you have, sir?"

"I'm fine for now," I responded. No need for a repeat of what happened on the trip over. I didn't need my beauty rest that badly.

"Very well. I'll be right back," she said.

Dudley and I sat next to one another in very cushy leather chairs. E.D. sat in one facing us and Kinky sat across the aisle from us.

Kayla came back with the drinks. The pilot's voice came on the loudspeaker.

"Good evening. Welcome aboard. I hope you had a pleasant trip to the Holy Land. Please sit back and relax. We'll be wheels up in just a few minutes on the way to New York. Kayla will take good care of you."

Definitely not Israeli.

E.D. and Kinky worked on their drinks. The plane started moving forward and Dudley and I closed our eyes. It was our bedtime, so why not? Dudley sleeps with one eye open anyway. I was out like a light. Getting kidnapped by terrorists, meeting the Prime Minister of Israel, and working at the new American Embassy opening in Jerusalem really takes a lot out of you. If, in fact, all of that actually happened. Now, heading back to Houston, I was starting to wonder if it all was just a dream to compensate for that ten-speed bike Santa never brought me for Christmas. The joke's on him because I'm Jewish. I may need therapy. The best therapist I've ever known is Jack Daniels. He really understands me. And his rates are very reasonable. I highly recommend him. And often.

I wasn't sure how much time had passed before I realized my partner had somehow managed to spill over into my seat and left a very moist goober spot on my trousers. I only hoped the evaporation process would take place before touchdown. Just as I was doing some wishful thinking I looked around and everyone was snoozing, except for possibly the pilot. "Good morning ladies and gentlemen, and Dudley," he said.

Dudley heard his name and said something. Everyone was now awake, but just barely, and smiled at Dudley's shenanigans.

"Unfortunately, we're going to have to make an unexpected stop for fuel. We were going to New York, but a very powerful winter storm is hovering over the airport. Traffic control has rerouted us. We'll be taking a detour to Washington, DC. We should be able to make up some of the lost time from

Washington to Houston. Sit back and relax, and Kayla will take good care of you."

Kinky and I shot a glance at one another. His eyebrows were raised as if to question the detour. Mine were as well, I found this very curious. If Dudley had eyebrows, they surely would have been raised.

"I'm sure it won't take that long, Careless," E.D. said. "You didn't have anything better to do than spend time with your favorite person, did you?"

"No, Kinky and I have a lot of catching up to do, so it's fine."

"Real funny, Careless. I was referring to myself," she said, looking somewhat annoyed.

"Oh, were you? I'm sorry." I did know but sometimes my smartassery gets the better of me.

About an hour later, we were flying over Washington, DC. It was midmorning, and all of the monuments were visible from our vantage point. We could even see the Capitol Building and the White House. Everyone was staring out of the windows. I could barely see anything out of mine because Dudley's big head was hogging up all of the space in front of the small window. Minutes later, we were on the tarmac.

"Welcome to Washington," Kayla said. "We're in line to be refueled. It could take several hours. Your company has just informed the captain that they have provided a car service to pick you up and take you out of the airport till the jet has been refueled. Please step this way." She opened the door and pointed the way out with her hand.

We all looked at one another and stood up. I stretched my arms and legs, and Dudley assumed the only yoga position he knew, which is downward dog. He also let out a loud yawn. He may have just created a new yoga position–yawning dog. We walked to the front of the cabin and deplaned.

"Something's amiss," Kinky whispered to me. His instincts were correct. And I just realized he was a big fan of Arthur Conan Doyle who wrote the wonderful Sherlock Holmes novels. I was sure we were both thinking of just how we were able to skip going through customs. Nobody gets to do that, except maybe the President of the United States.

Once off of the plane, we noticed three black Subourbons and half a dozen large men dressed in black suits, white shirts, black ties, black shoes, and wearing earpieces. Even their well cropped hair was jet black. Here we go again. They were either FBI or Secret Service agents who were sternly and silently waiting for us to enter the vehicles. Either that or there was yet another sequel to *Men in Black* being filmed. I was hoping it wasn't another sequel because everyone knows sequels are never as good as the original. On the other hand, I wasn't thrilled about the feds interfering with our travel plans. Or being surveilled–again.

"The package has been delivered," the lead agent said as he spoke into his sleeve. He showed no emotion. Neither did the others.

"Please come with us," he said.

It wasn't like we had a choice. We proceeded to the head vehicle, but Kinky, Dudley, and I were stopped by a rather large, well-built agent standing in front of us, blocking our way. I was clear to me he was probably on hemorrhoids. We stopped in our tracks. We didn't need this dude having a roid rage episode on us.

We turned and walked to the second vehicle.

Before we reached it, another agent pointed at Kinky and said, "You, in this one." Then he pointed at me and said, "You two, in that one." He tilted his head towards the third Subourbon. Kinky and I looked at one another. He nodded at me and got in. The agent closed the door behind him. I couldn't see through the tinted glass. I wasn't happy. Neither was Dudley, and he said something.

Dudley and I got in the third vehicle, and once the door was closed, the caravan lurched forward in rapid fashion. My guess was we were on the way to another visit with Supervisor Tirone. It was interesting how she and her agents could always find us no matter where we were or what we were doing. I suppose they wanted us all in separate vehicles so we couldn't corroborate our stories, not that we needed to. The joke's on them because little did they know that Dudley and I were able to communicate with one another. We could corroborate all we wanted to.

In ten minutes, I was shocked to see we were pulling up to the entrance of the White House. I thought we were either going to be heroes or in so much deep doo doo we would never see the light of day again. The lead Subourbon briefly stopped at the heavily guarded gate. It was well fortified and the heavily armed Secret Service agents looked to be prepared for a small-scale war. Steel bollards sank into the ground, and a heavy iron gate slowly swung open. After all of the vehicles passed through and the gate shut, the bollards rose up. Dudley and I heard the gate clank shut behind us. We were driven underneath a carport. I had seen it many times on the news when the President leaves the White House. I bet Kinky was a little nervous in the service right about now and pretty sure E.D. was as well. I know I was. But not Dudley. He was just curious.

The vehicles came to a quick stop and all the back-passenger side doors of each Subourbon were opened by Secret Service Agents standing by. We all got out and were escorted into the White House.

"May I ask what we're doing here?" I already knew but figured it didn't hurt to ask.

"Please step through here," the lead agent said.

We walked through a metal detector. Thankfully, we all passed. I think this was Dudley's first time through a metal detector. I was so proud of him. He always does well on tests. He's just smart that way. Then an agent explained that we were going to be patted down. Personally, this would be the most action I'd had in months, but it kind of reminded me of an overly exuberant TSA agent. A female agent was provided for E.D. A wand was passed all around her, I guess for electronic surveillance devices.

"If you'd like me to pat her for you," I said, "I'd be happy to." I mean, if she was going to get felt up from the belt, shouldn't I be the person to do it? I'm highly qualified for that. Nobody laughed. E.D. was not amused.

Just as E.D. finished her acupressure therapy session, the White House Chief of Staff walked in. I recognized him from TV interviews.

"Happy Holidays, and welcome to the White House. I'm the President's Chief of Staff. I hope you don't mind the unexpected visit to the White House, but the President heard you were in town and wanted to meet you. Would that be okay?"

I looked at Kinky getting his pat down from the hat down, and he had that "sure thing" look when he heard the Chief of Staff. He was surprisingly calm and quiet about what was going on. Even when he had to remove his black cowboy hat for inspection.

When it was my turn for the massage, a male agent approached me. I raised my hand and said, "Exscrews me, but may I have the agent that she had for the physical? I'm feeling very gender fluid right now and it would make me more comfortable."

The lead agent said, "I'm sorry, sir, but we have strict policies we don't deviate from." None of the agents even cracked a smile. But Dudley thought my non-binary moment was funny. So did I.

I received my Thai massage from the male agent, and then he thought about patting Dudley down. As he moved closer, I said, "I wouldn't do that if I were you." The agent got still closer to him, and Dudley said something to let him know to not even think about it.

"He doesn't like strangers," I said. "It has to do with something from his childhood when he learned about stranger danger." I had no idea if this were true but it sure sounded legit.

The agent stopped and looked over his shoulder for guidance. The Chief of Staff nodded, and the agent withdrew. Dudley wasn't going to bite him. But he wasn't fond of people he didn't know, and besides, it's not like he was wearing clothes. I mean, where on earth was he supposed to hide anything? Speaking of Earth, did you know my favorite planet is Uranus? I actually have to write that word in each one of my novels. It's a contractual obligation I legally can't get out of. Not that I've tried.

Once we all went through the process, the Chief of Staff asked us to follow him. We walked through many hallways that I'm sure the public never gets to see. No one spoke. We got to a smaller room where a woman sat at a desk. I couldn't believe this, but I actually thought we were standing outside of the Oval Office. There were two Secret Service agents standing outside of a large white wooden door. Kinky seemed pretty sure of himself. I know he was studying the situation. E.D. appeared to be giddy. I'm also legally obligated to use the word "giddy" in each novel. So, there you go.

The woman at the desk picked up the phone and held it to her ear. "They are here, Mr. President. Yessir." She put the phone down and said, "The President will see you now."

The Chief of Staff opened the door to the Oval Office and waved us in with his hand. Once we were in the room he walked in and closed the door behind us. There was a lot of history in this room. I could feel it. So could Dudley. Well, he actually smelled it. Sometimes smells tend to linger more than memories do. I had my hand on his shoulders, so I could sense his initial confusion. I silently explained it to him with my thoughts. He seemed interested.

"Good morning," the President said, "please come in. Miss, how are you doing?" He stood up from behind his desk. He straightened his tie and buttoned his jacket. He was much taller than he looks on TV. He did not extend his hand, but that was expected. I had heard he was a germaphobe and did not like handshake greetings.

"Good morning, Mister President. My name's E.D. Sweetie. It is such a honor to meet you and be here today."

"Oh, I know who you are. I follow your work. You do great work. Really, just great. I'm a big fan. Did you get some nice photos of the embassy in Jerusalem? I heard it was a nice affair. Just great. Really great. Amazing. The best. You know, many, many other presidents promised to move the embassy from Tel Aviv to Jerusalem. I was the only one out of all of them that kept my promise and did it. I hope you got some really nice big photographs of the event. Nice and beautiful."

I believed him. I could see how well he connects with people. Kinky and E.D. seemed to believe him as well.

"I did, Mister President," E.D. said. "I did. Thank you very much." Once again, she was giddy.

I've used the word "giddy" twice now, so I won't have to include it in my next novel.

"Please, have a seat. I'm sorry I don't have any bourbon or tequila for you boys. We don't serve alcoholic beverages to our guests. I don't drink alcoholic beverages, so we just don't offer them. May I get you some water?"

He was definitely well prepared, down to the detail of our favorite beverages.

"No, I gave it up," Kinky said with a grin, pulling out a fresh cigar and popping it between his pearly whites. "You know, I've been in the Oval Office before."

I'm pretty sure he was kidding about giving up Mexican mouthwash. But then it dawned on me he was talking about water. He was a little vague. I'll have to ask for clarification at a later date.

"I do know that, Kinky. You know, the last several Presidents weren't the only fans of yours. I'm a big, big fan. The biggest. I've read all of your books and love your songs. Especially your new CD, Circus of Life. And Kinky, I especially like the quotes you've given about me. I really appreciate that. You remind me a lot of myself. But maybe better looking, of course." The President sat down in a nice, very comfortable looking, old chair. He was smiling. He has a very warm smile. Very sincere. "Welcome back to the White House, Kinky."

"Well, thank ya very much, Mr. President," Kinky said in a very deep Texas voice, while sitting down in an equally comfortable chair. He took the cigar out of his mouth, quickly half pointed at the President, and placed it back in his smiling mouth. At least he didn't spark it up this time. We were all grateful for that.

E.D., Dudley, and I were in awe of Kinky. We hadn't known he had been in the White House before. He was even more famous than we realized.

"So, Careless and Dudley. The crime solving duo. You two have had some interesting cases. Really interesting. I don't think there's a mystery out there you two can't solve. I did like the Sold Out Without The Holdout, case but my favorite one was Burp Gun Bandit. I REALLY enjoyed that one." He looked at Dudley and me. Now I felt famous. Don't worry, it's not going to go to our heads. Still, I couldn't believe he knew about us. This guy does his homework and doesn't miss a beat.

"You know, I love dogs. Most people don't know that about me but they're wrong. It's fake news. Fake news. I love dogs. Would you mind if I pet Dudley?" he asked.

"I don't know, Mister President, he typically doesn't do well with strangers. We can try." I put my hand on Dudley's shoulder and asked him to walk over and be nice. I had about a fifty-fifty chance of that happening. You never know with him. He looked up at me and dutifully walked over and sat. The President patted him on the head. Fortunately, he did not say something.

"Good boy, Dudley," he said.

Dodged a bullet there. Dudley walked back over to me and sat by my side.

"I've heard you have a way with dogs," the President said. "I can see that's true. Very interesting."

"Yes, Mr. President, I speak dog." He smiled.

"All right, let's get down to business here, shall we? It has come to my attention that you guys may have something that belongs to the United States government. Now, I'm not saying you do or you don't, but if you do, we're going to need it back. You want to tell me about it? Because I already know a lot. A whole lot."

Nobody responded as we sat stone-faced.

"Come on! You don't know who you're messing with here. I like you guys. Don't make me get tough with you."

Spoken like a true New Yorker.

"Suppose we do have what you're referring to," Kinky said. "How would we know who it belongs to? And if we did know who it belongs to, how would we get it to the proper authorities?"

E.D. looked somewhat surprised. Dudley and I had our poker faces on.

"Those are really good questions, and I'm telling you, as your President, that you can trust me. You understand?" We were listening intently.

"Believe me, you don't want that falling into the hands of some very bad people. There are a lot of bad, bad, very bad people out there. Very bad."

"Speaking of which, we've had a lot of run-ins with some foreign nationals."

"We know about that. We've taken care of it. You won't have any of those problems again. Just think of it, if you don't have the item we're talking about, then you have nothing to worry about. No one will bother you once they know you don't have it."

That made sense.

"What about Copper Love, she seems to know everything about us," Kinky said. "Is she one of ours?" This was good. We were double teaming him.

"I really shouldn't be telling you about this, but I can trust you, can't I?" He surveilled our facial expressions. I guess he was satisfied.

"Are you ready? Copper Love is probably the most deadly Russian secret agent we've ever tracked. No one even knows what she really looks like. She's that good."

I halfway smiled. Only because Kinky really did know what she looked like. REALLY knew. But I digress…and quit smiling. All at the same time.

"You are very lucky to even be alive. The only reason you are still breathing is probably because she hasn't gotten what she wants from you yet. If I were you, I would steer clear of her. If you like breathing."

I like breathing. I was pretty sure E.D, Kinky, and Dudley did as well.

"All that was off the record. You understand that, right?"

We all nodded. Even Dudley. He can keep a secret.

"If we did have the item you are referring to," I said, "and if we were going to give it to you, would you call off Agent Tirone? She's really cramping my style."

"Who?" The President asked.

He didn't know who she was. This made a lot of sense. And not in a good way.

"Agent Tirone," Kinky said. "With the FBI? Dark hair, mean as hell. Supervisor?"

"Never heard of her," he said. He glanced across the room at his Chief of

Staff standing in the corner, listening intently. I swung my head around to see him fiddling with his cell phone, then looking up and shaking his head from side to side.

"We don't have an Agent Tirone in the FBI. Are you sure you're not mistaking her with another agent?"

"You're probably right," I said. "I'm sure that's it." I found this odd. From his facial expression, I believe Kinky did as well. I was sure the President or someone in his cabinet would either know or be able to locate an Agent Tirone in the FBI, especially if she were a supervisor. And I was pretty sure I had seen her on TV with the President. She was in the background. Maybe I had just imagined it. So, who was the person who took us into custody? More mysteries for us to ponder. But I believed I already knew the answer.

"Can we count on you to keep America strong?" the President asked. "What do you say? Your President is asking you for your help protecting our county."

I looked at Kinky and E.D. and we I all responded, "Yes," almost simultaneously.

"I knew I could count on you. Kinky, I'll have you back at the White House real soon. We'd love to hear you play your fantastic new songs. Okay?"

Kinky tipped his black cowboy hat and said to him, "Thank you for being American." The President chuckled.

"My Chief of Staff will show you out and he'll give you contact information so we can retrieve that item from you. Again, thank you for coming to see me." Like we had a choice. The President stood up from behind his desk and smiled. Everything was becoming very clear to me now. Somehow, we had been thrown into the middle of a spy and technology war. I guess we were just in the wrong place at the wrong time. Or were we? Maybe it was supposed to happen this way. Maybe this was the plan all along. Maybe I should stop trying to be so Zen and start the next chapter.

We followed the Chief of Staff past all of the Secret Service agents and back in the same direction we had come from earlier. I think we were all still in awe of being in the Oval Office and meeting with the President of The United States. I wondered if Dudley was the first canine to visit with a sitting president in the Oval Office. I bet he was. Just another feather in the cap of my best friend and soulmate.

We were led outside to a single dark Subourbon and headed back to the airport. They must not have minded us travelling together now that we had met with the President. And they must have thought we were going to give them what they wanted. Our driver was wearing a dark suit, white shirt, black tie, and sported an earpiece.

"Can you even believe what just happened?" E.D. said. "This has been the most amazing trip I've ever been on." She seemed very excited. We just nodded. The driver occasionally looked back through the rear view mirror to check on us. Dudley lay down with his head in my lap. I rested my hand on him and saw that he was tired. I suppose this trip had worn him out. He has been through quite a bit. He closed his eyes and drifted off. I could see his dreams. Oh yes, dogs do dream. Kinky was deep in thought. We were going to have to make some major decisions when we got home. Who did the L.A.M.B. chip really belong to? In my mind it was either going to America or Israel. But which one?

We made it back to the airport and were driven to a private entrance for private planes. We didn't have to get felt up from the belt up again by TSA agents or the like. The Subourbon came to a stop in front of the plane.

"Have a nice day," the Secret Service agent said. That was the first time we had heard him speak.

"What's your name, honey?" E.D. asked.

"Sam Malone, ma'am. Sam Malone." He eyeballed her in the rearview mirror. Then, just as quickly, he quit speaking while staring straight ahead. Short and to the point. I like that.

"Thank you for driving us, Sam Malone," she said.

"My pleasure ma'am. Have a safe trip home." He briefly viewed her through the rearview mirror, then looked straight ahead.

How did he know we were going home? We could have been travelling anywhere. These folks sure did know quite a bit about us.

We exited the vehicle and boarded the plane. Kayla, the sexy flight attendant was waiting for us.

"Welcome back. I'm so sorry for that unexpected stop and delay, but a few repairs were made, we are fueled up, and we are ready for takeoff. We'll have you back to Houston in a jiffy. Would you care for anything to drink?"

Kinky and E.D. sat in their own separate seats. Kinky ordered a Mexican mouthwash. E.D. ordered a Mimosa. Dudley and I sat in seats across the aisle from them and I ordered a Careless Coffee. I was ready to sit back and relax on the way home. I sipped my Careless Coffee and stroked Dudley's fur as he lay sleeping with his head in my lap. Just as I was about to doze off, my phone beeped at me alerting me of a received text. Kinky's phone beeped at the same exact time. The text was the contact information of the President's Chief of Staff. There were no secrets we could possibly keep from these guys. Well, maybe just one. Apparently, we couldn't hide squat from them. I looked at Kinky and nodded at him. He nodded back. E.D. was already fast asleep.

The captain announced, "Please prepare for takeoff." Kayla walked through the cabin and collected our drinks. I closed my eyes and drifted off, longing to get back home and get back to normal.

I must have been really out of it because the next thing I remember was the plane touching down and the captain announcing, "Welcome to Houston. We'll just taxi off of the runway, and get you good folks on your way."

"I called my friend," Kinky said, "Little Jewford. He'll meet me here and give me a lift back to the ranch. The Friedman's are anxious for The Kinkster's return." That was probably an understatement. "I'll call you when I get back."

As we got off the plan, Kayla waved goodbye and said, "It was a sincere pleasure serving you."

E.D. elbowed me and said, "I saw you making goo goo eyes at her." In my defense, she was hot and I am a guy. I grabbed E.D.'s and my bags and walked toward her car she had named Betsy. Kinky grabbed his bag and his guitar and walked to a car that was waiting for him. He put his things in the back seat and before getting in the car, looked at me and said, "I'll be in touch mate." They drove away, and so did we, leaving the airport and a lot of interesting memories behind.

40

E.D. drove us back to Big Rock Lofts. We just refer to it as home. It was kind of weird being back. I almost felt out of place. We hadn't been gone for that long, but so many things had happened, things just seemed strange. E.D. parked her car in the front parking lot. Dudley got out of the car and went straight to his familiar spots to do his business. It seemed like he felt right at home. E.D. and I walked in silence up to the old warehouse, converted into lofts.

She unlocked the door and we walked in. Sarge, as usual, was sitting on the sofa in the lobby. I often found him sitting there, either mentally travelling to some distant land or reading a book. He is an avid reader. Now I felt at home. It's strange the things that make you feel like you belong in a place. Sarge was one of those things. A familiar fixture, if you will. He was like a landmark. He didn't even hear us come in. I'm sure he was busy doing mental gymnastics. Probably with Leticia, I'm betting. I tried not to visualize.

Dudley immediately placed his nostrils in an opportune place and jostled Sarge back to reality. That startled him and woke him up. "Hey man, han, han. How's it going man, han, han." He reached down and patted Dudley on the head. Dudley was not amused and said something. Sarge promptly removed his hand.

"Where have you been? There sure have been a lot of people coming in and out of your places while you were gone. I called Birk, and he came over and spoke to them. I'm sure glad you're back." Sarge doesn't do well with change. Much like a dog, he needs and does best with a routine.

"Who was going in our lofts?" I inquired. E.D. seemed interested as well. I placed my hand on Dudley's back. He had already recognized who had been here by their smell. Therefore, I did as well.

"I don't know, man, han, han. It was some woman dressed in a black suit with black hair, and a bunch of men dressed just like her. She looked like she meant business. Birk talked to her. You should call him and find out who she was."

Agent Tirone. Of course. This was getting very interesting. Things were starting to become clear to me now, with the help of Dudley, of course. I don't know what I would do without him. I definitely would not solve as many cases, that's for sure.

"Okay, Sarge," I said. "Thank you for the info. I will call Birk once we've settled in and get to the bottom of this."

"You got it man, han, han. Welcome home." he said. With that, he went back into his trance we had disturbed him from.

"Who do you think he's talking about, Careless? Do you think he's just having an episode? You know, maybe he's been reading *Puff the Magic Dragon* again. Who knows?"

"No, this time, I think he's pretty accurate. I'll call Birk in a bit and find out more." Sarge can sometimes go off on wild tangents, but this was not one of those times.

We walked upstairs together and Dudley and I stopped at our loft, #158. It was good to finally be home. E.D. kept walking up the stairs to her loft which was directly above us.

As soon as we entered, I made myself a Careless Coffee and filled Dudley's food and water bowls. I expected him to be pretty hungry after his big journey. I sipped my coffee. He didn't come over to his bowls like he normally does. Instead, he wandered around the loft, sniffing here and there. I put my coffee down, walked over to him, rested my hand on his back, and followed him around. It didn't take long. The loft was small and compact. There had definitely been people here. Definitely Copper Love was one of those people. I suspected the same at E.D.'s place, but she would never know that because she didn't have the benefit of the super snooper, Dudley. The strange thing is, nothing was out of place. Everything was exactly as I had left it. Only because of Dudley did I suspect that everything had most likely been gone through.

I picked up the phone and called Birk. "Careless, I'm so glad you're back. You're never going to believe this. Sarge called me while you were gone because he saw people going in and out of yours and E.D.'s lofts. I came over quick like and sure enough, the FBI were in the building. They stopped me from entering your place, but when someone opened the door and walked out, I saw them combing through your things. They quickly shut the door, and I was told to leave the scene of an official investigation."

"Did you get any names?" I asked. I already knew the answer, but it never hurts to get firsthand knowledge.

"I sure did, Careless. An FBI supervisor by the name of Chelsea Tirone stopped me in the hallway as I was trying to enter your place. She had a badge and a gun. And she was as mean as an alligator. She asked me to leave the building. I wanted to see what they were doing but thought better of it. Sarge and I left and had a few beers at Henderson Heights. When we came back, they were gone, without a trace."

"That was probably a smart move," I said.

"What does that mean? Is there something you're not telling me? What's going on?"

"I'll explain later. My phone is beeping at me. Somebody's trying to cut in on your dance. I'll call you in a bit."

"Okay, Careless. Don't forget. Looks like you got yourself in a fine mess this time." He hung up and I pushed the button on the phone to see who was on the line.

"Careless, you are not going to believe this," E.D. said, sounding exasperated. I thought maybe she had figured out her loft had been rifled through. "Careless, I just listened to the messages on my answering machine. My boss called and wanted to know why I missed the flight on the corporate jet flying to Israel. She was pretty hot and said now they would have to pay to use stock images from the embassy opening in Jerusalem. What does that mean, Careless? We took the flight. I have the images. I even called the office to get permission for Kinky to fly back with us. What the hell is going on? I'm so confused right now." She was confused. I was not. "I just don't understand this. I know I didn't imagine any of this. What is happening, Careless? Help me out here. I'm just at a loss of words right now."

"I think I know what's going on, E.D. but it will take some time for me to explain it to you."

"Just hold that thought, Careless. Right now, my office is beeping in and I need to try to somehow explain that I have the images they need, so they won't have to pay someone else for them. I just hope I don't get fired. I'm in shock right now. I'll call you back when I get everything squared away." All I heard was a click as she quickly hung up the phone.

I called my office, and they told me everything was under control and there was no need to come in today. I told them Dudley and I would be there first thing in the morning.

I then called Detective Present and filled him in on everything that had happened. Just as he suspected, the jet we had flown on to Tel Aviv was most probably an Israeli Air Force jet. We would never know for sure, but we definitely didn't fly there on the company jet that E.D.'s office had arranged. It's almost like someone was perpetrating a big charade to force us to cough up the L.A.M.B chip. Detective Present told me he'd look into it, but not to expect anything because these types of people were extraordinary at covering their tracks. I was sure there would be no trace of anything. If this were a dream, it would have to be the most interesting one ever. And I was sure we had not all had the same dream.

I sat down on the sofa and drank my coffee. Dudley was busy finishing up his food and water. He noticed me sitting on the sofa so he gulped down the last bit his food and joined me. I was busy putting the pieces of the puzzle together. I was almost there but still missing a few pieces. Dudley noticed I was deep in thought. As he often does, he sat on the remote control and turned on the TV. I think he does it on purpose because he thinks it's funny. He looks around pretending to see who turned on the TV butt I know it was him. I just let him think he tricked me and ask him, "Who did that? Go find who did that." He looks around, snickers under his breath, and pretends to look for someone. The funny thing is he never finds anyone.

Eye Witless News was now blaring from the TV. They showed footage of yet another one of Little Rocketman's attempts to fire off a missile. It had blown up after leaving the launch pad. It surprised me to then see live footage of the President, whom we had just seen a day ago, crossing over the demilitarized zone between North and South Korea and shaking hands with Little Rocketman, Kim Jung Un. They walked together and spoke to one another in North Korea. It almost felt as if I've been living in an alternate universe. All of these recent events I've been seeing, I had never expected to happen in my lifetime. What next? Peace in the Middle East?

Dudley shifted his weight and, of course, changed the channel when his rear end moved. This was another one of his little tricks. He leaned up against me with all of his might. He slid himself down the side of my body like water flowing down the outside of a drinking glass when overfilled. He came to rest laying down on the sofa with his head in my lap. I rested my hand on him and drank my coffee. Now the TV was tuned to Eye Witless News Part II. They were showing a protest in the West Bank of Israel. Missiles were exploding in the air just as they were being launched. I guess whoever had the second

L.A.M.B chip must have worked out the kinks because it sure seemed like a lot of enemy missiles were malfunctioning. Coincidence? I think not.

Dudley started snoring. I was getting a bit tired myself and was about to doze off. The phone started having spasms. I looked at it and tried to decide if it was worth picking up. I lost the battle because of its perseverance. "Careless, it's Kinky. Kinky, here."

42

"Hey, did you make it back okay?" I asked. He sounded worried. I was a little concerned because he never really let anything get on his nerves of steel.

"Forget about that! The chip is gone. I got back and it was missing. I hid it behind the silver star on the Garrison Brothers Cowboy Bourbon bottle. I peeled the star away from the bottle, hollowed the back out, and re-glued it." He paused to breathe.

"I know."

"How could you possibly know that? No one was here when I hid it. I checked."

"Oh, someone was there. Louie was standing right next to you as worked your magic. And he ratted you out. But I have told no one. Who do you think took it?"

"I don't know, Careless. They took the whole damn bottle. I asked Floyd if he'd seen anybody, but other than his twenty-three cats he lives with, he saw no one coming or going. I just don't understand how they found it. I don't even know if it ended up in the right hands. And I forgot about that weird dog thing you do. I'm going to have a talk with Louie about that."

"Have you been watching the news?" I asked him.

"No, I just got in."

"Well, I'm not sure who took the chip, but I'm pretty sure it ended up in the right place. I think we're okay, Kinky. Go watch the news, and we'll talk later. I have to see a man about a horse."

"Okay, pal." He hung up the phone. Somehow, I knew after watching the news that, whatever happened, it was good for America and good for Israel. Why else would Little Rocketman invite the President to cross from South Korea into North Korea, shake hands, and stroll while talking. That had never happened before. This was one of the most interesting cases I had ever worked on. And as a bonus, I made a new interesting friend.

How many people have a friend named Kinky? That was a rhetorical question. There were still some loose ends to tie up. But right now, I just needed a little shut eye. I closed my eyes and joined my friend, Dudley. I'm sure we sawed some logs together until the next morning.

When we woke up, we went through our usual routine. I showered, fed and watered Dudley, and took him outside to do his business. We went to Papa's house for a hearty, yet very unhealthy breakfast. Dudley loved watching the old percolator coffee pot. His head bobbed up and down every time the coffee popped up in the glass opening at the top. He's entertained rather easily. I told Papa and Ross all about my trip to Israel that may or may not have happened. And I told them about meeting the President. I was pretty sure they may or may not have believed any of it. But Dudley and I know it happened.

We went to the office after breakfast. It was almost Christmas, and just like this time every year, people tended to slow down and try to remember why they were truly put on this earth. We were pretty slow at work and running a skeleton crew. Later that day, Dudley was upside down on his executive sofa with his legs stretched into the air. He was sleeping and his large jowls were hanging down, exposing his teeth. It was obvious from his clean white teeth that he had been flossing. I was happy about that. He always kept one eye partially open, while watching me. It was a neat trick. I'm not sure where he picked that up from.

My phone rang and I was kind of excited to get it because I was a little bored. "Carless, it's Kinky. It's Kinky. Kinky here," the voice said.

"Yessir, how may I help you?"

"Listen, I'm going to have a Christmas party here at the ranch on Christmas Eve. Why don't you bring your friends and come down? It'll be fun. We'll have a goooood time" he said as he stretched out the word good, to make sure I knew it would be fun. I then realized that for a man who smokes cigars, he has really good lung capacity.

"May I bring Dudley?" I asked him. I was hoping he'd say yes so I could bring him with my crew. We hadn't all been together since the last case, and that had been a while ago.

"Does the Dalai Lama practice Juddhism? That's Jewish Buddhism, you know."

"Yeah, I got that," I said. I took that to be an affirmative response.

"The more the merrier. See you tomorrow. You can stay here at the ranch if you need a place to stay."

"See you then." I hung up the phone.

Dudley was still sleeping on his back but was now wide awake with both eyes open. He seemed to know where we were going, without me even touching him. I guess he recognized Kinky's voice.

After work Dudley and I climbed in the Power Wagon and went home. When we pulled up I noticed Birk's Cowboy Cadillac in the parking lot. I parked next to it. The sheer size of his F350 Crew Cab Dually made the Power Wagon look like the size of a children's Red Flyer toy wagon. I'm not complaining because I was hoping he would drive us all down to Kinky's ranch in it so we could all be comfortable during the trip.

Dudley did his business for most of the way up to the old iron front door of the loft. He is actually quite a good businessman. When we walked in, Sarge was sitting in his usual spot, with E.D. standing on one side of the sofa with her arms folded, and Birk leaning up against the wall on the other side. They were all watching me and apparently waiting for something.

"What's the malfunction?" I offered up.

"Well, Careless," E.D. said, "we know that you know what's going on. I have filled in Birk and Sarge as to the details that I know of the last several days. Just like you always do after solving cases, we want you to tell us how the case was solved." She had a very determined look on her face.

"Yeh, and Sarge and I want to meet The Kinkster," Birk said. "Can you make that happen?" He seemed determined as well.

"I think I can make that happen," I explained to them. Birk and Sarge seemed pretty gleeful with that response. Kinky did say I could bring people to the Christmas party. So, maybe I'll just do that.

"Well, don't keep us waiting, Careless," E.D. said. "You know I hate waiting."

"A beautiful woman such as yourself should never be kept waiting," I schmoozed her. She smiled.

Dudley was getting bored and decided to start walking up the stairs to our loft. He was probably hungry.

"Tell you what, let's all go up to my place, I'll feed my friend here, make myself a Careless Coffee, and tell you everything I know. How's that grab you?"

"Sounds good," Birk said. "Let's hit it."

We walked up the stairs to our loft and Dudley sat and waited for me to open the door. Once in, I poured food in his bowl. While Dudley nosed his food around, I fixed myself a Careless Coffee. This time, a little heavy on the Garrison Brothers Cowboy Bourbon. I do love the Cowboy Bourbon. It packs a wallop, while remaining quite tasty. As I stared at the big silver star on the bottle, my mind started to wander. Who got the chip, and how did they find where it was hidden? I only wish I knew. I had an idea, of course, but nothing set in concrete.

"Uh, hello!" E.D. exclaimed. "Remember, beautiful women should not be kept waiting..."

"I'm sorry," I said as I snapped out of it. I sipped my Careless Coffee and leaned up against my old steel file cabinet they had provided me years ago that held copies of my cases. Who knows, one day, they could be turned into mystery novels. It could happen.

"Start at the beginning, Careless," E.D. said. "And don't leave anything out."

"You got it. On the way to dinner in Kerrville with E.D. and Kinky, someone driving an unmarked van almost ran into Kinky's car, the Yome Kippur Clipper, and E.D.'s car, Betsy. We met Kinky after we found and returned his dogs, who had been playing hooky."

"How come they name their cars, man, han, han?" Sarge broke in. It was a valid question.

"Shush, Sarge," E.D. said. "Please continue, Careless."

"Okay, when we stopped to inspect the cars to make sure they weren't damaged, we noticed an art gallery named the Copper Love Art Gallery. It looked as if there had just recently been trouble there. We walked in and sure enough, a huge skirmish had occurred. There was blood everywhere and what we thought were two dead bodies. However, we were mistaken. The person I checked on was dead. The one Kinky checked on was beaten and bloody, but alive. Kinky tried to help her, but right at that time the police arrived."

I paused to sip my number one favorite beverage. This was my favorite part where I would have them eating out of my hands. I also liked the silence. Silence is golden.

"Once we were interviewed by the local authorities, we went to dinner. By the way, the Chinese food was excellent, but I digress. The strange thing is that when I called Detective Present, he said there was no incident report regarding the gallery. There was just nothing, as if it never happened. After that, we were followed on the way back to Houston, and a Middle Eastern man actually walked up to E.D.'s car at a gas station, as if he were searching for something. Again, when I asked Detective Present to check the security tapes at the gas station so we could identify who was after us, there was some sort of 'malfunction' and no video." I paused again for another sip. Now they were sitting on the edge of their seats.

"Then there was the missing evidence, which was a pant leg section Dudley had extracted from the person who followed us to the gas station. I turned it in to be analyzed, but for some reason it could not be found. It seemed odd that every step of the way there were a lot of malfunctions and things going missing. Coincidence? I think not."

"He's right, all of that did happen," E.D. said. "I saw it with my own eyes."

"Shhhh…, please continue," Sarge said with a look of self-satisfaction plastered across his face. Speaking of self-satisfaction, I wondered how things were progressing with Sarge's girlfriend. E.D. did not look amused.

"When Kinky told me he had found a microchip in his jacket pocket, and after a robbery gone bad at a dry cleaner in Kerrville, I knew we had a problem. You see, Kinky had given his jacket to his friend, Floyd, to take to the dry cleaner. I realized that, while Kinky was checking to see if Copper Love was alive at the gallery, she came to and slipped the chip into his pocket. My guess was she knew the police were on the way and didn't want them finding the chip. She probably planned on recovering it later." I looked around. No questions or comments, so I walked to the sofa and sat next to my friend, Dudley.

"We later found out that the chip was actually something called the L.A.M.B. chip. It was a top-secret missile defense chip that we think had been stolen. The fight at the gallery happened when foreign nationals attempted to recover the chip. We never really knew who it belonged to, but several governments laid claim to it. Regardless, when the chip was not found at the dry cleaner, someone murdered the owner. We don't know who, but it certainly didn't appear to be a robbery, as it was made out to be." I made hand gestures with my free hand to make it more interesting and dramatic.

"Kinky had found the chip before sending the jacket to be cleaned and had squirreled it away in a secret hiding place only known to him, or so he thought. Copper Love had visited him and bugged his house. My house was also bugged. I knew from talking to Detective Present that the Feds were involved, and even though he warned me to back off, I didn't. It's not in my nature. My guess is that all of your places were gone through and bugged as well.

"The strangest thing was when Kinky and I were abducted and taken to a warehouse where FBI agents grilled us about the chip. The supervisor made us the object of her obsession. Her name was Agent Chelsea Tirone. She was a badass and super tough. Kinky said she even made him nervous in the service. I'm still not sure what that means, but it does rhyme. And I do like a good rhyme. We learned much later there was never an FBI agent named Chelsea Tirone. She doesn't exist. We have that on good authority. Here's what's going to blow your mind. Agent Chelsea Tirone and Copper Love are one in the same person." They all gasped. I know they didn't see that one coming.

I sipped my coffee and finished it. I make a good Careless Coffee. "Here's something else that will blow your mind. The flight attendant on the plane going to Israel we supposedly missed...also Copper Love. She was amazing with disguises. At the time, no one even had a clue. And about the plane, the one we were supposed to fly on to Israel, the one supposedly supplied by E.D.'s magazine, it was replaced at the last moment with an Israeli Air Force jet. Detective Present alerted me to that when I inquired about the tail numbers before we took off. We didn't miss the plane, E.D., we just got on the wrong plane. Or the right plane, depending on who's perspective it's from. Then flight attendant, Kelley, or Copper Love, searched our belongings after she drugged our drinks during the flight. I know this because Dudley remained awake and watched her. The call you thought made to your office asking if Kinky could fly back to the U.S. with us? It was intercepted by an intelligence agency, probably CIA. So you never really spoke to your office. You only thought you did." There was complete silence in the room.

"So where is Copper Love now and where's the chip?" Sarge blurted out.

"All good questions. Just to cap it off, the three of us, E.D., Kinky, and

I ended up meeting the President of The United States. I don't know of any other civilian dog who has ever visited the White House and met the President. You're famous now, aren't you, boy?" Of course, he said something. Everyone laughed.

"What about Copper Love?" Birk asked. "And who did you end up giving the chip to?"

"Right, well, it turns out that Copper Love was a Russian agent. Apparently, she is quite deadly and very good at dress-up. The only reason I knew she was Agent Tirone and Kelley, the flight attendant, is because of Dudley. You can't fool the nose of a Black Mouth Cur. Honestly, I don't know where Copper Love is. She vanished like bacon at an Overeaters Anonymous Convention. I doubt we'll ever see her again. At least never recognize her again."

"And why is that Careless?" E.D. inquired.

"You see, Kinky had the L.A.M.B. chip well hidden away. I was the only other person who knew where it was. And that was only because his dog, Louie, saw him squirrel it away. When I pet Louie, I knew exactly where the chip had been hidden. But I never told anyone. Sadly, someone found the chip while we were in Israel. And now it is missing. That's the whole story. I doubt we'll ever see anyone involved with this case again. Except the President. He said he would have Kinky back to the White House to entertain them."

"Who do you think got the chip, Careless?" E.D. asked. "You think a rogue nation got it?"

"I don't think so. After watching the news, my guess is either the U.S. Government or the Israeli Government retrieved it. Or possibly both, if they are working together. But we'll never know for sure. This may be my first case that goes somewhat unsolved."

Everyone seemed a little disappointed with the anticlimactic ending. I was as well, but it is what it is. Some things are just better left unknown. This might be one of those things.

After the telling of my little tale, the gang got somewhat restless.

"Hey," I said, "Kinky invited us down to the ranch tomorrow for a Christmas Eve party. Would any of you like to go?"

"Would we ever!" Birk belted out while looking at Sarge and E.D. for confirmation. Sarge and E.D. nodded in agreement.

"Terrific, Birk, would you mind driving, if you call what you do driving?"

"You got it, Careless."

"Let's all meet here at 10:00 in the morning. Don't be late. You know how E.D. hates to be late." I just said this to amuse myself. Even though it was true.

With that, everyone scattered and Dudley and I hit the sack. He did his usual routine. He waited for me to lay down, jumped on the bed, circled around several times, and lay his head on my chest. I rested my hand on him and started to doze off. He was excited about going on a road trip tomorrow.

The next morning, Dudley was eyeballing me. He was still and waiting for me to open my eyes. When I did, he got all excited like he hadn't seen me in years. His tail started spinning in circles and he began licking my face. I finally weaseled my out of his clutches and hit the head. I showered and got dressed. I fed and watered Dudley, who took his sweet time, and then I took him out back to do his business. While he was doing his thing, I went over in my head all that had happened during the last several days. I was sure I was missing something but I just couldn't focus my mind to pinpoint what it was. Maybe all the travelling had worn me out. It definitely had been a whirlwind Christmas.

When Dudley was finished we went back up to the loft and I packed an overnight bag. Dudley made himself comfortable on the sofa. I was thankful he hadn't eaten this sofa like he had done to its predecessor. The phone began having convulsions. He looked at it and thought about answering it–again, but I held up my index finger and shook my head at him. He backed off. I don't relish the thought of cleaning goober off of the phone.

I answered the phone, "Cerino's Pizza, how may I helpa you?"

"Real funny. Detective Present here. Something interesting came across my desk today, and I thought you'd want to hear about." He paused, maybe considering what type of pizza he wanted to order.

"Pray, continue," I prompted him.

"Do you remember that gallery you told me about, the one with the crime scene you and your friends stumbled into?" He paused again.

"Well, of course. Why do you ask?" This was getting interesting.

"Do you remember I told you there was no trace of an incident report?"

"I sure do," This was getting a little tedious.

"This morning, I saw an accident report. I had been searching the database for anything with certain names or locations after everything you've alerted me to. The art gallery you told me about, it was called The Copper Love Art Gallery, wasn't it?"

"It was indeed."

"There was a major accident this morning around Fredericksburg. A Mazda Miata convertible was T-boned and just crushed. There was hardly anything left of the Miata, and there was blood everywhere. And Careless, the car was registered to one Copper Love."

My mouth dropped open. Could this really be? Did this Russian agent's past finally catch up with her? I was just about in shock. Other than the L.A.M.B. chip going missing, this really brought the investigation to a head.

"One more thing, Careless. They took the driver who T-boned the Miata to the hospital. He's in a coma but expected to recover. Here's the weird part. There was no body recovered from the Miata." I could tell he was baffled and intrigued at the same time.

"Of course not," I replied. Just when I thought we were going to get some closure on this case, a monkey wrench was thrown into it.

"I'm sorry, Careless, there's not a whole lot I can do without a body. But based on the images, there is no possibility that whoever was driving that car survived. There's just no way."

"Thank you, Detective Present. I appreciate the heads up." Somehow, I wasn't as sure as Detective Present that no one could have survived the accident.

"I just wish I could have done more. Why don't you come in after Christmas and we'll compare notes? I also have a couple of cases we're going to need your help with. We'll go over them when you get here. Merry Christmas, Careless."

"Merry Christmas Detective Present," I said. I hung up the phone, perplexed. Dudley was still listening but was waiting to go downstairs to start our road trip.

I guess we'll never know what became of Copper Love. I almost wanted her to be alive. She had really become kind of a legend in my mind. I decided to name this case A Careless Christmas. I started to write that on the folder my notes were held in but stopped just short of writing the first letter. No, I think it should be A Very Kinky Christmas, in honor of my new friend, Kinky Friedman. Yes, that is what I will call it. I wrote that on the folder and placed it in the file cabinet with my other cases. I may need a new file cabinet soon. This one was starting to fill up.

I grabbed our bag and Dudley and I walked down to the lobby. Everyone was on time and waiting for us. We all climbed into the truck. Dudley and I sat in the co-pilot seat and E.D. and Sarge sat in the very spacious back seat. Dudley wanted to poke his head out of the sunroof, but it was too cold. He settled down and instead, he rode with half of his body in my lap, with the other half squished into the seat. I told the gang about the Copper Love accident. They offered up all kinds of conspiracy theories. But of course, no one had any definite answers. Was she still out there, carrying out missions for Mother Russia? We may never know.

We drove straight through to Kerrville and were approaching the ranch. I was always tickled when Kinky referred to the residents as Kerrverts. I don't know why but that always made me smile, in a juvenile way, of course. Now that I think of it, I think he lost his Kerrville mayoral due to Russian interference. Yes, I can see that happening. I hope somebody investigates it one day.

Passing by the Copper Love Art Gallery brought back memories. It was so different from what I remembered. I saw people walking in and out of the building and a sign in the front window showing it was open.

"Hit the brakes, Hoss," I said.

Birk did a real nice slide stop.

"What's the malfunction, Careless?" he asked.

"I have to make a quick pitstop. Would you mind letting me out right here? I'll just be a minute."

"I wouldn't mind at all. Let me park the truck, and we'll make that pitstop with you." The others all together muttered something to the effect of, "Yeah." Dudley, of course, said something. And he too insisted on coming with me.

Birk parked the truck and we got out and walked into the gallery. It looked exactly as it did the night of the crime, but without blood or dead bodies. In fact, everything was perfect. Almost too perfect. People were walking around looking at paintings, pointing at sculptures, and stroking their chins while pretending to care, secretly wishing they were someplace else. A little too pretentious for my taste but the artwork was pretty fantastic. I especially liked the painting hanging in front of me called "Cypress Trees On The River." Something about it haunted me. It seemed so familiar.

While I was looking at it, a very attractive red-headed woman with her back to me was talking to some customers about a painting they seemed interested in purchasing. Could it be? Was Copper Love still alive and back at the gallery? The anticipation was killing me. Dudley noticed a dog roaming around the gallery and decided to join him. Apparently, dogs like artwork as well.

Finally, she turned and faced us. "Hi, welcome to the gallery. Is this your first time here?" she asked. It was not her. The resemblance was uncanny, but it was definitely not Copper Love.

"No, actually, we were here once before, a little before Thanksgiving." I monitored her body language.

"I'm sorry, that's impossible. The gallery was closed in November for the Thanksgiving holiday until just a couple of days ago. We reopened for people wanting to shop for last-minute Christmas presents. I was away painting winter landscapes in West Texas."

"Great, yet another unexplained incident to add to the record," I muttered under my breath.

"We were definitely here," E.D. responded. Birk and Sarge looked bewildered, which is usually the case.

"I'm sorry, I'm Copper Love. I own the gallery. I think there has been some kind of confusion. Are you sure it wasn't another gallery? There is one just up the block that looks very similar."

"You're probably right," I said. "Did you say your name is Copper Love?" E.D. appeared perplexed.

"Yes, I own the gallery. Some of the paintings are mine, but I do represent several other very talented artists. Would you like to have a look around? I can tell you about anything or any artist in the gallery."

"Yes, we would love that. Would you mind me asking you a couple of questions?"

"Not at all, go ahead," she said.

"Is that your dog over there hanging around with my hoodlum friend, Dudley?"

"Why, yes. That's my dog, Clovis. He goes everywhere I go. He comes to the gallery with me every day. He sure does seem to like Dudley. Normally I find him just lying by my easy chair."

"Oh, everybody loves Dudley. One last question, what type of car do you drive?"

"Well, that's kind of an odd question. But I did drive a red Mazda Miata convertible. I call her Ruby Tuesday."

Great, another person who names their car!

"She was stolen from in front of my house last night. Clovis and I love driving around with the top down. I reported her stolen to the police, but I haven't heard anything back yet. I hope they find her. I love that little car."

I refrained from asking her if she enjoyed driving topless. It took a little more effort than I expected.

We all looked at one another. "I'm sure they'll find her," I said. "Would you mind if I pet Clovis? I just love dogs."

"Sure, he's super friendly. He loves people. Listen, I have to go help out a few customers who look interested in some paintings. You guys look around and if you see anything you love, please come find me. We're having a fifteen percent off Christmas sale right now."

Before she could walk away I said, "I really like this one." I pointed at the "Cypress Trees On The River" painting.

"I'm so sorry. That painting was purchased several days ago by a client who purchased it as a surprise present for Kinky Friedman. Have you ever heard of him? He's pretty famous around here."

This was getting way too coincidental.

"Yes, as a matter of fact, my friends and I were on the way to his ranch for a Christmas party before your gallery caught our attention."

"Really? How odd? What are the chances of that happening?"

What indeed?

"Hey, would mind taking the painting with you? I was going to deliver it myself after I closed the gallery today. You'd be doing me a huge favor. I'll even give you a twenty percent discount on anything you're interested in purchasing."

"It would be my pleasure."

"Great, I'll just wrap it up for you. Why don't you browse and see if something jumps out at you?"

"You got it." I walked over to Clovis and Dudley and put my hands on each of their backs. I saw from Clovis that her human really was the true Copper Love. And they had been travelling in the Ruby Tuesday until last night. Clovis would sit by her side as she painted landscapes. Very beautiful landscapes. And he did go to the gallery with her every day when it was open. Well, this was interesting. I wondered if the Russian agent pretending to be Copper Love, or whatever her real name is, was still alive.

The gang was watching me. I nodded to them to verify that Copper Love was who she said and that she was telling the truth. Dudley and I said goodbye to Clovis. He walked over to Copper and sat right by her side as she described a painting to a customer who seemed interested in it. She glanced at me and quickly excused herself. She picked up Kinky's painting and walked over to me.

It looks like you guys are ready to go. I'm sorry you didn't find anything this time. But please do come back. The discount offer still stands. Thank you so much for delivering this painting for me." She handed it to me.

I nodded as I accepted the painting and we left the gallery with just as many questions as we had come with.

We got in the truck and drove all the way to Kinky's ranch. Everything was lit up with Christmas lights. Birk parked the truck and we got out. The Friedmans ambled up, and Dudley joined his little friends. He especially hit it off with Mr. P, the white poodle.

When we walked in there were several people walking around. Kinky was playing his guitar and everyone seemed to be having a good time. I put the painting down in a little room off to the side and joined everyone.

"Come on in," he belched out while leaning his guitar against a wall. "Can I interest you all in some Man In Black Tequila? Why, it's the best damn Mexican mouthwash you ever had. It's gooood."

Birk and Sarge introduced themselves and then had some Mexican mouthwash. They were pretty thrilled to meet him. I poured myself a Jack Daniels since the Garrison Brothers Cowboy Bourbon had been stolen. Back to the basics. Nothing wrong with that. Sometimes you gotta dance with the one who brang ya.

Everyone was having a great time. About twenty minutes later, Kinky walked up to me and said, "I Just wrote some new songs. You want to hear them?"

"You bet," I said.

"Willie Nelson is going to sing with me on some of them." He seemed very touched to be singing with Willie.

He went to the little room where I had put the painting. This is where he kept his guitars and cigars. Hmm...that would be a great name for one of his next songs. Everyone else seemed preoccupied with Christmas festivities and didn't notice our departure.

He had an old electric typewriter on his desk and a handwritten notebook filled with his songs. He was about to pick up a guitar when he noticed the painting I had left for him.

"Wait, what is that?" he asked, pointing at it.

"That, Kinky, is a painting I was asked by Copper Love to drop off to you when she found out I was on the way to your Christmas party."

He didn't seem too surprised about me seeing Copper Love and unwrapped it.

"Why did she ask you to bring this? I don't know anything about it."

"She said one of her clients bought it and asked her to personally deliver it to you as a present."

"Interesting," he said. "This sure looks familiar."

"Yes, I thought the same thing. Wait, I know that place. Do you see that branch that resembles a rhinoceros head? I know exactly where this is. What do you say we take a little trip in the Yome Kipper Clipper?"

"Let's go," he said. He stood up, grabbed some keys off of his desk and walked out of a back door. I followed him. No one noticed our exit. We even were able to sneak past Dudley, who normally never lets me out of his sight. He was a bit preoccupied with the Friedmans. We drove for a couple of minutes to a river crossing, right next to where a humongous cypress tree stood.

"Let's stop here," I said.

He pulled off of the road and parked. We got out and walked around the very old, majestic tree. Sure enough, his bottle of Garrison Brothers Cowboy Bourbon was leaning up against the backside of the tree. It wasn't visible from the road. It was empty but appeared to have a note inside of it. There was another full bottle right next to it.

"How did you know the bottle was here?"

"I didn't. But the painting caught my attention. There was a branch on one of the trees that looked to be in the shape of a rhinoceros head. Walk over here and look at the tree from this angle. You see that branch down low on the tree? I noticed it the first time we drove here, when we were bringing back Winnie and Louie after they ran off and went exploring. She wanted us to find this place."

Kinky picked up the empty bottle and peeled the silver star off of the front of it. He separated the chip from it and held it up close to inspect it. I thought for a minute we were back in business, until his lips formed a clever little smile.

"What? Is it the chip?" I asked.

"Oh, it's the chip all right. Except it's the old Compaq computer chip Copper Love stole from me when she thought it was the L.A.M.B. chip. Clever girl."

I smiled. She was clever.

"About that, she wasn't actually Copper Love. The real Copper Love is still working at the gallery. She's there right now."

"I'm well aware, Careless. Well aware. I've been to the gallery. We have a lot to go over. But first, let's read the note, shall we?"

"We shall."

He opened the empty bottle and slid out the rolled-up note.

"Your country thanks you," he read. "And my country thanks you. Natan wants you to remember what he told you. He wanted me to leave you another bottle for the one that is now empty. In our county, it is an insult to refuse a gift."

"Well, how you like that?" Kinky asked.

"I like it just fine. Let's go back and gargle some Mexican mouthwash and Cowboy Bourbon," I said.

"What a great idea. I was just thinking that. Turns out Copper Love, or whatever her real name is, was actually an Israeli double agent. Who would have guessed? I suppose this case is officially closed."

"Sure seems that way, Kinky. At least closed enough." I agreed.

I knew one thing, Kinky and I were going to get along just fine. Let the Mexican mouthwash flow.

When we go back, nobody except Dudley and the Friedmans noticed we had been gone. They were anxiously awaiting our return. The Friedmans all flocked to Kinky, and Dudley sat by my side, where I hoped he'd always be. Kinky walked over and sat in his favorite chair. He sparked up a cigar and Mr. P took his rightful place, jumping up in his lap. Kinky stroked his fur while blowing smoke up to the heavens, watching it delicately ascend. He seemed deep in thought.

I walked up to E.D. and was about to fill her in about what Kinky and I had discovered. Before I could utter a word, she held up her index finger to her pursed lips and shushed me. Then she pointed above us. Hanging from a rafter was a sprig of mistletoe. Finally, my big chance with E.D. had arrived. I had been waiting for this moment for so long. A Christmas miracle was truly about to occur. I closed my eyes and waited. I didn't have long to wait. Just as the eagle was about to land, I felt a very large golden-colored hound dog jump up between us to receive the mistletoe kiss. I opened my eyes just in time to see it. It seemed to be playing in slow motion. Foiled again by my best friend. I smiled and everyone had a good laugh. It was indeed A Very Kinky Christmas.

COPPER LOVE
by Kinky Friedman

Copper Love is gone but her memory's living on
In every tree and rock at Echo Hill

And the river flowing by puts a teardrop in my eye
And tells me that her spirit's with us still

Copper Love is gone but this is her song
May we sing it as long as we live

And may this melody bring peace to you and me
And help us to love and forgive

Oh, Clovis was there lying by her easy chair
He could hear strange voices on the phone

He'd waited there all day till the sun had went away
Copper Love was never coming home

Copper Love is gone, wherever they go
Who help so many so much

And we're all left behind where spiritual decline
So, Copper, please keep in touch

Oh, Clovis was right there lying by her easy chair
He could hear the people crying on the phone

He'd waited there all day but he'd once been a stray
And he knew that Copper'd found another home.

A DOG IN THE SKY
by Kinky Friedman

Goodbye Mr. P you meant the world to me
But you just can't keep an old dog from running off to die

Goodbye Mr. P it was always you and me
Now you are my dog in the sky

Now you're safe my little friend, until we meet again
Across the bridge where skies are always blue

And I believe that when we die there's a dog up in the sky
And I believe my precious one that dog is you

You could hardly hear, you scarcely see
Now my little old man is free

I'm an old man myself, all my dreams are on the shelf
But you just can't keep an old dog from running off to die

But there's one thing that I know, it ain't the pot of gold
No, Mr. P, it's the rainbow

You could hardly hear, you could scarcely see
My old man is free

Goodbye Mr. P it was always you and me
I can't forget you even if I try

Goodbye Mr. P it was always you and me
Now you are my dog in the sky

Thank you, dear reader, for partaking in another one of Dudley's delightful tales. He tells me he's not sure how many more books he has left in him, so he asked me to dedicate his story to the following people:

Kinky Friedman is probably one of most talented and prolific authors, singers, songwriters, and philosophers of our time, with a heart of gold that is metaphorically the size of Texas. His parents Min and Tom graciously touched almost as many children's lives as there are stars in the night sky at Echo Hill Ranch. If you don't have Kinky's books or CD's, it's never too late to make it a financial pleasure for him.

Copper Love, her last name says it all. She was so in tune with animals and nature. She was the horse whisperer before there was a horse whisperer. She spoke horse.

Dear sweet Mr. P broke a lot of hearts when he was called home. He was the epitome of a good boy. Rest easy, Mr. P.

My Dudley, who was my best friend and soulmate, not a day goes by that I don't utter your name.

As always, the proceeds from this book will go to animal shelters and rescue groups who save and care for Dudley and Mr. P's cousins, who through no fault of their own end up homeless, wanting only a human of their own.

THANK YA VERY MUCH!